The Lady in Black

Frank J. Infusino Jr.

Author of
The Final Word and
Murder at Fort Revere

The Lady in Black
Copyright ©2021 Frank J. Infusino Jr.

ISBN 978-1506-905-49-5 PBK
ISBN 978-1506-905-52-5 EBK

LCCN 2021920402

November 2021

Published and Distributed by
First Edition Design Publishing, Inc.
P.O. Box 17646, Sarasota, FL 34276-3217
www.firsteditiondesignpublishing.com

No one believes that she is there,
Just following me everywhere.
I can never be at my rest,
it's always me and silent guest.

P.J. Reed
The Lady in Black

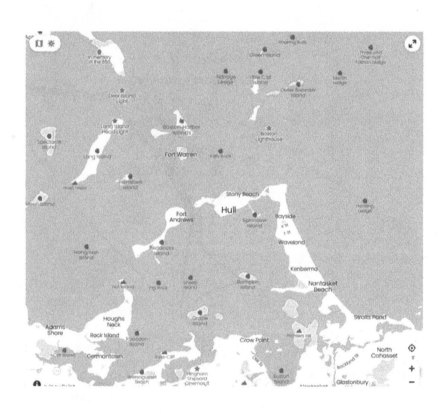

The Legend

September, 1862

The petite woman draped in oversized black robes stood on a makeshift wooden scaffolding shivering in the biting cold, her face a mask of fear and remorse; a frightened child masquerading as an adult. Forlorn and helpless, she awaited her fate; death by hanging.

A military tribunal convicted her of treason for spearheading a brazen escape attempt from a Confederate prisoner of war camp located within the granite walls of Fort Warren, an island bastion guarding the entrance to Boston Harbor.

The tragic saga began when the eighteen-year-old newlywed, disguised as a man, slipped into the fort to rescue her husband, a Confederate cavalry officer. In a driving rain, and choppy seas, she steered a small dinghy a mile alone from the tip of the Hull peninsula to the massive fortress. A merchant, and southern sympathizer, who delivered rations to the island, had smuggled in a note alerting the prisoners of the date and time she planned to arrive.

Once reunited with her husband and his comrades, she outlined a daring plan; dig a tunnel to the arsenal in the center of the compound, obtain weapons, overpower the garrison, and flee or capture the vital fort for the Confederacy.

Older veterans, content to ride out the war in a safe place run by a benevolent commandant, scoffed at the idea. They refused to risk getting killed or maimed in a preposterous venture proposed by a would-be Joan of Arc. Their skepticism was not shared by a handful of younger men eager to rejoin the struggle for independence.

But the skeptics proved right. The plan unraveled not long after work began on a tunnel. A vigilant sentry detected a noise beneath his feet, warned his comrades and led an armed detail to intercept the escapees. In the ensuing melee, the woman's unreliable percussion revolver, which she had brought to aid the breakout, exploded, killing her beloved.

The looming execution angered the rebel prisoners assembled in a staggered U-configuration around the scaffolding. Many glowered, others paced with fists clenched, some kept their eyes riveted to the ground. A detachment of Union troopers stood between them and the gallows with rifles at the ready, bayonets fixed, prepared to thwart any interference. Most of the soldiers, young trainees who had never fired their guns in anger, were as fearful as the Confederates were irate.

The commandant's sympathetic gesture to grant the woman's request to be hanged as a woman---she wore black monk's garments he found among the props used for on-site theater productions---did not soothe the enraged prisoners. Sensing a revolt, Colonel Justin Dimick, placed a hood over her head and gave the signal that sent the woman plunging to her death. She was buried in an unmarked grave in an undisclosed location on the island.

* * *

The hanging of a southern belle on an isolated fort in the waters of Boston Harbor might have become an overlooked footnote in the chaos of the Civil War, but for the actions of wily veterans who seized on a widespread belief at the time that the spirits of the dead "survived" and could communicate to the living, sometimes in strange ways.

To keep the memory of the hanging alive, and no doubt to scare young recruits, they spun tales of having heard and seen a mysterious form, shrouded in black, scurrying through the tunnels of the fort moaning and crying for her dead husband. Some reported objects in their barracks moved without reason; lanterns blew out when no wind existed. Footsteps appeared in the snow coming from nowhere and ending at the site where the gallows once stood; evidence of a life-force among them.

Nineteen-year-old Private Alfred Turner, a new Union recruit, was mesmerized by such stories. Turner grew up in Salem, Massachusetts, listening to town elders regale children with descriptions of witches, demons and ghosts. It wasn't a stretch for him to believe the spirit of a wronged woman haunted the fort.

On a frigid December night, three months after the execution, he marched along the parapet above the parade ground, one of two sentries on watch. An hour after midnight, the temperature hovered around thirty degrees and an icy wind drove Turner to dip his chin into the top of his overcoat as he completed his rounds. To him, the howling gusts sounded ominous, like the wailing of a wounded creature. He ducked for shelter, and safety, behind one of the massive 15-inch Rodman guns deployed on the fort's walls for defense.

After several minutes, Turner regained his nerve, and jumped out from behind his hiding place. Rifle cocked; he barked a challenge to stop to a menacing shape floating towards him. When the "thing" ignored his warning, the terrified youngster fired.

"Jesus Christ, Turner," the other sentry shouted as a .58 caliber mini ball whistled past his ear. "Are you crazy?"

Turner stared dumbfounded and shaking, his terror replaced by shame and humiliation. He escaped being court-martialed when his pal agreed to support his claim that he tripped and his musket discharged.

Though Turner's actions were those of an innocent youth motivated by fear, the incident was twisted to confirm reports that the spirit of a grief-stricken lady stalked the island, and when angered, even attacked a soldier. Over one-hundred years later, the fable, by then entrenched in New England folklore, muddled a murder investigation, and bewildered a cynical detective struggling to make sense of bizarre occurrences that saved his life.

PART I

Murder

Murder is just a horrible crime.

Stacy D. Spell
Captain, LAPD

Does it make any sense?
No. But murder never does.

Lieutenant Joe Kenda
Homicide Detective

Chapter 1

Present day September

Alyce Crimshaw, a park ranger with the Massachusetts State Department of Conservation and Recreation, guided twelve students on a field trip through the cavernous tunnels of Fort Warren. The teenagers were in the Advance Placement U.S. History class at Bridge Hill Academy, an elite college prep school in Cohasset, a coastal town about ten miles away. Two staff members and their wives, along with their teacher, chaperoned the group.

The forty-year-old Crimshaw, strands of her blond hair jutting out from her wide-brimmed iconic ranger hat, stopped from time-to-time to recount the history and describe the intricate construction of the island fortress. The kids crowded around her as she spoke.

"Fort Warren," she explained, "was part of the Boston Harbor defense system for eighty-six years from the Civil War to the end of World War II. Decommissioned in 1947, it's now a National Historic landmark. It once served as a prison for many high-ranking southern military officers and politicians including vice-president of the Confederacy, Alexander H. Stephens. It had a reputation for humane treatment, unlike many camps such as the notorious Confederate stockade, Andersonville."

Crimshaw's audience, most headed to the Ivy League, paid rapt attention. Their bright, eager faces reinforced the ranger's hope that the current generation was not all doped out, social media addicted robots.

Not everyone hung on Crimshaw's every word, though. Teacher Michael Dimick, whose great, great ancestor, Colonel Justin Dimick, served as the fort's first commandant, stood at the back of the gathering. He could recite Crimshaw's monologue verbatim, this being his sixth outing to the island. He wasn't bored though. Crimshaw did a superb job and he always requested her as their docent. He hung back to strike off on his own to explore the labyrinth of rooms and dark corridors. He hoped to discover the grave of the Lady in Black to validate the tale and prove the skeptics wrong. He had seen a room earlier that he couldn't remember checking.

The class marched deeper into an arched chamber which Crimshaw identified as a "casemate," an armored enclosure for artillery weapons firing through embrasures, or openings, in the walls. Some casemates, she said, were converted to cells for prisoners, housing around twenty-four men each.

After a few questions about how guns maneuvered in such confined spaces, everyone, except teacher Dimick, who continued to lag behind, followed Crimshaw further into a vaulted corridor, called the Dark Arch, which became pitch-black as they moved away from the casemate apertures.

Crimshaw shined her Maglite on her face, so she could be seen by everyone. The effect produced an eerie glow giving her a "ghostly" appearance. The more impressionable students shivered and clung to one another for support aware of the stories of the spirit of a condemned woman prowling the fort in search of her dead husband. And, as if on cue, a deafening scream pierced the silence and a black cloaked form swept through the area knocking two girls aside and storming past Crimshaw.

The intruder shook the teens, some of whom stifled cries, but Crimshaw waved them on to a more lighted area, put up her hands and smiled. "Don't be alarmed," she said in a relaxed, deliberate voice. "We often get pranksters trying to scare visitors; schoolboys who've read or heard about our resident ghost. I'm sure you know the tale?"

They did. Dimick used the intriguing story, and his family's connection, to generate interest in the field trip, not an easy task with high school kids entering their senior year. Their fear allayed, the students debated the truth of the legend, arms waving, voices raised, some giggling.

Crimshaw regained the group's attention, raising her voice above the din, and regaled them with a vivid account of chasing one thirteen-year-old boy from Hull, who jumped out at one of her tourist groups like the person who just barged through them. Her candor and gentle manner reassured the youngsters, and they settled down to enjoy more of Crimshaw's spirited narrative of the fort's history.

The disruption of the field trip was a calculated diversion. While Crimshaw worked her calming magic, the "intruder" wended his way back toward a small, windowless room off the central passageway which he observed Mike Dimick enter. He slipped into the room unnoticed; the teacher had his back to the narrow entry and stood in the middle of the room oblivious to anything but his examination of the chamber, unaware of the uproar that had occurred ahead of him. He focused his small flashlight on the floor and stomped on it for any signs that something or someone might be buried beneath.

Recognizing that Dimick was engrossed in his task, the intruder, moving with the quickness and agility of an athlete, grabbed the teacher from behind, whipped a knife across his neck and stabbed him as he fell.

At that moment, Dakota Johnson, a female student infatuated with her teacher, and hoping to have some alone time with him, came looking for him. She stopped outside the dark room when she heard a commotion. As her eyes adjusted to the darkness, she screamed. Dimick lay face down on the damp ground clutching his neck. A menacing shape hovered over him for several seconds brandishing a knife, stepped over the fallen body and dashed from the room brushing against the petrified girl.

Unhinged by the scene she had just witnessed and the specter of a mysterious stranger who touched her, Dakota Johnson unleashed deafening shrieks that caught the attention of her classmates and the chaperones who had gone ahead. The group, led by Crimshaw, charged back toward the noise, astonished and stunned when they saw a body sprawled on the concrete, their classmate cowering against a wall: a surreal scene.

Boys and girls hugged each other for comfort. Two became hysterical when Dakota blurted, "Somebody…something… hurt Mr. Dimick. It had a knife. It had a knife. It touched me. Oh! my god. Oh! my god. Help me."

She collapsed into Crimshaw's arms, sobbing. The ranger handed the girl off to a female chaperone, so she could determine the extent of Dimick's injuries. She flashed her Maglite over his body. His throat was slashed and blood oozed from a wound in his side, his eyes and mouth open. A foul odor permeated the room.

The man was dead.

* * *

The shadowy figure who attacked Michael Dimick had ducked into an alcove to avoid the onrushing students. He gulped for air, heart thumping, hands shaking. He stumbled off in the opposite direction when the group stormed by. He stopped to discard his robes and the murder weapon, stuffing them in a green trash bag secreted in a crumbling fireplace cavity. He placed the articles on an inside ledge out of sight.

Dakota's screams, and the ensuing commotion, attracted other tourists in the midst of their self-guided tours. They approached the location with trepidation, heads on a swivel, parents clinging to children No one noticed the new addition to their ranks who stood on the rear fringe when Crimshaw cautioned them to stay back before plucking a radio from her belt to call for assistance.

A murmur rose from the frightened onlookers when they overheard Crimshaw explain who had been killed and under what circumstances. She avoided details of Dimick's wounds in deference to the crowd that included toddlers. She didn't want to create panic and make it difficult for the scattered rangers on the island to maintain control. Nevertheless, the cluster of people exchanged furtive glances. Parents pulled their kids close.

The teens from Bridge Hill Academy mingled with the other sightseers, all riveted to the spot where they stood, afraid to stray from the safety of the small band. Some gossiped; a few confessed their concerns. The legend of the "Lady in Black" dominated conversations. The killer, acting shocked and upset, a frown creasing his face, shared his own fear and misgivings. One woman put an arm on his shoulders to console him.

He was ecstatic.

His masquerade convinced these morons that a supernatural being had a hand in the slaying. The empty suits and vapid women of the "Fourth Estate" would fall all over themselves injecting the idea of a vengeful spirit from the past committing a modern-day atrocity. Hell! It wouldn't be any more bizarre than the ridiculous theories floating around the country these days---lizard aliens intent on enslaving humans or baby-eating Satan worshipers secretly running the government.

He did his best to suppress his joy; he was not a monster. Dimick had to be stopped. The authorities chose to turn a blind eye to his behavior. He didn't;

couldn't. It was personal. And his retribution was not complete. His eyes drifted to a future target.

Chapter 2

Ranger Crimshaw's call for assistance was routed to Sergeant Timothy McCann of the Boston Harbor Patrol. The BHP shared jurisdiction with the Coast Guard, Massachusetts Port Authority, U.S. Customs & Border Protection and the state police.

McCann, a graying veteran, pounded a beat on the streets of East Boston for twenty-years before transferring to his present assignment. An Irishman patrolling an Italian community created the potential of stirring animosity among the residents. Old prejudices die hard. But McCann, a bear of a man, affable and gregarious, won over the locals with his glib tongue, affinity for Cannoli's and Santarpio's pizza, heralded as one of the top two pizza joints in the city. McCann's expanding paunch motivated his decision to move to the seas bordering Boston; riding a boat much easier than climbing up and down hills.

His girth did not dull his knowledge and instincts. His officers, unlike those from other agencies claiming control over the islands, were in a better position to respond to emergencies, though the sergeant couldn't recall murder being one of them on his watch. As a thirty year-veteran, the last ten with the BHP, he didn't spend time ruminating over past situations. He dispatched two high speed intercept boats to Fort Warren with orders sealing off the enclave; let no one enter or leave. Next, he called the Boston PD homicide unit.

His phone-call connected to a beleaguered Captain Brian Olson. For the past three weeks, a spate of killings in Boston between rival gangs vying to dominate the drug trade, overwhelmed his men and women. The Columbia Point Dawgs, Revere Bloods and Latin Kings left bodies strewn across the city. His team slogged through multiple shifts with corpses piling up daily. Olson did not want to add a slaying offshore to his team's workload.

Fortunately, he had an option.

Under Massachusetts General Laws, the eleven-district attorneys in the commonwealth conducted the investigations of all homicides. Boston, Springfield, Worcester and Pittsfield were exceptions, their departments cleared to work their own cases. In all other municipalities, locals deferred to the state.

In some instances, with mutual agreement, state police detectives assisted their counterparts in the exempted cities like Boston. Olson contemplated such a scenario. One where he would hand off the Fort Warren homicide to the "staties" with his department assisting on an as needed basis.

Hull, the nearest town to Georges Island, fell under the province of the Plymouth County District Attorney and the detectives within that office. Olson knew the Plymouth County D.A., Sharon Stonehouse, whom he met at a law enforcement conference in Worcester, Massachusetts, conducted by the FBI.

Olson called the D.A.'s office, and after a ten-minute wait, was patched through and greeted warmly. The two law enforcement officers exchanged pleasantries, and updates on their daughters who both attended the University of Massachusetts, Amherst, before Stonehouse cut to the chase. "I suspect this is not a get reacquainted call, Brian."

"Very perceptive. No doubt why you're the D.A."

Stonehouse chuckled. "Okay. Spare me the BS, Brian. What can I do for you?"

"We've had a murder at Fort Warren on Georges Island, which we would ordinarily handle."

"Yes," Stonehouse said, and waited for Olson to drop the shoe.

He didn't disappoint. "To be honest. We're swamped now and could use some help."

"What do you have in mind?"

"Well, your guys did a super job with the priest homicide in Hull and breaking up the Mexican cartel human trafficking scheme. I hoped your team could take the lead on this. I'd owe you big time."

Stonehouse hesitated, then acquiesced: "Always happy to help out our Boston brethren."

Olson sighed. "This helps a lot Sharon. I appreciate it."

"What's the status of the case."

"Well. It just happened. The island is sealed off; visitors detained. It's late and not enough housing to keep everyone overnight, though."

"I assume you'll send the body to the Boston morgue?"

"Yes."

"Who's the victim?"

"A private school teacher taking his students on a field trip."

"Yikes! Who kills a teacher?

"Someone he pissed off."

"Yup. And odds are, the murderer is someone with his group or someone aware of the trip; kids, parents, school employee?"

"That's for the investigators to determine," Olson said, an unspoken rebuke in the tone of his voice. "Might be another situation altogether."

"Right," Stonehouse responded, chastised. "Getting ahead of myself. If the Harbor Patrol and rangers interview the tourists, record their personal data and take fingerprints, my unit will follow-up tomorrow if that works for you."

"It does. Not ideal. But the best we can do under the circumstances. We'll transport any suspects to Boston and hold them for your people."

"Okay, Brian. I'll call as soon as possible and let you know who will supervise the investigation."

"Much obliged, Sharon. Can't thank you enough."

"No problem, happy to help," Stonehouse said, and broke the phone connection.

She leaned back in her chair for a moment before phoning Captain Ed Catebegian, the commander of the detectives assigned to her office.

Chapter 3

In this age of cell phones and social media, the attack on Michael Dimick at Fort Warren made headlines. Late afternoon television news programs and their internet affiliates carried the story hours before the tourists departed Georges Island.

Under **Breaking News,** all the major outlets gave sketchy reports. The myth of the Lady in Black worked its way into several accounts. Some Bridge Hill students who tweeted or posted on Facebook and Instagram revealed that prior to the murder, their field trip had been interrupted by a screaming figure in black robes. Most dismissed the incident as a prank; others were not so sure. New England folklore was rife with tales of spirits inhabiting historic buildings and ancient graveyards. Tours at these sites were organized to reinforce such beliefs.

Jennifer Holcomb, an enterprising young TV reporter, after some quick online research, recounted the legend of the young woman executed as a spy during the Civil War roaming Fort Warren in search of her dead husband.

Over the years, Holcomb declared, reputable researchers, soldiers and park rangers described encounters with the lady. She quoted from a story on Civil War ghosts where one woman claimed, as a child, alone in a darkened room, she came face to face with the mythical woman "who had a kind face." Others swore they had been enveloped in cold or touched by an unseen entity as they explored the dim tunnels of the fort. One man, fishing in the channel behind Georges Island, alleged that one night "fanatical screams" came from the island.

Others made similar claims.

"The murder victim, Michael Dimick," Holcomb stated, "long professed to be a distant relative of Fort Warren's first commandant, Colonel Justin Dimick, the officer who ordered the hanging of the legendary Lady in Black.

"We have all heard and read about bizarre incidents which defy explanation," Holcomb pronounced in a solemn tone. "Was the slaying of teacher Michael Dimick the action of an unhinged psychopath or an act of revenge by a wronged woman?"

She paused for effect, looking straight into the camera, eyebrows raised.

"We may never know," she said, mimicking pitchman Rod Serling, of the 1960s TV show, the Twilight Zone, who warned viewers before each episode they were about to enter a new dimension of sight and sound whose boundaries were limited only by their imagination. Audiences loved the program; tuning in to marvel at the strangeness of the universe and to be frightened out of their wits.

The popularity of the program highlighted the blurred boundaries between the real and the imagined. Throughout history, humans have grappled to explain experiences occurring on the margins of reality. Hence, footsteps echoing in an empty room are attributed to "ghosts," while unexplained objects in the sky become alien saucers from another planet. Holcomb's unsubstantiated and fanciful commentary, for which she was later rebuked and suspended by station management, reinforced those beliefs and threatened to complicate the murder investigation to come.

The public reaction, at least as reflected by the sensationalized news accounts, exceeded the killer's expectations; the reason he assumed the persona of a dark spirit. Watching Holcomb's unhinged narrative on his TV in a room devoid of personal items, he smirked.

No one ever went bankrupt underestimating the intelligence of the average citizen.

Chapter 4

Ed Catebegian

Captain Ed Catebegian, watching a news report about the murder at Georges Island on the thirty-seven-inch wall mounted TV in his office, shook his head, sat back in his chair and laughed. The female reporter, a Barbie Doll clone with frizzy hair and bright red lipstick, intimated a ghost reputed to haunt Fort Warren had a hand in the slaying. He stopped laughing when the Plymouth County D.A., his supervisor, called to notify him that his team would handle the investigation. Ghosts, he mumbled to himself. Crazies would come out of the woodwork and complicate or impede their inquiry.

Catebegian, nicknamed "Big Cat" during his college football days for his size, agility and quickness as a defensive lineman, was a newly minted captain. He attained his rank six months earlier due, in part, to his leadership of a task force investigating the double murders of a Hull Catholic priest and the town's police chief. In the process, his men and women uncovered a fraud and human trafficking scheme engineered by a Mexican cartel.

Catebegian was a team player. He learned the benefits of that on the grid-iron and carried that experience into his years as a patrol officer and detective. He owed his promotion to the hard work of the unit he assembled and, more specifically, to one Vince Magliore, a brilliant detective but a pill-popping, insufferable, insubordinate jerk who could piss off Mother Theresa.

Magliore worked the Hull case as an unpaid consultant on medical leave from a police department in southern California. The Hull police chief, a boyhood pal, insisted Magliore join the investigation because of his knowledge of the area and personal relationships with the victims.

Despite Catebegian's reluctance, he brought Magliore on board. The man's instincts and dogged persistence helped nail the killers, though he narrowly escaped losing his own life as events unfolded.

When Magliore resigned from his job in California, Catebegian secured him a position as a "probationary" lieutenant. He threw this lifeline based on Magliore's agreement to seek professional help to overcome his addiction to painkillers, a habit he developed while recovering from wounds suffered in the line of duty.

With the Fort Warren homicide thrust upon him, Catebegian didn't hesitate. He'd use Magliore, who had grown up in nearby Hull, and his partner, Theresa Lopez, to spearhead the investigation. They were both tenacious investigators; Magliore the veteran, Lopez a thoughtful, by the book, newcomer. Catebegian did worry that Magliore, brash and abrasive, might be a poor example for the young woman. And his drug use posed a problem as well if his mandated rehab failed.

Determining the positives outweighed the negatives, Catebegian picked up his cell phone and tapped in Magliore's number. A ridiculous recording greeted him:

"Vince here," the voice announced. "If you're calling to confess a crime, give me the details and I'll arrest you as soon as possible. If not, leave your name and number. I'll get back to you when I finish my pasta. Ciao."

Not amused---actually he was---Catebegian left his own message: "This is the boss. Get your sorry ass to my office, forthwith."

Catebegian broke the connection, but couldn't suppress a smile.

* * *

While Catebegian organized his team, Plymouth County D.A., Sharon Stonehouse, held a press conference in the media room at her office in Brockton, Massachusetts. Representatives from the major TV channels were present as well as reporters from local newspapers and the Boston Globe and Herald.

Stonehouse explained to the group that, at the request of the Boston Homicide Division, state detectives would be handling the murder at Fort Warren. She named Captain Ed Catebegian as spokesperson in the matter and said he would deliver future updates, although he would not be present today. She declined to name other detectives involved before opening the meeting to questions.

A Globe reporter asked the first question: "Any suspects at this time?"

"Two or three persons of interest," Stonehouse said.

"Can you tell us who they are?" a correspondent from the Herald inquired.

"No," Stonehouse replied, without elaborating.

After four other mundane questions, one from the local Patriot Ledger representative triggered laughter and hoots. "Any truth to the rumor that an unexplained person or entity might be involved?" he asked, deadpanned.

Stonehouse stood slack-jawed and crossed her arms. "Please don't give credence to such nonsense," she said, and walked out of the room.

Captain Ed Catebegian, watching the live broadcast, groaned. The Dimick investigation was deteriorating into a media circus. An "oldies" music buff, Catebegian thought of a 1970s Judy Collins song: **_Send in the Clowns_**.

God help us!

PART II

The Investigation

The truth must be quite plain,
if one could just clear away the litter

Agatha Christie

A crime scene tells you what happened,
it doesn't tell you who made it happen.

Lt. Joe Kenda.
Homicide Detective

Chapter 5

Vince Magliore

Present Day

I killed a man.

He deserved it. But I'm no murderer. I'm a cop. The man I killed, also a cop, *was* a murderer. He slaughtered other lawmen and their relatives, including my partner, as payback for having been fired. Led us on a wild, desperate chase through three southern California counties until we trapped the son-of-a-bitch in a cabin in the San Bernardino Mountains. My colleagues waited for the word to close in. I didn't. I slipped into his hideout unseen under the cover of darkness and shot him in the head.

No one knows that.

The coroner ruled the bastard committed suicide as hordes of lawmen moved in and burned the building to the ground. I suffered a leg wound crawling away from the scene when flares and ammunition exploded and shrapnel pierced my thigh and calf. I took a medical leave, returned to my hometown of Hull, Massachusetts, and intended to recuperate and get my mind straight.

That didn't work out.

The Hull police chief, a high school classmate, dragged me into a blackmail scheme, a homicide investigation and a human trafficking conspiracy. Two of my childhood buddies were slain and a woman I love landed in a hospital bed, in a coma, unlikely to recover.

You can't make this stuff up.

* * *

My name is Vince Magliore, by the way. I'm thirty-nine years old, single, never married. Some call me dashing and debonair---after chugging a few beers. Most of my friends, or colleagues, use other adjectives to describe me, like asshole, for example.

I'm sitting in the reception area of the office of Ms. Mavis Fisher, a shrink recommended by Randy Hundley, my high school compadre and the murdered Hull police chief. I felt good when I killed the deranged LA cop, but since then, I've been an emotional basket case and just a short time ago stopped taking prescription opioids to block out the pain of my wounds and the memory of my act of revenge. That's why I'm in Fisher's office. She's a psychologist, not a psychiatrist but, in my opinion, a "headshrinker" nonetheless.

I've been sitting for fifteen minutes ignoring the latest issue of People Magazine when Ms. Fisher enters the waiting room from a door adjacent to the receptionist's desk. Her smile is warm, enticing, a woman to whom you could spill your guts. She appears to be in her late forties, slender, about three clicks shorter than me; I'm six-two. She looks professional in a pressed pink blouse and gray skirt ending an inch or two above her knees. Her auburn hair frames an unlined face. Not my image of a shrink, but what do I know. She welcomes me with a soft but firm handshake, if that makes sense, and guides me into her office with her left hand in the small of my back; no doubt to prevent me from bolting, which I considered every minute of my wait.

Fisher's beige carpeted office has a couch and two stuffed chairs with a glass-topped coffee table in between. A mahogany desk in front of a window, blinds closed, is free of clutter except for a white phone on the top right. A wall to my left holds two certificates authorizing her service as a psychologist along with a Bachelor of Arts diploma from Smith College. Two landscape paintings and an iconic photo of the old Roller Coaster at Paragon Park in Nantasket Beach adorn the other walls. No doubt why local boy Randy Hundley liked her.

Fisher directs me to one of the chairs while she takes the one opposite. Guess I don't yet qualify for the couch. She crosses her legs, grabs a notebook from the coffee table, places it in her lap and asks, "Do you mind if I take notes? It helps me to focus later on what we discussed. They remain confidential at all times."

I don't respond, mesmerized by the expanse of thigh exposed when she crossed her legs. Not very discreet with my gaze, Fisher fixes me with a stare I associate with my fourth-grade teacher——a combination of a glare and a smirk. I had a permanent seat beside that teacher's desk. Not quite a dunce stool in the corner, but close.

"I'll take your silence as a yes," Fisher says.

Chastised, I sit up straighter and grin like a dumbass. With a slight shake of her head, she asks, "What brings you here, Mr. Magliore?"

That's when I bolt.

* * *

I can hear Hundley laughing his ass off until his belly aches and tears roll down his cheeks. He'd say, "What a dumb shit. I hook you up with the one person who can help you, and you run out of her office like a quarterback evading an onrushing linebacker."

He'd use a simile like that; we were high school football teammates. And yes, I understand the difference between a metaphor and a simile. I paid attention in English class when not ogling my girlfriend, Angela, who sat across from me.

But I digress. I'm sitting in my car in the parking lot of the clinic alternately banging my hands and head on the steering wheel. I'll either give myself a concussion or knock some sense into my pea brain as my commanding officer, Captain Ed. Catebegian, often refers to my mental prowess or lack thereof.

I'm screwed. My new job with the Massachusetts State Police is contingent on one thing---that I begin and complete drug rehab therapy. Catebegian is aware of my addiction, but doesn't know the underlying cause. I have no choice but to return to the office and hope Mavis won't throw me out on my butt.

Not an auspicious beginning.

I'd grovel at Fisher's feet, but she'd no doubt suspect I was trying to peek under her skirt.

Chapter 6

Magliore

I drag myself out of my car and trudge back to Mavis Fisher's office head down, shuffling my feet like a man headed toward the gallows. When I enter the waiting room again, the receptionist raises her eyebrows. Two of the patients, who were in the room when I darted through, shoot me knowing glances no doubt thinking I'm as loony as them.

"May I help you?" the receptionist asks, her voice dripping with sarcasm.

"Can Ms. Fisher see me again today?" I ask, struggling to maintain eye contact. "I want to apologize for my behavior."

She folds her arms across her chest and fixes me with a withering stare. She's about to deny my request, when the door to Fisher's office opens. The doctor comes into the reception area trailing a woman who exits in four or five long strides, head down.

The doctor regards me with an imperceptible smile and says: "Ready to try again, Mr. Magliore?"

I clasp my hands in front of me and nod in the affirmative.

She directs her assistant to add me as the last patient of the day, turns toward one female in the room, and beckons her into the inner sanctum.

I sit in one of the straight-backed chairs against the wall, pull out my cell phone and access my emails to avoid the daggers shot my way by the receptionist.

An hour and a half later, Fisher again welcomes me to her office. We take the same seats as before.

"Well, Mr. Magliore," she begins, "perhaps I should start with a different question this time."

I relax, the tension draining from my body. "Why don't I tell you my story, and we can go from there," I offer.

Fisher nods and I describe in detail my partner's slaying at the hands of a demented LA cop, the subsequent manhunt, my role in killing the guy, my wounds and later addiction to painkillers. I omit my recurring vision of that cop's face lurking in my bedroom at night.

Fisher scribbles notes on a yellow pad, which unsettles me, but I plunge on with the expectation of doctor/patient confidentiality.

I finish and glance at Fisher like a puppy waiting for a pat on the head. I expect the type of absolution a priest delivers in the confessional; three "Our Fathers," three "Hail Mary's." On your way son. Sin no more.

Fisher's expression, eyes focused on her notes, mouth tight, jaw firm, indicates a pardon is not forthcoming.

She smiles and re-crosses her legs, again flashing an expanse of thigh, perhaps testing my ability to focus. Though tempted, I keep my eyes riveted on hers.

She looks pleased before asking a variation of the question that prompted me to flee our first meeting.

"What do you hope to gain from these sessions, Mr. Magliore?"

As a lapsed Catholic, I seek the next best thing to absolution: "Peace of mind," I murmur, looking away.

"And how do you expect to achieve that?" she asks.

"You're the professional. You tell me," I blurt without thinking. A frequent habit of mine.

Unoffended, Fisher's expression doesn't change. No doubt she gets that reaction from jerks like me all the time. Nevertheless, I apologize before she can respond.

"Sorry. I'm an idiot."

She grins before saying something unsettling and unexpected. "I think you're suffering from a form of Post-Traumatic Stress Syndrome (PTSD).

PTSD?

Most people associate PTSD with returning veterans struggling to cope with their combat experiences. In World War II, they called it "shell-shock" or "battle fatigue." General George "Blood and Guts" Patton almost lost his command because of his insensitivity to the condition. To be fair, though, he was not alone among the brass in the belief that those displaying symptoms, without physical wounds, were cowards, dodging the front lines. Now the majority of us understand any traumatic episode can trigger PTSD: a car accident, a rape, surviving a natural disaster. My partner's murder and my subsequent revenge for that act would qualify as triggering events, though I never made the connection.

I look at Fisher, eyes wide, relieved in some way, but unsure of the future.

"So, Mr. Magliore, from the way you told your story, I gather you're feeling depressed, angry, guilty or all of the above."

"That covers it."

"Your use of drugs an effort to dull the memory of the episode?"

"Yes."

"Having difficulty with relationships?"

I stifle a laugh. "Yes. But I had trouble connecting way before that. Something I call the "Magliore Curse.""

Fisher covers her eyes with her left hand to hide a smile, fumbling to hold on to her note pad.

"Okay" she says," but you struggle more now with trusting people. Afraid to let your guard down for fear of being exposed."

True.

"So. Can you help me?" I ask.

"Yes, but you must be honest about your feelings, or we'll be wasting our time."

"Can do," I say, sounding more confident than I am.

Fisher's eyes betray her skepticism, but she indicates a willingness to proceed.

"There are two primary ways of treating PTSD," she explains. "Psychotherapy or counseling and medication."

"Medication's out," I blurt.

She holds up her hand, palm towards me. "I'm not recommending that. Psychotherapists, and I'm not one, you understand, use both Cognitive Processing Therapy (CPT) and Prolonged Exposure (PE). They may sound complicated, but they're both just techniques to develop communication skills to cope with your trauma. Talking about it and reflecting on it often can move you to the point where the memories or flashbacks you experience no longer upset you."

My eyes glaze over. "It does sound difficult."

"It's not," she emphasizes. "If you're willing to discuss the traumatic event and analyze your reaction to it, we can attain the peace of mind you seek."

I do want relief from the frequent flashbacks thoughts and dreams about violating my oath as a police officer. My new job gives me a second chance, but the ache from my leg wounds is a constant reminder of two things: my act of revenge and my drug addiction.

I played college football, endured numerous injuries and took the medication team doctors prescribed, in those days, Percocet; didn't become addicted. The pain was short-lived; unlike the mental anguish I undergo every day from my lapse in judgement and criminal actions.

I'm out of options if my sessions with Mavis Fisher don't help.

I make an appointment with the receptionist to come back the following week. She doesn't smile when I explain I'm to return weekly, at least for the next month or two. She hands me a reminder card without looking up. For once in my life, I don't aggravate the situation by making one of my inane comments.

I step out into the parking lot. The air is crisp, leaves beginning to take on a golden-brown hue. The earthy smell is invigorating. Reminds me of walking down main street in Hingham in the fall after attending a football game, thrashing through piles of fallen leaves on the sidewalk; a simpler time when leaves and other debris could be burned on the front lawns of homes. No one had heard of a "carbon footprint."

I interrupt my brief reverie to check for calls or text messages. I had turned the cell phone off while meeting with Fisher. I hate it when people disrespect the privacy of others in offices or restaurants by making or taking calls and discussing personal issues as if no one else is present.

There is a terse voicemail from my boss, Captain Ed. Catebegian, ordering me to his office, forthwith, which in cop lingo means without delay.

Nice. He can't wait to see me.

I think of him as my hairless Chubaka, a bald hulk, whose grunts are not as shrill as the Star Wars character and more decipherable. I don't tell him this, of course, since I value my life.

Hah!

Chapter 7

Lopez and Catebegian

I stroll into the office of Captain Catebegian without knocking. His head is drooped on his chest, eyelids at half-mast. I stand rigid for a minute or two until he becomes aware of my presence. He glowers as I intrude on his quiet reflection, or afternoon snooze. Take your pick.

"Don't you ever knock, Magliore?" he asks, as his head snaps back, and he struggles to appear alert.

I ignore the question, slide into a straight-backed chair facing his desk and present my best Cheshire Cat grin.

"What?" he says, now more irritated than ever. "And wipe that shit-eating grin off your face."

I say Cheshire, he says shit-eating. Tomato/tomahto. I don't go there.

"Just eager for my next assignment," I say, and sit up straight like a dog anticipating a treat. I skip the tongue hanging to one side and the paws/hands in front of my face.

"Well, we do have a new case." Big Cat says. "A teacher on a field trip with his class to Fort Warren on Georges Island was killed."

"Georges Island? Is that our jurisdiction?"

"It is now. Boston Harbor Patrol kicked it to us because of our outstanding work in solving the Hull murders and breaking up that Mexican cartel's human trafficking ring."

"You think they're blowing smoke"

"Doesn't matter. Our leader says it's ours."

"Our leader" being the Plymouth County district attorney.

"Fine with me," I say. "The salt air will refresh us."

Big Cat's eyes widen, his lips curl upward. "Not us kimmosabe," he says, using the famous phrase by Tonto, the Lone Ranger's Indian companion. He's wrong, of course. He's Kimmosabe and I'm Tonto in our equation, but I keep silent, contradicting the boss is never a good idea.

Catebegian continues to rub it in, though. "I'm a Captain now. You and Lopez will handle the grunt work while I take the credit if you solve it and point fingers in your direction if you don't."

He has discovered the perks of moving up the chain of command.

"At your service exalted one," I say.

I'm ready to get up and head for the door before the Cat can unleash a torrent of expletives or worse, the paper weight on his desk, when my new partner, Detective Terry Lopez, appears in the office doorway and raps on the door jamb.

Catebegian waves her in and stares at me with an expression that says: "Someone respects protocol, or at least demonstrates manners."

I disregard the unstated rebuke and smile at Lopez as she comes into the room. She dips her head in response.

Lopez is about five-nine, slender, not sleight, in her early thirties; black hair cut short, soft brown eyes, mischievous as she exchanges glances with Big Cat and me. She wears black jeans and a white blouse; her service revolver and handcuffs clipped to her belt at the base of her spine.

Lopez is new to the detective bureau. As an outsider, she assisted our investigation of the Hull murders. Her tenacious follow up of cigarette butt evidence led to the discovery of the killers and their connection to the Cartel de Jalisco Nueva Generacion (CJNG).

We have not partnered before. I wasn't an official member of the unit either, just an unpaid consultant, added at the insistence of my friend, Randy Hundley.

Lopez chooses to stand instead of taking the seat next to me. I don't take it as a rebuke or as a sign I give off an offensive odor. I slapped on enough deodorant and after-shave this morning to produce an aura of cleanliness---or drive those with allergies to give me a wide berth. Catebegian often smoked cigars---when not chewing tobacco---sometimes in confined spaces like a car, so he tolerates my aroma. Lopez is oblivious, or avoids giving me the opportunity of commenting, knowing I will snap off a snarky comeback.

Smart lady.

Cat looks from Lopez to me.

"So, do either of you believe in ghosts?"

Chapter 8

Ghosts!

Big Cat once chewed tobacco every day. Maybe over time the nicotine addled his brain.

"What ghosts?" I ask, giving him my best impression of a comic's straight man like Bud Abbott in the old Abbott and Costello routine, "Who's on First?"

Undaunted, Catebegian continues.

"Witnesses to the murder on Fort Warren claim a dark clad figure ran from the scene. It revived an old legend about a lady in black roaming the island seeking her husband who died during the Civil War. Even a TV newswoman repeated the story."

The hint of a smile creases the corners of Cat's mouth. He looks from Terry to me expecting a response.

I raise my eyebrows, but keep quiet. Lopez, face crimson, clasps her hands in front of her. "You know I'm Hispanic right?" she asks.

"So," I say, in a brilliant retort.

"Well, belief in the supernatural is woven through Mexican culture. My mother swears La Planchada cured her of an illness during a hospital stay."

"What's La Planchada?" asks Catebegian, crossing his arms on his massive chest.

"Not what, but who," Lopez corrects. "La Planchada means 'ironed lady' in Spanish. According to legend, she was a nurse who fell in love with a doctor who spurned her. She died of a broken heart, and now lurks in hospitals. She appears in a meticulously ironed old-fashioned nurse's uniform, hence the name, La Planchada.

"Her spirit emits a glow and floats through emergency wards. After her appearances, patients report feeling better. Doctors cannot explain their improvement. My mother insists this happened to her. She once suffered from flu-like symptoms that baffled her physicians. La Planchada hovered over her bed, smiled, and she recovered."

The overhead fluorescent lights add a gleam to her eyes as she recounts this fable.

Big Cat and I steal glances at each other.

"And you believe this?" I ask.

"Well," Lopez says, dipping her head, "sometimes ghost stories have a practical objective rather than a literal meaning. For instance, when we misbehaved, my mother threatened that La Llorona, the "crying woman" would come and punish, or kidnap us. She murdered her children to be with a man who rejected her. So, the legend says, she's condemned to wander the earth searching for the children she killed, and sometimes takes others to be with her. You can bet we changed our behavior to avoid being a victim of La Llorona."

I'm impressed with Lopez's use of the terms "meticulously" and "literal" in her stories---smart gal---but ignore that and stumble ahead in my usual callous disregard for the feelings of others.

I say in disbelief, "Yeah. And my parents threatened me with the 'boogeyman' hiding in the closet, or under the bed, to pounce if I acted up. But I've checked. He doesn't lurk in either place anymore."

I catch myself before plunging further down that rat hole. In my drug induced hallucinations, the face of the man I killed sometimes looms over me while I sleep; perhaps a reflective moment of guilt.

Lopez shrugs off my outburst. "There are things in the universe we cannot explain," she says, pointing at me. "And I bet you believe in the supernatural too."

"What?" I stammer.

"You're Catholic, right?"

"Yeah"

"So. The crucified Christ died, was buried, and ascended into heaven at the right hand of God. He now controls the world. An astonishing tale don't you think?"

My mouth drops open and for one of the first times in my life I'm speechless. It takes me a minute to regain my composure. "That's, that's not supernatural," I protest.

"Oh! A guy rises from the dead, watches over us, and an army of Angels helps him."

I'm stunned as if Lopez had smacked me upside the head. My eyes glaze, face reddens. I haven't set foot in a church in years, but the lessons of my youth and years spent as an altar boy are difficult to shake.

Big Cat cuts me off before I attempt to defend my beliefs.

"Enough," he says, his voice rising. "Find out who committed the murder at Fort Warren."

He stands up as a way of dismissing us. As we move to leave, he shouts, "But don't tell me it was a ghost, La Planchada or La Cucaracha or any other mystical being."

I hide my smirk from Lopez.

Chapter 9

Lopez and Magliore

Lopez and I leave Catabegian's office and agree to meet at the Brew Haus in Weymouth to grab a bite and discuss the case. The captain gave us a folder with available details.

A hostess leads us to a booth across from the rectangular bar that stretches the length of the room. We navigate through many empty tables at the late afternoon hour as we are escorted to our seating. We take opposite padded bench seats and both order a house draft beer, which the waitress later brings in two frosty mugs.

We raise the mugs, but neither of us offers a toast.

"I'm sorry I busted your chops in the captain's office about the ghost thing," Lopez says, offering a smile.

She's a few years younger than me, I guess, but even a dunce like me knows never to ask a woman her age.

Her white teeth are set off by clear olive skin; the top two buttons on her blouse, unfastened, display ample cleavage. I pushed aside thoughts of another woman since Kate Maxwell, my girlfriend, was shot and remains hospitalized in a coma. Yet, glue my eyes to Lopez's chest.

She catches me staring. My face feels hot.

"Are you blushing because you're looking down my shirt?" she challenges.

"Guilty," I say

"Vince. You're smart, funny, easy on the eyes, but we're not going to hook-up as they say these days. I'm your colleague as well as a woman, worked my ass off to get here, harder than most. I ignored the sexist remarks and the unintentional brushes against my breasts; the unwanted hugs that lasted too long; warded off the pats on the butt without protest. So, you're not getting in my pants, capiche?"

Capiche!

I smile; another closet Italian.

"Duly noted, Detective Lopez," I say, managing a weak grin, my face on fire.

"Also, I know about Kate. I'm not going to be your rebound option," she adds.

She lifts her mug, takes a deep swallow and keeps her eyes riveted to mine.

I sit back, turn away and consider her comments. Like most women in law enforcement, hell, women in any occupation, she puts up with a lot of bullshit. I don't intend to be another in a long line of assholes treating her like a piece of meat.

I hoist my mug. "To us, as colleagues and damn fine detectives."

We drink and make small talk for the next couple of hours as the bar fills up. Murder and ghosts don't enter the conversation.

I take care of the check, wave away her protests, struggle to get to my feet; find my legs unstable, my vision blurred.

"Okay Italian Stallion" ---I had regaled her with my detailed knowledge of the Rocky films--- she says, as she wraps her arm around my waist in an attempt to steady me. I outweigh her by fifty pounds; she strains to keep me upright, gives up after a few tries and eases me back into the booth.

"No way you're driving tonight," she declares, breathless from her effort to help me. "I live close by. You can sleep on my couch."

Her voice sounds far away. I can't protest. I don't remember anything else until I awake in an unfamiliar room to the aroma of brewed coffee and bacon frying.

* * *

I still wear the clothes from the night before. A blanket covers my shoulders; a pillow cradles my head. I'm rubbing the nighttime funk from my eyes when Theresa Lopez walks into the room wearing a short blue robe and matching slippers. She waves a white spatula in her right hand. "How do you like your eggs?" she asks.

Bacon and eggs are my favorite meal any time of day but the thought of eating makes me nauseous. My stomach's doing flip-flops; my head throbbing.

Lopez sizes up the situation. "How about some black coffee?"

My hang dog expression says yes. She does a smart about face, and heads back toward the kitchen. As awful as I feel, I can't help ogling the tight muscles in her legs as she retreats; the robe too short to cover her buttocks. To me, that slight dimple between a woman's butt and thighs is super erotic. My little soldier, with a mind of his own, stirs, despite the scolding Lopez delivered to me at the bar the previous night; my resolve not to push her for sex weakens.

She comes back into the room with two cups of scalding java, hands me one and sits in a stuffed chair facing me. Her robe raises up. I catch a glimpse of white.

Lopez catches me gawking, shakes her head, places her cup on a low table between us, stands and sheds the housecoat, revealing a white bra and panties.

She scoots around the table and braces in front of me, legs not more than six inches from my face. She smells of fresh soap; her skin soft and smooth.

Her next words stun me: "Okay, Magliore. If this is what you want, go for it. But know this. If you do, you will never see me like this again. And when we go back to the office, I will ask Catebegian for another assignment and a new partner. You can explain why."

My face reddens. I remember the time my fifth-grade teacher caught me trying to peek up her skirt and banished me to the principal's office. Later, she made me tell my mother--in front of her-- what I had done.

Lopez's bold move is as humiliating. Thank God my mother isn't around. I sit back holding my coffee in both hands and mumble, "Scrambled."

"What?" Lopez demands, confused.

"I like my eggs scrambled."

"Wise decision," she says, slips her robe back on and stomps back to the kitchen. I avert my eyes this time.

We're still partners.

* * *

As partners, we're going to Fort Warren to inspect the murder scene. We've lost several hours to kick start our investigation since the murder happened yesterday afternoon. No problem. I'm not a disciple of the popular belief that the first forty-eight hours are critical, and chances of solving a murder after that time decline dramatically. I subscribe to former Colorado Springs Homicide Detective Joe Kenda's philosophy. "In murder cases, it's not about speed," he contends. "Speed doesn't help. A murder case is a spinning top on a table. It's perfectly balanced...put pressure on the wrong place, it goes off the table, and you never get it back."

Kenda should know. He solved ninety-two-percent of the over three-hundred cases he handled. A spectacular record. For us, whether we believe in the forty-eight-hour theory, or not, it doesn't matter. We start today; no choice.

Lopez called ahead and requested the Harbor Patrol pick us up at Windmill Point at the tip of the Hull peninsula, a narrow, jagged spit of land snaking into the Atlantic, a mile from our destination.

Still groggy, despite the excellent breakfast, and in my wrinkled clothes, I assure Lopez I'm well enough to go out to Georges Island. I'm not looking forward to a choppy boat ride though.

I still keep a room in Hull at the home of Karen Hundley, my former high school classmate and widow of the town's murdered police chief. I beg Lopez to stop there on the way, so I can change clothes.

She nixes the idea, taking pleasure in my discomfort and seeking payback for my crude behavior earlier.

"No stops," she notifies me in a tone brooking no rejoinder. "We're late already."

In no position to argue, I endure silence on the drive to Hull.

Two Harbor Patrol officers are waiting on Pemberton Pier at Windmill Point when we arrive. The pier, less than a hundred yards from the high school located across the highway, is on the bay side of the town sheltered from the turbulent Atlantic.

We park in front of a small restaurant and join the officers on a twenty-seven-foot-long high-speed intercept vessel named "Protector." The pilot executes a U-turn and navigates through the Hull Gut, a deep-water channel between the end of the peninsula and Peddocks Island, once a fortress like Fort Warren but of later vintage. Seagulls screaming like banshees' dive bomb us as we head out to sea. A couple of hardy fisherman in hip huggers standing on the rocky shore wave as we pass. They look like miniatures with the giant white wind turbine that provides electricity to the town whirring behind them. The day is clear. The Boston skyline visible to the west---a Norman Rockwell scene.

The trip is so quick I don't have time to up-chuck my eggs and bacon. I do turn a deep shade of green. Lopez looks pleased.

The boat officers, not involved in the investigation, drop us off at the Georges Island pier. We walk a short distance to a red brick visitors center to meet Rangers Alyce Crimshaw and Emiliano Santana. Harbor Officer Zack Holt, who helped interview people after the Dimick homicide, is also present.

Crimshaw takes the lead.

"We detained fifty-one people at the time of the murder," she explains. "Sixteen with me including chaperones. Emmy, referring to Santana, shepherded a contingent of twenty Japanese tourists, twenty-one with their interpreter, on the north side of the island when the murder occurred. Emmy supervised them at all times, even escorted them to the restrooms for breaks as a group. That leaves fourteen unsupervised by our staff; three sets of parents, two with kids under six years old and four others on their own---two college kids exploring together and two older men doing the same."

She takes a breath before continuing. "Officer Holt interviewed the adults, including the male and female college students. He recorded their personal information and used a mobile scanner to take their fingerprints which he ran through local and national criminal databases. Two matches popped; one male parent arrested on a DUI two years ago and one of the single men cited for disturbing the peace during a bar altercation last year. No other hints of criminal activity, certainly not murder."

She offers additional information on two of those questioned. "The college students, a Jennifer Lewis and Hayward Paulson, attend Boston University and were here to research a Civil War project. They planned to write an article for the school newspaper debunking the "Lady in Black" story. But after the incident both appeared shaken. I suspect their expose, if they ever publish it, may take a different slant.

Both Lopez and I laughed.

"The high school kids and chaperones stayed with me including lunch and scheduled bathroom breaks," Crimshaw reports. "I recorded their names and school contact information but didn't question them further. My gut tells me none of them did it."

Gut instinct works sometimes but not always; depends on how long you've been on the job. Crimshaw is a park ranger not a trained investigator. We'll grill the kids later.

"So, they all remained with you the entire time?" Lopez probes.

Crimshaw shrugs. "Well, the chaperones, as adults, take snack or restroom stops as needed, but according to their statements, did so with their spouses or as a group."

"So, you didn't always have eyes on them," Lopez presses.

"True," Crimshaw admits with a sigh.

In, an attempt to get off the hot seat, she turns and grabs a folder from a table covered with brochures on the Civil War, the Boston Harbor Islands and Fort Warren.

"This contains a summary of our interviews, the fingerprint results and their contact info," she says, handing the binder to Lopez.

"We believe we can eliminate the parents as suspects, the Japanese and the high school kids with me," she adds. "The married couples swear they hung together the whole time. No reason to doubt them; no apparent connection to Dimick. The college students appear innocent enough. We'll leave the in-depth research on them to you."

"What about the two older guys?" I ask.

"Claim they came together and explored together," she says, pursing her lips. "I believe they're gay.

"Not that that has a bearing on anything," she adds, looking away, embarrassed.

"Thanks, for the update," I say, ignoring the gay reference. "We'll review everyone's statements and follow up where necessary."

Crimshaw nods.

"I assume you searched everyone?" I ask.

"Yes. We separated the men and women and examined them individually in the reception center. Found nothing pertinent. The college girl had a couple of joints in her purse, which I confiscated."

Lopez and I laugh, thank Crimshaw for the help and request to see the crime scene.

We all follow her into the fort across a wooden bridge and through a dank hallway. We cut across the parade ground and enter the former prisoner's quarters through a narrow opening. Once inside, we're awed by the cavernous tunnels and intrigued by the numerous, dark passageways to smaller rooms. A killer could disappear here and stash a weapon in any one of a number of nooks and crannies.

"Going to be difficult to find the knife or whatever the assailant used," I say, making a sweeping gesture with my arm.

Crimshaw nods. "We're bringing in a group of police cadets from Boston to help. The island will be closed until we find something or turn up empty-handed."

The likelihood of their success is remote. The murder didn't seem like a spur of the moment act; killer did some prior planning and no doubt scouted out a secure place to hide his paraphernalia.

"This is it," Crimshaw says interrupting my thoughts. The bleak crime scene is cordoned off with standard yellow tape.

Lopez and I pull out Maglites borrowed from the rangers, slip on gloves and booties and duck under the flimsy barrier and into the room. The dirt covered cement floor is strewn with small pebbles. A brown patch of dried blood lay close to one wall. We hug an opposite wall and play our lights over and around the room. It will take a floodlight to illuminate the area to the point of finding anything worthwhile; a job for the state CSU boys and girls.

We exit the room, discard our gloves and booties and walk down the tunnel for fifty yards or so; stop in a stretch illuminated by sunlight streaming in through apertures in the wall. That's the nature of Fort Warren; some areas dark and foreboding, others well lit.

We thank Crimshaw for the brief excursion and prepare to return to the reception building when I ask another question.

"Could the killer escape the island on a concealed boat?"

Crimshaw's face flushes. She lowers her eyes and answers in a soft, unsteady voice. "Didn't have to be concealed."

"What," I say, incredulous.

"We allow private craft to moor offshore on a first-come, first-served basis and row in by dinghy. We also maintain slips adjacent to the pier that need to be reserved."

"Why didn't you tell us earlier?" Lopez inquires, in a less biting tone than mine.

"No staff member recalls any boat leaving around the time of the murder."

"But there were some here?"

"Yes."

"And gone by the time Dimick's body was discovered and everyone rounded up."

"Yes," Crimshaw replies. Her voice quivers. "I just didn't think it relevant. I'm sorry. We're not used to dealing with murder."

She's distraught. No use badgering her about the omission.

"Is there any record of who those boats belonged to?" I ask.

Crimshaw shakes her head, turns and marches away, a hand clasped over her mouth.

We stand without conversing for two or three minutes until Lopez breaks the silence. "You think forensics will turn up anything?"

"Can't say. Those people are experts and sometimes perform miracles, but it will be tough to extract evidence from the murder scene.

"If the cadet search uncovers the weapon, and I don't hold out much hope of that, we might recover prints or extract DNA. But now, based on what Crimshaw revealed, it's conceivable the killer carried it with him and escaped by boat."

Lopez shakes her head. "A huge risk. He might run into somebody, ranger or tourist, as he made his way to the shore or pier. Odds are he stashed it.

"And that person," she continues, "if not among the people detained, knew Dimick would be here, lay in wait, saw an opportunity when Dimick and the girl ditched the field trip and separated from the group."

I nod and add, "Someone from the school? Or an acquaintance with a grudge? Somebody Dimick pissed off."

"Yes," Lopez says. "But I don't buy the idea of the killer waiting to follow Dimick to the island, killing him, then escaping by boat. Gotta be a student or staffer from the school and on the field trip. We need to question Dimick's colleagues and his friends. Find out if he had any enemies. Two of the male chaperones taught with Dimick. Maybe they weren't bosom buddies. Crimshaw admits they were free to roam around. One of them does the deed, blends into the crowd when chaos ensues. No one gives him a second look."

I offer another perspective. "How about the wives? Women are capable of murder."

Lopez disagrees. "Slitting a throat is not a woman's method of committing murder. They have been known to stab someone in a fit of rage, but they prefer poison or pills, bashing someone over the head with a blunt object, even drowning and asphyxiating them."

"Really? You know this how?"

"I read a lot. You should try it sometime."

I fall back as if in shock, but press my point. "I'm not prepared to eliminate anyone, male or female, gay or straight, student or parent. Except maybe the Japanese."

Lopez laughs. "I'll buy that. They wouldn't know Michael Dimick from Michael Jackson."

I don't touch that line but I'm ready with one of my own.

"This could be like looking for a ghost," I say, deadpanned.

Lopez rolls her eyes.

I thought it was funny.

Chapter 10

Magliore

Soon, I'm not in the mood for jokes.

On the way back from Fort Warren, I got a cell phone call from a physician I befriended at the South Shore Hospital. My girlfriend, Kate Maxwell, died.

I show up at the hospital in a fog of grief and disbelief, and find Kate's room empty, her parents standing in the doorway clutching each other for support. Neither speak, their anguish overwhelming.

My feet are leaden as I walk up to the distraught couple and put my arms around them. My tears join theirs, my shoulders shake, mourning for what might have been. The encounter is brief. We part in silence, and I don't linger. I drag myself down the corridor and out through the metal swinging doors.

Kate had been wounded by an angry, deranged Quincy, Massachusetts cop who held her responsible for the murder of his lover, the Hull police chief. The chief was investigating a construction company with ties to a Mexican Cartel engaged in fraud and human trafficking. Kate, an executive in the firm, knew nothing of their scheme. But since two of the cartel's henchmen killed the chief, she paid the price along with her bosses. She has been in a coma since the shooting thirteen months ago, never regaining consciousness despite the prayers and constant vigil of her devoted parents. God sometimes doesn't answer such appeals, or he does, just not in the way we'd like.

Kate's death hit me like a runaway truck. My relationships with women over the years have been sporadic and unfulfilling. My fault, or theirs, for expecting things from me I couldn't or wouldn't give---like unconditional love. I tell myself I was willing to offer that to Kate. Now, we'll never know.

I'm not a Neanderthal, though expressing affection is not one of my strong points. Perhaps it's my job. Cops distrust people. Or maybe it's the residue of my parents' lack of showing outward expressions of love. Or might be I'm an asshole, as many of my friends and colleagues suggest. Whatever the reason, I've blown through many relationships. The "Magliore Curse."

I did have a long-term connection once, if you can call six months long-term. In high school. Her name was Angela, a cheerleader; Italian, black hair and eyes. Wonderful smile that lit up her face and made her eyes dance. She had curves in all the right places, as eighteen-year-old girls do. Breasts pert and firm. She let me fondle them once or twice; never let my hands drift to other places---which of course made me want her even more. Our romance ended when I went off to college in California to play football. She stayed in Hull, went to work. We lost touch. She attended our last high school reunion with some other guy. We never got to talk. A brief hug our lone contact.

I feel bad making Kate's death all about me. Her parents were so distraught I worried about their survival. Her father acted brave but his eyes revealed the depth of his anguish. He won't recover soon from the death of his only child.

I offered no words of condolence to them at the hospital, none seemed appropriate. After our group hug, I walked away without looking back, another chapter in the book of my life finished.

I'm enraged with no immediate outlet for my wrath. The man who shot Kate is dead, a misguided soul. The cartel organization he helped take down is in tatters. I don't regret my role in their demise, but grieve for the consequences.

It isn't long before I realize one battle has been won, but the war is far from over.

Chapter 11

Magliore

Kate Maxwell is being interred in a small cemetery in Duxbury, a town thirty-five miles south of Boston where she spent her childhood and where her parents still live. A sign on a concrete stanchion supporting ornate metal gates on the roadway leading into the graveyard notes the site can trace its origin back to 1637; old, yet not unusual in New England. Not far away, the Myles Standish burial ground, the oldest maintained cemetery in the United States, dates to 1634. I know this stuff as a local history buff, but it's doubtful few, if any, of the other mourner's care about the age of the place. They came to show their respect to Kate's parents and to mourn her passing.

Many friends and relatives crowd around the grave site as the minister offers final comforting words to her devastated mother and father who sit clinging to each other as he speaks.

Captain Catebegian and I stand four rows back from the casket, not wanting to intrude on the ritual or draw attention. I was her significant other at the time of her death, but we hadn't been together long. Catebegian's connection is through me. Nevertheless, we thought it appropriate to attend the graveside services. We skipped the church ritual.

Like most in attendance, we bow our heads as the clergyman finishes with prayers of condolence and hope. For some reason, I glance to my left, to the access road adjacent to the grave site. Two men in blue striped suits stand along a row of parked cars, arms folded, staring in our direction. From my experience, they look more like thugs than grieving friends of Kate or her family.

Maybe long-lost cousins.

Hah!

I suspect they're hit-men for the Cartel de Jalisco Nueva Generacion, the Mexican cartel I helped break up when investigating the murder of my friend, Randy Hundley. He stumbled on to the cartel's construction fraud and human trafficking scheme when vetting them as the contractor for a proposed Hull redevelopment project. His snooping cost him his life and now Kate's.

As I consider my options in the face of this potential threat, the two guys get back into their black Chevy Suburban, maneuver out of their parking spot, and drive away.

I could be wrong about who they are, or they decided a gathering with many witnesses not a proper venue to take me out. Or, the sight of Catebegian, a formidable adversary at six-six, two-sixty-five, scared them off. Whatever their purpose, they left, but their presence here was troubling. A not-so-subtle warning that bygones are not bygones as far as the cartel is concerned, and I better watch my back.

I expect we have not seen the last of them. Their friends tried to kill me once before, attempting to make it look like an auto accident. Forced me off the highway and into some trees on the edge of a lake. Though banged up, I suffered no serious injuries.

Lady luck was with me. I hope she continues to stand by my side, real or not, dressed in black or not.

I don't count on it.

Chapter 12

Magliore

My head is thumping like a drum and bugle corps is marching through it; my eyes are scratchy, my nose running. I'm not a drinker; wine with dinner, a beer or two with friends, seldom touch the hard stuff. I made an exception today. The day of Kate's burial. Spent the afternoon downing shots of whiskey at a sports bar in Hanover and stopped at a package store after that and bought a bottle of Jim Beam. I drove back to the cemetery in Duxbury where Kate is buried and now sit alone, back against a tree, on a grassy embankment overlooking her grave site.

Kate is interred in a new section. The older one lies to my right behind an aging four-foot-high fence. The barrier is leaning over as if too tired to stand guard anymore. Lichens cover many of the old gravestones, some have toppled and lay in pieces, others are weathered, obliterating their inscriptions. The men, woman and children entombed beneath them are long forgotten, and the messages left behind of interest to historians, the curious, or nuts like me. I like wandering through old cemeteries inspecting the engravings on the grave markers.

Man! This whiskey is smooth. Lucky I'm sitting down, or did I fall down. Can't remember, don't care. Feel warm inside.

But I digress. I got interested in tombstone inscriptions while vacationing on Cape Cod with friends one summer. Took a girlfriend at the time, can't remember her name, into a cemetery to be alone. Captivated by the etchings, she started reading them aloud. Although inebriated, we were both touched and amused by the epitaphs. Some sad. Some funny. Most reflecting the hardships of the time.

Many children died in infancy in the sixteen and seventeen hundreds. I still recall one. The kid was less than a year old.

> My life in infant days was spent
> While to my parents I was lent
> One smiling look to them I gave
> And then descended to the grave

People today would be offended, I suspect, if someone used that poem to memorialize their child. Not P.C.

The gravestones seem to be dancing with some levitating now and then. Whiskey can make anything possible. I clench my eyes closed to stop the movement, and try to recall a gravestone inscription that reminds me of Kate, her life and mine. After some trouble focusing and another swallow of golden brew, it comes to me:

Remember me as you pass by
As you are now, so once was I.
As I am now, as you must be,
Prepare for death and follow me.

I remember you Kate, your smell, your laugh, your smile, your perfect skin, your red hair. I'll follow you in death someday, but not soon, I hope, although in my line of work longevity is not guaranteed. Not that anyone would care.

Shit. I sound like a lonely sap; which is what I am. I need another swig of whiskey to buck up my sorry ass spirits.

Well, Catebegian would miss me. He'd lose his favorite whipping boy. Deep down I think he likes me, but that might be the booze talking. I'm rambling but no one's around to shut me up.

Shit. The whiskey's gone.

* * *

I hold up the bottle to inspect it, to ensure no liquid remains, when it explodes in my hand. Bark from the tree I'm resting against disintegrates. Fragments shower my head and shoulders. I stare at the shattered remains of the Jim Beam until my addled brain sends me a delayed message. Move idiot. Somebody's shooting at you.

Despite my slowed reflexes, I roll down the mound I'm perched on and land behind a moss-covered obelisk, one of those monuments with a square base and a pyramid shaped top. Good cover now, but I'm a tad slow. A bullet grazes my left arm ripping through my shirt but not drawing much blood. Rounds from automatic rifles ping off the tombstone, chipping pieces of stone. I hug the ground. Bullets whistle overhead and tear up chunks of turf near my face.

Though blinded by dirt clogs, I'm able to find and grasp my Smith & Wesson M&P 45 in a holster secured to my belt at the small of my back. It's accurate and reliable but small potatoes compared to the high-powered weapons pinning me down. I reach out and fire off a couple of rounds to keep my attackers at bay while I blink and pull the muck from my eyes.

Being used for target practice sobers me up. I realize I'm carrying my cell phone. The Massachusetts State Police maintain a barracks in Norwell. Troopers from that station patrol Duxbury as part of its sixty-eight square miles of coverage. Norwell is twenty-five minutes north, too far to provide immediate help. A squad car may be closer than that; at least I hope so.

I punch in the number of the barracks from my contact list as bullets buzz over and around me like a swarm of angry bees. The female dispatcher answers on the second ring and I shout out my situation over the din. "This is detective Magliore. Badge 1965. I'm under fire at the All-Saints Cemetery in Duxbury. Need assistance ASAP."

I cut off before she can question me and dart to another four-foot-high marker six feet from my location. The move catches my assailants off guard for a second or two before another volley rips through my left pant leg, this time drawing blood and stinging like hell. My pants become saturated with blood as my thigh oozes red.

My adrenaline kicks in to stave off the pain. I peer around the right side of my cover and return fire still unsure of their exact location or how many there are. I have two ten round clips to hold out for a while or take out a couple of the bastards if they rush me.

Me and Davey Crockett.

I prepare to snap off another two rounds when sirens echo in the distance; troopers on the way or responding to another call. Perhaps the goons attacking me won't know which and panic. I steal another look around the edge of the tombstone, and when I don't draw incoming, make a bold move although some, like my boss, might label it stupid.

I jump up, assume a firing position—like they teach us on the range--legs bent, arms outstretched, but not rigid, and spray bullets in a small arc from left to right, then dive for cover again. Sweat tinged with dirt drips into my eyes. I tense waiting for the next fusillade.

No response.

Nothing but silence.

My muscles ache. Head throbs.

I wait. Weak from the loss of blood.

Still quiet.

No movement.

The sound of sirens draws closer.

I chance it again and stand up, sweeping the terrain with my eyes in a one-eighty arc anticipating a volley of bullets.

Nothing.

I holster my weapon as three police cruisers---two from the Duxbury PD and one from the state police---pull up at the cemetery entrance. Officers from the three cars all exit, guns drawn. I hobble toward them hands in the air, badge displayed in my right palm. I get within ten yards of the group when one cop yells, "Hold it right there."

Not the reception I expect. The hard expressions on their faces tell me a wrong move might spook them.

"Detective Magliore," I shout, "Plymouth County D.A.'s Office. I called this in."

One of the Duxbury officer's orders me to get on my knees disregarding my explanation and identification. My heart races and my legs wobble.

"I don't think I can officer," I explain. "I'm weak and I've been hit."

I had ignored my wound, adrenaline staving off the pain, but now my pant leg is saturated with blood and the ground beneath my feet turns a reddish brown. Before I can say anything else, I collapse and lose consciousness.

* * *

For the second time since returning to Massachusetts from California, I awake in a bed in the South Shore Hospital in Weymouth. Also, for the second time, I open my eyes to the sight of Ed "Big Cat" Catebegian standing in the room, arms folded, mouth twisted in a half grin, half grimace.

He's a menacing figure with his shaved head, scar on his right cheek. Once an inveterate tobacco chewer, he's trying to kick the habit by chomping on massive amounts of gum. A wad now pushes against his lower lip. Reminds me of those TV closeups of baseball managers on the first step of a dugout surveying the field, cheeks puffed to the max, brown liquid dripping down their chins.

Disgusting!

Catebegian offers his usual uplifting encouragement. "Who did you piss off this time, Magliore?"

He warms the cockles of my heart.

"I swear I don't know, Cat," I say.

With no hint of a smile, he responds: "Captain to you detective."

"Yes, exalted one," I say, trying to melt the ice in the room. Catebegian remains stoic. Perhaps as a captain he's under more pressure than he had been as a lieutenant. I didn't want to add to it. He went to bat for me when I applied to the state police. My drunken escapade doesn't help my chances of sticking around or his standing in the department. I regret putting him in a difficult spot.

"I can see the wheels turning in that brain of yours, Magliore, what are you thinking?" he says, shaking me out of my brief reverie.

"A hell of a lot of firepower used against me," I say. "Did the CSU turn up anything?"

"Many spent cartridges from AK47 assault rifles, the favorite weapon of cartel gangs and terrorists. Since I doubt you've had time to antagonize any terrorists, could be our friends in the CJNG are still unhappy with you. They showed up at Kate's funeral hoping to get a shot, no pun intended, at you, or me, for that matter. They backed off. Too many witnesses, I suspect. You gave them a second opportunity by showing up blitzed and alone at the cemetery.

"I thought we crushed those guys when we destroyed their New England operation, Captain, sir," I respond, showing proper deference to my superior.

A slight upward movement of Catabegian's lips indicates the ice might be melting.

"The cartels are a multi-headed hydra," he says. "Cut off one and another grows. The way to snuff them out is to kill the immortal head in the middle like Hercules did and bury it under a rock. In our case a jail."

My turn to smile. "Wow! I didn't know you were a mythology buff."

"There's a lot you don't know about me, Magliore and if you keep this up, I doubt you'll learn much more."

Couldn't argue with that, but I hadn't done anything in several months to put a target on my back. Had to be residual from our dealings with the Jalisco Cartel.

And if I'm a target, those around me are also at risk. Catebegian won't back down but my new partner, Theresa Lopez, doesn't deserve to be placed in jeopardy.

Nevertheless, my juices are boiling. "This is personal, Captain. These sons of bitches ran down my friend Randy Hundley like a dog in the street. They didn't pull the trigger on the gun that killed Kate but their actions put her in harm's way. They'll regret pissing me off. I repeat an Italian expression worthy of Michael Corleone: "*Vendicarsi*. I'll take my revenge. Count on it."

Catebegian shakes his head. "Remember the old proverb, my friend, before you begin a journey of revenge, dig two graves. One for your enemy and one for yourself.'"

Now he's a philosopher.

Unmoved, I retort. "They'll be more than one grave for sure, but none will be mine."

Such hubris often gets me into trouble.

Chapter 13

Miguel Chavez

Miguel Chavez was pissed.

The two Sicario hit men sent to dispatch the meddling cop, Magliore, failed and they were now hiding out in one of his stash houses in Connecticut. Later he would get them transported back to Mexico.

His first instinct was to eliminate them. He didn't suffer fools. His men must know a botched mission came with consequences, for them as well as their targets. Mistakes cost lives. Their fiasco alerted the cop to be on guard and might lead him to start snooping around their operation again. They didn't need this distraction.

Yet, as a new father, Chavez, experienced a once unknown feeling--- compassion. He opted to give the young men another chance, make them sweat it out, give them as many shit jobs as possible to earn back his trust.

Miguel Chavez was a Regio, *Regionales*, (regional officer) for the Cartel de Jalisco Nueva Generacion, (CJNG) one of the six cartels the Drug Enforcement Administration (DEA) tagged as having the greatest drug trafficking influence in the United States along with the Sinaloa's, Beltran Levya and Juarez and Gulf organizations. Miguel ranks above the Los Capos (Captains) who supervise lieutenants and other lower gang members. As a Regio, he oversees the New England area and is responsible for controlling illicit drug distribution.

In retrospect, he regretted the attack on Magliore. It jeopardized his mission of returning CJNG to dominance in the American northeast after their failure dabbling with construction fraud and human trafficking. That disaster left them vulnerable to their rivals, the Sinaloa's, who attempted a take-over of their drug operation. Chavez beat back that attempt by employing some local gangs and paying them with cocaine, meth and oxycodone knock-offs cut with fentanyl.

He now managed dealers throughout New England and made headway with college and high school students, sometimes recruiting teachers with a taste for his product. Magliore was not worthy of his attention unless he threatened their operation. If he posed any risk, Chavez would direct his *Soldatos* to take him out.

Chavez had a bolder plan in mind. He would concentrate on that. Nevertheless, he posted a man outside the hospital where Magliore was recovering to shadow the cop; report back. Not make a move unless so ordered.

* * *

Miguel faced greater problems than an interfering police detective. He slammed his fist on the kitchen table in his rental home in Lynn, Massachusetts, spilling his morning coffee and jolting the *Soldados* sitting with him. He was angered by a Boston Globe story entitled, **Huge Drug Bust in 3 states nets 25 cartel members**.

The article read as follows.

> **A multi-agency task force of the state police, FBI, DEA and Homeland Security raided five stash houses in Massachusetts, New Hampshire and Maine and arrested 25 men and women associated with the notorious CJNG Mexican cartel.**
>
> **Brenda Jordan, the newly appointed Special Agent-in-Charge (SAC) of the Boston Office of the FBI, reported that along with the individuals arrested, the raids netted over 150 pounds of methamphetamine, 100 pounds of cocaine, 15 pounds of heroin and 800 fentanyl tablets disguised as oxycodone.**
>
> **Fentanyl, said Jordan, is one of the world's deadliest narcotics, fifty times more potent than heroin and deadlier because street pushers have no clue what is a safe dose. Nor do they care. Doctors prescribe it in micrograms, not the milligrams dealers use to mix it with other substances; as little as two milligrams can kill.**
>
> **Fentanyl is responsible for the catastrophic increase in overdose deaths in New England, Jordan continued, particularly in the small towns of New Hampshire and Maine.**
>
> **DEA agent, Phillip Murray, added that raids such as this go a long way to disrupt and dismantle organizations like CJNG which smuggle drugs across the Mexican border, and prey on our most vulnerable citizens. Investigations of drug trafficking are ongoing, Murray said, and they expect to make future arrests.**

Miguel Chavez dropped the newspaper to the floor, took a sip of his now cold coffee and looked from one associate to another. Each lowered his gaze to the table and shifted in their chairs waiting for the explosion.

None came.

Chavez kept his voice calm, a twitch in the eyes betraying concern, nothing more. "We must find a better way to get our product across the border and distribute it. We cannot let the authorities defeat us. Our future depends on our success. Understand?"

Both men nodded. But they were soldiers. Soldiers followed orders, supplied muscle. Any trouble from the big boss, "El Mencho," any retaliation for the loss of money, for product, would fall on Chavez. They would continue to march under someone new if it came to that. It was how things worked.

They left Chavez and headed to the nearest restaurant for breakfast to await instructions, from Chavez or another big-shot. Didn't matter. Breakfast burritos would be tasty either way.

* * *

After his two associates left, Miguel Chavez leaned back in his chair and rubbed his brow. He fought his way up the chain of command of the CJNG to become a trusted member of the leadership structure, a Regio. "El Mencho" himself selected him for this assignment. The American northeast was ripe for the picking; demand for their products high. They had forced aside their primary challenger in the region—the Sinaloa's.

The fucking FBI Special Agent in Charge quoted in the Boston Globe nailed it though. The raid on their stash houses hurt; their pipeline disrupted; valuable Diablos (drug dealers) taken out of the equation. The damage must be repaired and the flow of drugs started again. The Sinaloa's were sure to try to take advantage, regain their lost territory. A bloody fight loomed. Chavez's position, his life, hung in the balance. "El Mencho's" loyalty was not unconditional. Profits outweighed friendship.

Chavez continued to wrestle with the problem when his girlfriend, Camila, stepped into the kitchen wearing a bathrobe. She stayed up most of the night with their newborn, her eyes slits, her face paunchy, hair askew. Though not married, they had lived together for five years and had a baby girl.

Camila shuffled over to the table with a fresh cup of coffee, replacing the now cold brew in front of Chavez. She placed her arm around his shoulders, sat on his lap and kissed his forehead. Her closeness and body warmth relaxed Miguel. He pulled her tight to him, buried his head in her ample bosom like he had as a boy with his mother seeking comfort or forgiveness.

"We will be okay, Mio," Camila whispered, stroking his hair.

Chapter 14

Miguel Chavez

Miguel left Camila to attend to their baby and drove to the shoreline. Lynn was a blue-collar town, a suburb of Boston. Once home to shoe factories and iron works, now striving to become a center for art and culture. The house he rented was nondescript, in a quiet neighborhood close to a park, small front yard, swimming pool in back, unused and covered. Neighbors offered a wave, a smile, but no welcoming basket of fruit or bottle of wine.

Perfect.

Miguel needed and wanted privacy. He liked Lynn for its proximity to Boston and the ocean. The rental property was a ten-minute drive from the Lynn Shore Reservation where he could walk along the beach, sit at a picnic table to think or bask in the sun or a cool offshore breeze.

Miguel survived the mean streets and alleys of Ciudad, Juarez, Mexico by sheer force of will and a knack for entrepreneurship. He bought things. He sold things. His enterprises brought him to the attention of cartel operatives---dealers, gunmen for hire.

Bright and resourceful, he elbowed aside rivals and now honchoed the drug pipeline to northeast New England. But the recent setback delivered by the American authorities challenged his survival skills and toughness. He needed an audacious plan.

One must take chances to succeed.

His organization utilized the many ways to smuggle contraband into the United States: cars, product stashed in hidden compartments and driven across the border by mules (people desperate for cash); private planes landed at remote, forgotten airfields; miniature submarines (elaborate and ingenious, but unreliable); intricate underground passageways like that used to facilitate the prison escape of "El Chapo" Guzman of the Sinaloa Cartel.

Problems existed with all methods, of course. Mules were intercepted, cars searched and drugs seized, planes tracked and airfields monitored, tunnels uncovered and filled in, mini-subs floundered on their own or were captured by the U.S. Coast Guard.

Miguel considered boats to be the safest method---fishing boats in particular. Fishermen plied their trade every day; their craft common on the high seas. As long as they're registered, the Coast Guard ignored them.

New England's extensive coastline, from Cape Cod, Massachusetts, to Bar Harbor, Maine, offered many safe inlets to land and offload their goods. As he looked out into Boston Harbor, the sketch of an idea percolated in his mind. Bold and precarious, it might not last forever, but would get the flow of drugs started again and give him time to develop a more formidable, lasting strategy.

Along with the newspaper article about the recent massive drug bust, another item described a murder at Fort Warren on Georges Island, a place he and Camila visited as tourists before the baby came. He remembered the dark archways and rooms, perfect for stashing product. And something else he had in mind.

The story made reference to the ghost on the island, folklore which still captivated the imagination of visitors and frightened some. Miguel smiled. This phantom might aid his plan. Although of Mexican heritage and familiar with family tales of the supernatural, he dismissed such yarns as fantasy, but would use anything to his advantage.

He fished in his wallet and retrieved the card given to him by one of the rangers at Fort Warren who spoke fluent Spanish. He, Miguel and Camilla talked about Mexico and family. The lawman, his guard down, let slip his parents crossed the U.S. southern border illegally years ago. Never became citizens, an oversight the ranger would come to regret. Miguel and his friends would pay Emeliano Santana a visit, convince him to cooperate. Threaten him if he balked. An inside man at the fort was critical to the success of his budding plan.

Chapter 15

Emeliano Santana

Emeliano, "Emmy," Santana, thirty-five, divorced, lived alone in a rental property in Cohasset. He was named after Emeliano Zapata, a Mexican revolutionary leader who championed peasant farmers and organized the overthrow of the country's dictatorial government. Santana's parents prayed he would also be a leader someday, perhaps a modern-day champion of immigrants working to enter the United States.

Emeliano didn't care about Zapata, the Mexican Revolution or Mexicans in general. Born in the United States, he spoke Spanish at home or when his job required it. He obtained an associate's degree from a community college to further his career. He distanced himself from Hispanics as much as possible and sought out and married an Anglo woman, although that didn't work out.

On an overcast Monday afternoon, Emeliano pulled into the long driveway off Forest Avenue leading to his rental house. He stopped in front of his garage and exited his vehicle surprised when another car he didn't recognize came to a stop behind him. Three men in suits emerged from a black Chevrolet Suburban and approached him, the shortest of the three in front. The other two hung back, their hands at their sides, looking like secret service agents without the recognizable ear pieces.

The smaller man introduced himself as Miguel Chavez and handed Santana a card identifying him as the area representative of Elite Shipping and Transportation.

Santana, puzzled, thought he recognized the man, but couldn't place him. He had no dealings with any shipping companies and prepared to ask why they were contacting him when Chavez spoke: "We have a business proposition for you, Mr. Santana."

Santana shrugged, still confused. "I'm a park ranger. What can I help you with?"

"You are assigned to this Fort Warren in Boston Harbor, are you not?" Chavez responded.

"Yes but…." Chavez held up his hand before Santana finished his sentence.

"We need a secure place to ship some goods north," he said.

Santana shook his head from side to side. "The island is an historical preserve owned and regulated by the Massachusetts Department of Conservation and Recreation. They don't do transactions for private companies."

"We understand *señor*. That is why we come to you."

Santana's eyes widened. Now he understood the three "businessmen" were proposing something illegal. He wanted no part of it.

"I'm sorry, I can't help you," he said.

Chavez smiled and his eyes bore into the park ranger. "Oh! Yes you can. There are three reasons for you to do so."

A trickle of sweat wended its way down Santana's spine. He stepped backward fearing the men might attack him.

"Your mother and father are undocumented, are they not? A shame if La Migra got their names."

Santana's parents had been smuggled across the border so his mother could give birth to him over thirty-five years ago. He trembled and clasped his hands in front to calm himself. He assumed they were safe by now.

"And your wife," Chavez continued, could have an accident. "This country's roads can be treacherous."

"We are divorcing," Emeliano blurted.

"Si. But you still care for her do you not?"

Emeliano hung his head. He still loved his estranged wife, the break-up not his idea. He wanted no harm to come to her sensing the threat these men presented. Trapped, the safety of his family depended on his cooperating. He needed time to think. He nodded and dropped his eyes to the ground.

"I will do whatever you ask," he said.

Chavez beamed. "We will contact you soon, *señor.*"

He and his companions retreated to their car, completed a U-turn and departed, leaving Emeliano standing in the driveway shaking.

Crushed and paralyzed by fear, he had few options. The police, colleagues, supervisors, all out of the question. After much agonizing, he settled on the one person he trusted; Mavis Fisher, his therapist. He had a scheduled session with her the following afternoon.

He hoped the thugs didn't have him under surveillance. If so, he might endanger Mavis.

* * *

Santana fidgeted in his overstuffed, wing back chair, rubbed his hands together as if washing them in a sink, crossed and uncrossed his legs, kept his eyes riveted to the floor, remained silent.

He sat in Mavis Fisher's office for his scheduled session. He began therapy three months earlier after his wife walked out, blindsided by her decision. After a year of marriage, she left a note on the dining room table informing him she didn't love him anymore; no contact with her since, except through her lawyer. His talks with Mavis helped, yet now he faced an even greater problem. The threats posed by the three goons who visited him a few days ago.

Fisher waited. Most patients couldn't stand silence and blurted out their concerns and fears after a moment or two. Emeliano kept quiet for so long she prepared to ask a probing question when he bolted upright, fear in his eyes. "I don't know what to do."

The flare-up didn't disturb Mavis. Emotional outbursts during therapy not uncommon. Her patients sought help after a great deal of soul-searching and encouragement by friends or relatives or when their problems became overwhelming.

"Did you confront your wife, Emmy? Is that why you're so upset?"

Santana got up and paced back and forth, head bowed, arms around his chest, hugging himself. He stopped and turned toward Fisher. "This does not concern her," he said, in a dismissive tone.

Fisher remained calm, unoffended. "Can you tell me what it is, Emmy?" she asked, continuing to use his nickname to create a closer connection.

"That's just it," he said, "I'm not sure I can explain. And I'm afraid I'm being watched. I may be putting you in danger."

Fisher had been threatened before, several times by irate husbands terrified their beleaguered wives might be sharing intimate secrets or revealing physical or emotional abuse. As a result, Fisher established a close relationship with the Hingham police which included a direct line to the watch commander who could dispatch units to her office within minutes. Her secretary once utilized it when an enraged husband stormed into the office brandishing a gun. Officers arrived in under five minutes and deescalated the situation without injury to anyone.

In this case, there was no immediate threat, no reason to sound an alarm. Fisher needed more information, something specific.

"Why do you think I'm in danger, Emmy?" she probed.

He shook his head, wrung his hands together, looked away, distraught, uncommunicative.

"I don't know Ms. Fisher. I don't know."

"Please tell me what you can, Emmy. I can't help you if you aren't forthcoming. Is it work related?"

Emeliano blanched. "I shouldn't have come here," he stammered. "I shouldn't have come."

Sadness and fear reflected in his eyes, he walked to the door, opened it and left.

Fisher sensed trouble ahead for Emeliano. She considered contacting the authorities, but didn't want to escalate the matter, put him at risk or violate doctor/patient confidentiality. Her gut feeling did not constitute evidence of an impending criminal act.

Emeliano served as a park ranger at Fort Warren. An article in the Quincy Patriot Ledger, a newspaper chronicling events on the South Shore of Massachusetts, reported a grisly murder there. Could that be the basis of his stress? He paled when she mentioned work.

But speculating in her profession was never wise. She couldn't help him without more information; sensed he was in no condition to give it. Yet, waiting for him to return, if he returned, might be too late. These situations put therapists, like priests, in a bind. They often had knowledge that should be shared with the police, but the rules governing their profession forbid it.

Fisher, no priest, would report any evidence she possessed that might prevent a crime or harm to an individual, whether a patient or not. In this instance, she was stymied. Dealing with troubled individuals was the core of her work . She couldn't contact authorities at the first hint of concern.

Was this different?

She sat alone for over fifteen minutes, struggling with what to do, if anything. One option she bandied about was unorthodox and borderline unprofessional, more than dubious if honest with herself.

She leaned forward in her chair, rested her elbows on her knees and held her head in her hands. Her solution to one person's problems might create another for one of her other patients. A lawman with issues of his own.

Chapter 16

Lopez and Magliore

After my brief hospital stay---I'm a difficult guy to kill---Lopez and I resume our investigation of the Mike Dimick murder. I'm grateful Captain Catebegian didn't sideline me. My wounds proved less serious than feared. Lots of blood, but no bones splintered or vital organs punctured. I'm good to go albeit with a slight limp and enough stitches in my arm and leg to cover a baseball.

We start at Bridge Hill Academy where Dimick taught U.S. History. We'll concentrate first on the students and staff on the field trip to Fort Warren before interviewing the two Boston University students. They may remember something they didn't think about or report when questioned by the park rangers. College kids are supposed to be bright and perceptive, right?

Two of our colleagues will follow up with the adults on Georges Island that day, although a preliminary check indicated none had any apparent connection to Dimick. We agree that the Japanese tourists are not suspects. The wild card is the possibility someone unknown to us moored a boat offshore and escaped detection.

Bridge Hill Academy is a $60,000 a year college prep private boarding and day school, grades 9-12, founded in 1951 by William Bridger, a railroad magnate and philanthropist. The school has six-hundred students and seventy-five faculty, is located in Cohasset and accepts kids from across the United States and ten foreign countries. Twenty percent of its graduates are accepted to the Ivy League each year with many going on to high level government positions.

I read this Wikipedia description of the school on my iPhone aloud as Teresa Lopez maneuvers our unmarked police vehicle through the school's open ornate metal gates. The tree lined road into the campus, bordered by some soccer and football fields, leads us to a red brick edifice with a white colonnaded entry---the Administration building.

We park in a visitor's lot and walk to the thick glass entrance doors. I pull a door open for Lopez, my usual chivalrous self, and bow from the waist as she sweeps by, rolling her eyes and jabbing me in the stomach with her elbow.

The elegant foyer is dotted with stuffed leather chairs and couches with table lamps beside each one. Six students sit on or stand around the furniture; four boys dressed in blue blazers, gray pants and red striped ties, two girls in pleated blue and gold skirts, white blouses and blue sweaters.

The dress code appears not to cover skirt length. Both young ladies' butt cheeks are exposed. Guess if your parents are paying upwards of sixty-grand to attend such a prestigious school, such transgressions can be ignored.

Lopez sees my eyes widen and gives me a scolding look. The kids eyeball us as we pass and stroll toward the office identified by an engraved wooden plaque on the door as that of Dr. J.D. Watt, Headmaster.

Again, I open the door for Lopez, this time without the bow. She brushes by me into an expansive reception area. Several padded chairs line one wall, bookshelves cover another. An immense oak desk dominates the middle with a neatly coiffed, stylishly attired fifty-something woman sitting behind it. Her name plate reads Loretta. She smiles as we approach and inquires: "Detectives Lopez and Magliore?"

Our fame precedes us.

We dispense with showing our badges and follow her as she gets up, knocks on a door behind her, announces our arrival, steps aside and motions us in.

The headmaster, in his early sixties, is slender, a few clicks over six feet tall. He's wearing a blue, pin striped suit and red tie and sports a full white beard and mustache. He stands as we enter, shakes our hands and directs us to sit at a round table adjacent to his desk.

"We are all devastated by Michael's death," he says, opening the conversation. He avoids the term murder. "This is a small, close-knit school everyone is shocked especially those on the field trip with him. May take a long time for them to recover."

He pauses before assuring us he'll help in any way, as will the staff.

"Thank you for that sir," Lopez says and goes straight to the point. "Did Mr. Dimick have any enemies here? Someone angry enough to kill him?"

Dr. Watt recoils in his chair as if shot. "You think someone here murdered him?" he asks, his eyes wide, his lips pressed together, his head moving from side to side as if trying to rid himself of such an impossible notion.

"We explore all possibilities' sir," Lopez responds. "You understand."

"Of course. Of course," Watt stammers. He recovers his composure after a minute or two and leans forward, elbows on the table. "I can't think of anyone who disliked him enough to do him harm. Not really."

Lopez pounces: "What do you mean, not really?"

"Well," Watt says. "At last year's Christmas reception, Mr. Dimick and another teacher, Arthur Lawson, engaged in an altercation. They had been drinking. Lawson accused Dimick of inappropriate behavior toward his wife. They exchanged harsh words. Lawson pushed Dimick. Other faculty members intervened. I ordered both men to leave and they did so."

"Did you investigate the accusations?" I ask.

"No! No! I didn't," Watt asserts. His eyes widen as he realizes that might not have been a great decision. He attempts to lessen the impact of that mistake.

"I regarded it as an alcohol fueled incident," he says. "Mrs. Lawson never came forward with a complaint. I did confront the men in my office later. They both apologized. I deemed the episode closed."

Watt sits back in his chair and continues. "Perhaps with all this sexual harassment stuff going on these days, the "Me Too" movement and such, I should have spoken to Mrs. Lawson. I Didn't. Reluctant to put her on the spot, I suppose. My fault. Her husband is a quiet, gentle soul. Murder. I can't believe it.

"Not so gentle at the party," I say.

Watt lowers his gaze to his desktop.

"Any indication that Mr. Dimick and Mrs. Lawson were, in fact, involved?" Lopez asks.

"No. No rumors. No water-fountain gossip. The squabble between the two men a misunderstanding. We all moved on. I thought nothing more about it."

I change the line of questioning. "What about Dimick and students?"

Watt exhales. "Mr. Dimick was a handsome man. More than one female employee fawned over him. Some of our girls had a crush on him."

"You didn't answer the question, Dr. Watt."

The headmaster sighs. "The father of one of the girls in Mr. Dimick's AP History class complained about him spending an inordinate amount of time alone with his daughter. She stayed after school often seeking extra help."

"Did you follow up on the complaint?"

"Yes, of course. To ensure that nothing untoward occurred, and quite frankly, to cover our backsides. I requested our law firm look into it. They employ investigators."

"Did they file a written report?"

"Yes. I'll give you a copy. The gist was both Mr. Dimick and the young lady claimed they had no relationship beyond that of student and teacher. The girl confessed being smitten by Dimick. She took every opportunity to spend time with him but swore nothing sexual ever happened between them."

"Did the investigator believe her?"

"She suspected the girl might be holding something back but her father's presence at the interview stifled the girl's responses. No faculty or support staff interviewed could offer any information on a sexual relationship between the two.

I warned Dimick to avoid being alone with the girl, or other female students. He concurred; the investigation ended. The dad agreed not to take it further, though not convinced the relationship was innocent. He confided to me that he didn't want to drive his daughter away. He and his wife were experiencing marital difficulties, and he feared that would make matters worse."

"So! It's possible something was going on?" I say.

Dr. Watt shrugs.

"Who was the girl?" I ask.

Watt hesitates, wrings his hands, lifts his eyes upward as if thinking about his answer, says, "Dakota Johnson."

The girl with Dimick when he was killed. No surprise there. Like Watt did with the teacher-on-teacher quarrel, we move on.

"Ranger Crimshaw said twelve students attended the field trip to Fort Warren, right?" Lopez says.

"Yes. Twelve is our class size here at Bridge Hill. Allows for individual attention and stimulates debate and discussion, one of the many factors making this school such a fantastic learning environment," says Watt, ever the salesman for his program.

"And four chaperones," Lopez adds.

"Yes. We encourage as many adults as possible to supervise these trips."

Dr. Watt opens a folder on the table in front of him and blanches.

"Is something wrong?" Lopez inquires.

The headmaster looks from Lopez to me and back to Lopez. "Teacher Brett Kilgore and his wife, Eleanor, chaperoned the kids as did Mr. and Mrs. Lawson."

"The same Mr. Lawson who scuffled with Dimick?"

Watt nods.

"Doesn't it seem odd to you that they would go on the field trip given the dust-up with Dimick?" I ask.

"Yes and no," replies Watt. "The classroom teacher arranges for the chaperones."

"So Dimick was comfortable with them accompanying him, or at least didn't object."

"Seems so."

"We'll need to speak to both of them and the students. Dakota Johnson first."

"Of course," says Watt. "I've arranged for the kids to stand by. I'll provide a substitute for Mr. Lawson who is teaching now. You can meet with the students in my conference room next door."

* * *

A heavy rectangular oak table, with ten padded straight-backed chairs surrounding it, dominates the headmaster's meeting room. The pictures of former headmasters dating back to the school's founding in 1951 cover one wall. A huge portrait of William Bridger, replete with handle bar mustache, hovers over those leaders.

Floor to ceiling glass windows opposite the photo wall present a sweeping view of a quad with concrete benches and Maple and Birch trees. A boy and girl lay side-by-side on the grass reading near the edge of a small pond in the central area. Postcard stuff or an enticing cover photo for a brochure touting the benefits of attending Bridge Hill. Who wouldn't want to send their precious child to such a tranquil, charming environment?

As long as you have sixty grand a year to spare.

"Picturesque," Lopez says, admiring the scene.

A knock on the door interrupts her reverie. Dr. Watt enters followed by Dakota Johnson. She wears the school uniform of blue and gold skirt, cut to upper thigh length, white blouse and blue sweater. She takes a seat at the end of the immense table. We flank her.

I defer to Lopez who introduces us, explains why we're here and encourages her to relax.

Fat chance!

Johnson puts her hands on the table and studies us with inquisitive green eyes as she chomps on a wad of gum. Her blond ponytail bobs up and down as she tosses the gob around in her mouth.

"Dakota," Lopez begins, "please tell us what happened at Fort Warren. We know this is difficult but it will help us find whoever hurt Mr. Dimick."

The girl's eyes are cast downward as she launches into her narrative. "Mr. Dimick liked to go off on his own to explore the creepy tunnels, and stuff. He told us before the trip he might do this; to find the Lady in Black's grave."

"Didn't that seem strange?" Lopez asks.

"Not to me. Mr. D. loved the fort and all its passageways, rooms and hideaways. He told us stories about them all the time. He was sure he would find the burial place."

She stops; gazes out the window lost in thought; shakes her head, perhaps dismissing things she doesn't want to remember. Her body stiffens anticipating the next question.

Lopez interrupts her reverie. "Why did you leave the group, Dakota?" she asks.

"I got worried. I thought he was gone a long time?"

"So, you saw him leave?"

"Yeah! We were standing together when he left."

Lopez seizes on that comment to change direction. "Your father suspected you and your teacher were too close, didn't he?"

The girl's face hardens; her eyes narrow. "My dad tells me what to do all the time. Tries to control me. Protect me, he says. Nothing happened."

Lopez hones in. "What are you saying, Dakota? Did Mr. Dimick try to do something to you?"

The question strikes home. Dakota begins sobbing, her body convulses. She lays her head down on the table, tears cascading over her cheeks.

Lopez extends a reassuring hand to her shoulder, gives her time to let it all out. Dakota's emotional release indicates she's been holding her feelings in check for a long time. Her secret.

She lifts her head and swipes the sleeve of her sweater across her face. We have no tissue to offer.

"I adored Mike, Mr. Dimick. He was so cool; so good looking, kind and smart. I'm almost eighteen. I wanted to spend the rest of my life with him," she says.

"Did you share your feelings with him?" Lopez presses.

She shakes her head; tears continue to fall. "Not in so many words," she admits.

Dakota is like many teenage girls obsessed with a suave, mature teacher. The exact opposite of the pimply faced boys lusting after her body. She did everything to show Dimick her feelings; would have given herself to him, couldn't accept that he didn't reciprocate. Maybe he gave her signals that he was interested. We'll never know.

Lopez pivots back to the day of the murder. "Okay, Dakota. We understand how much this hurts, but we need you to tell us what happened that day at Fort Warren. Be as specific as you can."

Dakota sniffles, swipes the back of her hand across her nose: "Like I told you. I left the other kids when Mike was gone so long. I thought something may have happened to him. When I got to the room, someone---something--- dressed in black ran out and pushed me aside, almost knocked me down. I screamed and kept screaming until Ranger Crimshaw came running up and comforted me. That's all I remember. I swear."

"Did the person who hurt Mr. Dimick say anything. Make any sound?"

The girl shakes her head. "I don't remember. I was so scared."

"Could you tell if it was a man or a woman?"

"No! No! Please. I don't want to talk about it anymore."

"Okay, Dakota," Lopez says, again putting her hand on the girl's shoulder. "Thank you for speaking with us. If you can think of anything else, no matter if you think it important or not, you will tell us, right?"

Dakota nods. "Please don't tell my father about my feelings for Mike. Please. He'll get mad and yell."

We both assure her anything she told us would be confidential though that isn't technically true. Later, we'll submit a written summary of our interview to our boss, Captain Catebegian. We aren't obligated to share the contents with her father. Dimick's dead. No purpose would be served by revealing such details to her parents. Why exacerbate their remorse at not knowing their daughter's feelings for a respected teacher.

We still have to probe the other students, determine if they know anything about Dakota's relationship with Dimick. Might have a bearing on his murder, might not. Someone wanted the man dead. If not an irate parent or pissed-off colleague, who?

Some kid with a grudge over some slight or off-hand comment? These days anything can set a teenager off as we've seen reported in the news almost on a daily basis.

I don't enjoy interviewing kids. Depending on their age, the law requires parents to be present causing them to clam up, afraid what they say may anger mom and dad even if it's nothing incriminating. And then there are a few turds I'd like to grab by the neck and shake the living shit out of.

Of course, I feel that way about some adults too. I control these impulses most of the time. Catebegian would prefer I never exhibit them.

Chapter 17

Luis Garcia

The Chevrolet Suburban following Lopez and Magliore, driven by CJNG *El Capo*, Luis Garcia, continued on past the entrance to Bridge Hill Academy when the two detectives drove onto the campus.

Garcia watched the TV news broadcast about the murder of teacher Michael Dimick and read the subsequent Boston Globe article reporting the state police would assume responsibility for the investigation. The reporter included the names of the investigators assigned to the case, highlighting Magliore's previous exploits in solving two murders in Hull and battling a Mexican cartel. Garcia didn't participate in that operation. Those who had were no longer breathing.

The inquiry into Dimick's death threatened to disrupt CJNG's drug pipeline in New England. The teacher, a small but important cog in distributing their product to young people in the area---not just his school would be replaced, but that would take time better spent on other challenges.

Garcia had no clue who killed the teacher or why; no one in their organization. Yet, if the detectives traced the source of the drugs back to their man in New Hampshire, it could complicate things. Remote chance, but shit happens. Best be prepared.

Garcia didn't support taking out Magliore or his female partner. CJNG didn't need a spotlight shined on their activities. Neither could it sit back and let disaster happen. Keeping an eye on the detective wasted resources, but was necessary. They'd move on him as a last resort.

Garcia drove from Bridge Hill Academy to Route 3A and to a Starbucks in Cohasset. The coffee chain wasn't everywhere like Dunkin' Donuts, but he preferred their bold brew and scones. Coffee would help him think and to develop a plan of action for his boss, Miguel Chavez, a bright and cunning leader, but a hothead. Garcia was his sounding board and a steadying, calming influence.

Once inside the Starbucks, Luis ordered a Pike, Tall---they were out of bold---and a blueberry scone, which he carried to a small table by a window and sat. He sipped his drink and relaxed. Despite some recent setbacks, their operation was going well. Miguel's bold plan to acquire guns , which he revealed to Luis in a private conversation, was promising, though Luis expressed doubt. Why screw up a good drug business with a plot that might backfire and destroy their entire network.

Miguel ignored his concern; that's why he runs the show, and Luis is second in command. Some men lead, others follow. He understood his place.

He leaned back in his chair, took a bite of his scone and another sip of coffee, and turned his thoughts back to Magliore; a speed bump in the road. They'd run over him when the time came.

He snickered at his own feeble joke.

Chapter 18

Lopez and Magliore

We question the other eleven members of Dimick's AP class after Dakota Johnson leaves and uncover no useful information other than most share being frightened by the incident. Two girls thought Dakota and Dimick "fooled around"---their words--- but offered no evidence to back up their claim, except teenage girl intuition.

One student though, is a pain in the ass. Obnoxious demeanor and smells like he bathes in cologne; the stench overpowering. Both Lopez and I push our chairs back from the table. He doesn't notice or care.

Rory Belanger is the captain and leading scorer on the lacrosse team he tells us; the first words out of his mouth. Also, he's been accepted to Princeton, his father's Alma Mater, and was last year's prom king. His grandfather is president of the Bridge Hill board of trustees.

Modest lad.

He's a handsome, strapping young man, biceps bulging under his white shirt, neck muscles resembling ropes. Most people think I'm ripped---I work out, when possible, at the gym---but I question whether I could take the kid in a fight. Something I contemplate as he rambles on in his self-congratulatory soliloquy.

He offers nothing new regarding the incident with Dimick except to emphasize he's Dakota Johnson's boyfriend and suspected the teacher of having a sexual relationship with his girl. He didn't use that term though, but rather an expletive to describe what he imagined was going on. More than one obscenity to be exact. His face is red and he clenches and unclenches his fists as he speaks.

It's clear he loathed Dimick. Could he have killed him? He had the opportunity and motive.

I sense he might lash out if pushed and incriminate himself.

I push.

"Did you kill Mr. Dimick, Rory?" I ask, fixing him with a challenging glare and leaning in to him across the table.

He's startled by my invasion of his space, but the explosion I provoke never comes. He exhales, folds his arms across his chest and counters my glare with one of his own.

Lopez, caught off guard by my antagonistic behavior, intervenes, thanks Belanger for meeting with us and dismisses him.

Rory stands, smirks, and strolls out of the room, triumphant.

Incredulous, Lopez shakes her head. "Did you actually want to goad that boy into a fight?"

I dip my head, chastised, but I believe the kid has the temperament to have killed his teacher.

The tension in the room ebbs but not the lingering aroma of Belanger's cologne. Lopez windmills her arms in a futile attempt to rid the room of the stench.

* * *

Lopez is still going through contortions to wave away Belanger's aroma when a knock on the door attracts our attention. Dr. Watt sticks his head inside and notifies us teacher Lawson is waiting.

We signal the man in. He enters wearing his graying hair shoulder-length and sports a red bow tie trying to appear laid back but at the same time professorial. He's at least three inches shy of six feet, slender, weighs less than one-hundred fifty-pounds, I guess; pushing his colleague at the Christmas party was not a great idea. Dimick could crush him like a grape.

Lopez and I both smile and indicate he sit in the chair between us. He dips his head and does so.

"Thank you for meeting with us," I say.

"Did I have a choice?" he asks. His body stiffens, his mouth twists into a lopsided grin.

I overlook the snarky remark and begin. "You chaperoned the field trip when Mike Dimick was killed, correct?"

"Yes," he replies. "But I did not see anything. My wife and I left the tour to get a cup of coffee. We heard Dakota's screams on the way back, but by the time we got to the scene the ranger held everyone away."

"I'm curious why you agreed to chaperon at all. We understand you and Dimick did not like each other."

Lawson grins. "So, Dr. Watt told you about our argument at the holiday shindig?"

Neither Lopez nor I react to his statement, so he plunges on. "I loathed the man; a pervert and homewrecker."

"Any proof of that?" Lopez chimes in.

Lawson, an expert at facial contortions, glares at us as if we don't understand his brilliance.

"He leered at my wife, touched her at every opportunity. Stared at female students the same way."

"In what ways did he touch your wife?"

The cockeyed grin again. I'm ready to punch him. But being a gentle soul, I wait for his answer.

"He'd rub her back and shoulders, hold her hand and kiss her on the cheek by way of greeting."

"Did your wife complain about this?"

Lawson sits back. "Why are we talking about my wife. Isn't this about Dimick's murder?"

Lopez and I remain silent.

He gets the message. "What? You think I had something to do with Dimick's death. I told you, we weren't there when it happened. Talk to my wife, the kids, the ranger."

We aren't making any progress with this jerk.

"Thank you for your time, Mr. Lawson," I say, by way of terminating the discussion. "We may want to meet with you again, though."

Lawson pushes his chair back, stands and bolts for the door without any further comment.

Lopez and I glance at each other. "He had motive and opportunity," she says. "Could be our guy."

I don't agree, though I'd like nothing better.

"The weasel doesn't have the balls," I say, as my face reddens at the use of those words. I've made a determined effort to avoid coarse language in front of my female partner. Reverse sexism, I suppose.

Lopez calls me on it. "I've heard the expression before, you know. Don't patronize me."

I steeple my hands and bow my head in her direction.

She flips me the bird.

Chapter 19

Dakota Johnson

Dakota Johnson was shaken by the meeting with the two state police detectives, embarrassed that she confessed her obsession with teacher Mike Dimick. He didn't share her feelings, but like many of the other male teachers, ogled her at every opportunity. She encouraged it, flaunting her sexuality by wearing the tightest sweaters and shortest skirts that tested the limits of the school's dress code.

Truth be told, she and Mike hadn't progressed beyond a hug or two after class, though she pressed him to go further. She wanted to experience what sex would be like with a real man, not the slobbering boys who fawned over her.

Dimick's death devastated her. She worried her father would discover her passion for him and her desire to run off with him when she turned eighteen. She didn't know how that would happen unless she blurted it during one of their many fights.

Distraught, she yearned for something and someone to comfort her. On her way out of the interview with Lopez and Magliore, she called a classmate who could do both; asked him to meet her in her dorm room.

Dakota resided in Williams Hall, one of five student residences on Academy grounds. Williams was one of two new dormitories added in the last year with the help of generous endowments from former students or wealthy benefactors who support the private school movement in the United States.

Stan Williams graduated from Bridge Hill in 1960 and Harvard Law six years later. After a career as a high-powered attorney for a Washington D.C. law firm and lobbyist for arms dealers doing business with the U.S. military, he retired as a multi-millionaire, some say billionaire and settled in Cohasset. He now serves as the president of Bridge Hill's board of trustees. His grandson, Rory Belanger, is a senior at the school.

Dormitories, like Williams, house eighty-per cent of the school's population, most of whom live out of state or too far in state to commute. Dakota Johnson lived in Hingham a few miles away, and could have commuted, but persuaded her father that staying on campus would better prepare her for college life. As an only child, Dakota often wangled her way with her parents, especially her father, who doted on her.

The residence halls at Bridge Hill were not co-ed; boys forbidden to even visit girls above the lobby. Of course, the kids found ways to circumvent those rules. Boys eager to join their girlfriends, say on the third floor where Dakota lived, would enter through the window of a conspirator on the first floor, exit that room and creep up the stairs. The proctors, older men and woman, avoided patrolling the corridors at night although contracted to do so.

When the friend she called knocked on her door and entered, Dakota's first words were, "Did you bring the stuff?"

* * *

The young man smiled, dipped his shoulder to shrug off his backpack, unzipped a side pocket and pulled out two baggies. One contained several blue pills and the other a white powder. He also opened the middle section of the pack and took out two mini-bottles of Jim Beam.

Dakota's eyes widened and she licked her lips. "Let's party," she said, reaching for one of the bottles.

The boy held her back with his left hand while dangling the bottle in the air with his right. "Not till you take off your sweater."

Dakota still wore her school uniform, the short skirt showing off her toned thighs. She learned early in life that flaunting her charms turned many boys and men to jelly. Her visitor no exception. She'd get what she wanted by displaying a little skin. A small price to pay.

She smirked, stepped back and wriggled out of her sweater. Taking her time, she unbuttoned her blouse and dropped it to the floor, following that up by reaching behind her back, releasing the clasps of her bra and letting it fall at her feet.

The young man's eyes bulged as did something else on the lower part of his anatomy. He twisted the cap off of one of the bottles of whiskey and handed it to Dakota who took a long swig. He did the same with the other bottle and pushed Dakota back onto one of the beds in the room. Dakota kept hold of the bottle as she lay on her back and continued to sip as her classmate explored her body with his hands and tongue.

Dakota stopped him from trying to pull off his pants and hers. "Easy big boy," she said. "We have all afternoon. My roommate's visiting her parents until tomorrow. Let's do some crank."

Still aroused, the boy rolled off Dakota but understood the drugs he brought would make it easier to get his way later. He emptied some white powder on top of the desk in the room, gave a short straw to Dakota, and they each inhaled the substance up their noses. They finished the booze and most of the meth, became so high neither remembered how they wound up on Dakota's bed naked, their bodies entwined. They fell asleep in each other's arms.

The young man awakened first, saw that the digital alarm clock on the desk read 12:05 a.m., and realized he had to race back to his room before being discovered by proctors who monitored the halls in the morning. He dressed, bent to kiss Dakota one last time on her breasts and thighs, and exited the room. In his haste, he left the remnants of the drugs and booze on the floor.

Dakota became aware of the door closing and sat up. Still groggy, she stumbled to the desk and discovered the remainder of the meth and the baggie of blue pills. She opted for a pill.

A mistake.

The tablet she ingested was knock-off oxycodone laced with fentanyl. Genuine oxycodone is an opioid medication prescribed for moderate to severe pain. Fatal side effects can occur if consumed with alcohol. Counterfeit oxy cut with fentanyl can be deadly in miniscule amounts. Taking it with alcohol is like putting a gun to your head.

Dakota didn't know or care. For a long while she had been taking whatever her friends or boyfriend provided. The highs were exhilarating and made dealing with her father easier. She lay back on the bed, asleep in less than a minute. She didn't hear the door open and someone slip inside.

Chapter 20

Miguel Chavez

Miguel Chavez did not think of himself as a thug, gangster, hoodlum or any other pejorative to describe those working for cartels. He was a businessman, nothing more. People craved his product; he provided it. Competitors sometimes had to be dealt with harshly, even eliminated, but as a last resort. As "El Mencho," said: "bodies are bad for business."

Miguel intended to establish CJNG as the primary cartel in the northeast United States. In doing so, he hoped to gain access to the Junta Directiva, the executive committee of top drug lords. Might even become "El Mencho's" successor.

His upward mobility in the organization depended on achieving two objectives: Flooding the market with drugs, and acquiring firearms in bulk for his Soldados; a unique, unheard-of prospect.

Most drugs funneled into the United States come through Mexico, while most guns smuggled into Mexico come from the U.S. Mexicans can legally purchase weapons only from a single, government regulated shop in Mexico City, controlled by the army.

Guns flowing south do so irregularly and never in mass quantity. Sometimes, individuals make purchases at gun stores in the United States, and lug them across the border. At other times, women with no criminal history, recruited by cartels, procure weapons and transfer them to smugglers who sneak them into Mexico a few at a time, so they don't raise the suspicions of authorities.

CJNG utilized these methods, of course. But Miguel fixated on finding a way to acquire multiple guns at one time giving his people a decided advantage over their rivals.

Chavez did his homework and discovered several top manufacturers located in the northeast United States. Smith & Wesson maintains facilities in Springfield, Massachusetts, Houlton, Maine and Deep River, Connecticut. Sig Sauer operates a multimillion-dollar facility in New Hampshire. Sturm, Ruger, the biggest supplier in the country producing assault rifles and pistols along with hunting rifles, has its headquarters in Southport, Connecticut, and a manufacturing plant in Newport, New Hampshire. Its website proclaims, "Ruger offers consumers over 400 variations of more than 30 product lines...a rugged reliable firearm to meet every shooter's needs."

Miguel chuckled to himself.

Wonder if they had cartel Soldados in mind?

Sitting in his rental home, Chavez contemplated a bold plan which would make him a legend among the Mexican cartels and catapult him to the pinnacle of CJNG. He identified Sturm, Ruger as his target company. He considered a raid on their facility, but several obstacles loomed as he sought to develop a strategy to do so.

First, security. Did such a place employ perimeter protection as well as trained interior guards like off-duty police officers; or typical rent-a-cops for show? Or no guards at all?

Second, breaching a facility's defense did not ensure success. Once inside, the guns had to be located. Some might be out for display in a showroom, most would be secured in locked storage rooms or vaults perhaps with impenetrable electronic locks.

Third, it must be assumed there would be alarms tied to local or state police in the event of a breach or a natural disaster, which could make their stock vulnerable to looters. This made it unlikely Miguel's men could enter the building or buildings, find the guns and flee before the cops arrived.

Perhaps because of these hurdles, no report anywhere indicated an assault on a weapons manufacturer in the United States had ever occurred let alone succeeded.

Miguel considered abandoning the idea until he stumbled onto an Internet article: "Guns stolen but never reported." It happened several years ago, but outlined the blueprint for a plan.

The thefts happened while the firearms were in transit, exposing a huge vulnerability in the supply network. Security and reporting requirements were lax. Weapons that disappeared while being transported did not have to be reported at all, and many times weren't. Private carriers such as UPS, FedEx and Conway trucking handled some gun shipments while others traveled by rail.

Insiders engineered most heists; disgruntled or corrupt employees working at the production sites or for the freight companies. They either tipped off the thieves about dates and times of transport or participated in offloading the cargo themselves; paid in drugs, money and sometimes guns for their personal use. Miguel Chavez could furnish all three for those willing to participate in his scheme.

He was back in business. His first step was now much easier than organizing a dangerous attack. Just identify people at either Storm, Ruger or their shipping company who might have a taste for his product or a desire to fill their pockets with cash.

While less risky, this plan required patience and tact. Choosing the wrong employee could blow up in their faces and destroy everything Miguel had achieved.

Luis Garcia, his second in command, was best suited for this mission. He'd dispatch him to Newport pronto.

Chapter 21

Lopez and Magliore

Lopez and I leave Bridge Hill after our interviews with students and staff and drive to Michael Dimick's residence in Hingham, a split-level condominium not far from the shipyard shopping center, a former working boatyard during World War II. Once a crumbling lot with vacant, decaying buildings, it was now occupied by a Wahlburger's restaurant, a Trader Joe's and a movie theater among other retail shops. You could also catch a ferry to downtown Boston or Fort Warren from an adjacent pier.

A judge granted us a warrant to search the condo, which is in an upscale new development. Pine and red maple trees line the road into the complex. A small park and two tennis courts adjoin the clean and well-maintained buildings; pricey digs for someone on a teacher's salary.

We have keys to Dimick's residence; picked them up as part of the personal items taken from his body at the Boston morgue, our first stop after getting this assignment. The autopsy hadn't been completed at the time; a huge backlog of cases took precedence. We viewed the body and took custody of an evidence bag containing his affects, which included his wallet and driver's license.

The front door of the condo opens into a spacious living room replete with a 75-inch wall-mounted TV faced by a leather sectional. A free-standing low bookshelf includes biographies of Presidents Washington, Jefferson, Lincoln, Kennedy and Obama. Multiple histories of the Civil War, World Wars I and II and Vietnam complete the array displayed. Not an unusual collection for a history teacher.

A sprawling throw rug covers the wooden floor in front of the sectional. On the wall opposite the TV, an iconic picture of kicker Adam Vinateri driving home the field goal securing the New England Patriot's first Super Bowl holds prominence. A door to the left leads to the kitchen while stairs to the right head upward. Lopez tackles the first floor while I search the second.

Two rooms dominate the upstairs, one of which is an office. An Apple lap top computer rests on an oak desk pushed against one wall under a window. When I turn it on, a screen-saver pops up revealing three unlabeled folders. They're not password protected unlike the Gmail identified by the mail icon.

The first folder stores lesson plans for Dimick's AP History class; the second, files downloaded from the Internet, and the third, photos.

Scenic shots of Bridge Hill Academy and the town of Cohasset cram the photos folder along with group classroom snapshots of Dimick's students. There are two of Lawson and his wife and one of Mrs. Lawson alone smiling demurely. One picture shows Dakota Johnson in her cheerleader's outfit and one of she and Dimick with arms around each other on campus. Nothing salacious or relevant to our investigation at first glance.

I try but fail to access the Gmail account, not surprising since my technical expertise begins and ends with turning electronic devices on or off.

Lopez joins me as I pound the desk in frustration and frowns at my juvenile behavior. She waits until I calm down before reporting finding nothing of substance downstairs.

She elbows me aside and tries accessing Dimick's Gmail; also fails. Though happy, I present a stoic face. Lopez isn't fooled, refrains from commenting. Defeated, we agree this is a problem for the tech geeks.

I choose to finish exploring the office while Lopez takes the bedroom. The middle desk drawer, in addition to pencils, pens, post-it notes and scissors, contains a Phillips head screwdriver Dimick may have used for making minor repairs; kept it here because these units have no attached garages, which would be the logical place to keep any tools.

I join Lopez when further rummaging through the desk turns up nothing related to Dimick's murder. Searching someone's bedroom always feels intrusive to me; a private place reserved for intimacy. Dresser drawers contain underclothing and items one would not want a stranger to see. Nevertheless, it's also a place important evidence is often found. People seem to think hiding valuables, documents, even weapons under panties, pajamas, or socks is safe. Go figure.

Lopez examines Dimick's bureau while I peruse the walk-in closet. Sandwiched between two suits and three sports jackets, is a women's skirt and blouse. Before I can to call out to announce my discovery, Lopez shouts, "Hey. Look at this."

I stick my head out of the closet door to see her hold up a pair of panties.

"Big girl's or little girl's?" I ask.

"Could be a teen-age girl but more likely a woman based on the size."

"Yeah! There's a woman's outfit in here."

"So Dimick had a girlfriend who stayed over or changed here," Lopez says.

"Could it be the glamorous Mrs. Lawson?"

"If so, gives her hubby a motive for murder."

"If he knew?" she adds.

I nod; the three primary motives for homicide are money, sex and revenge. In Lawson's case, at least two of these apply.

This raises two questions for a future discussion with Mrs. Lawson: Was she involved with Dimick and did she stay with her husband the entire time on the field trip at Fort Warren?

* * *

I turn my attention back to the closet. Six shoe boxes, all empty, rest on the floor stacked in front of a gray heating vent cover. This struck me as odd. First, there's another vent in the bedroom close to the ceiling. Two vents in a room of this size is superfluous. Second, the position of the boxes block air flow and could create a fire hazard.

I take a knee and examine the vent. The area around the two screws securing it to the wall is scratched from constant use. Who opens and closes a heating vent often unless there is a problem, or if it is used for something else?

I remember the screwdriver in the desk drawer, retrieve it, kneel down again and remove the vent screws. Pulling the cover off reveals a plastic Tupperware-type container stashed inside a small oblong space. I slide it from the enclosure, open it and am confronted by another surprise; multiple storage baggies filled with small blue tablets scored with an "M" in a square on one side and a "30" with a line down the center on the other, a counterfeit version of oxycodone hydrochloride. I recognize them from my days abusing painkillers.

Stashed behind the container is a packaged burner phone.

I call out and ask Lopez to join me. Her eyes widen when she sees my discovery. "Holy shit," she blurts.

"Yeah! Mike Dimick had a sideline---drug dealer."

I've been clean for over nine months, yet seeing the pills produces an anticipatory reaction. I shiver, lick my lips and my face reddens like an addict awaiting his next fix.

My physical response alarms Lopez. "Are you okay, Mags? You look like you're having a stroke."

Before I can answer, we hear the click of the front door lock and both draw our weapons. I flatten myself against the wall to the right of the door while Lopez hides behind the opened door.

Within a few minutes, the stairs creak as our visitor climbs toward us and enters our room. Lopez slams the door behind the intruder and I execute one of my best downfield tackles driving him to the floor. A deafening scream pierces my ears. Our party crasher isn't a male.

I roll her over and discover I'm on top of the frightened Mrs. Lawson; her skirt bunched high up on her thighs revealing pink underwear. She's not happy.

"Let me up you bastard," she shouts as she struggles to wiggle out from under me and pull her skirt down at the same time.

I straddle her body, stand up and offer her a hand she slaps away. She rolls over and pushes herself up. "Who are you and what are you doing here?" she demands, in a tone designed to put us on the defensive.

I'm dumbfounded. My partner comes to the rescue. "We're state police detectives investigating the murder of Michael Dimick. Why don't you tell us who you are and why you're here?"

Lawson's face flushes, she plops down on the edge of the bed, her body convulses as she whimpers and moans. She's immobilized for two or three minutes before regaining her composure.

"I'm Sandra Lawson, uh, a friend of Mike's."

She wipes her eyes with the sleeve of her blouse and stares at the floor, face reddening in embarrassment.

"Such a friend that he allowed you to leave clothes here?" Lopez presses. "We don't want to accuse you of obstructing justice, Sandra, but we will if you don't answer our questions truthfully."

Lawson bites her lower lip. "I loved him; intelligent guy, liked having fun. We enjoyed each other's company."

I wonder if that fun included popping pills, but don't go there.

Lopez changes direction. "You and your husband chaperoned the field trip to Fort Warren, right?"

Lawson nods.

"Did he remain with you the entire time?"

Lawson is shocked, her face reflecting surprise and fear. "You don't think? No. He couldn't, wouldn't."

Lopez homes in. "He suspected you and Dimick were having an affair, right?"

Lawson dips her head. Wipes her nose and eyes again. "I don't love Arthur. Don't know why I married him. He's smart and has been kind to me. Until…until the last two months."

"When he found out about your tryst?"

"He didn't have proof. Mike and I denied it, of course. Arthur and I have been fighting a lot. He got into a shoving match with Mike at our school Christmas party. Not like him. He's a gentle man."

"So, I ask you again, Sandra. Was your husband with you the whole time you chaperoned the students at Fort Warren?"

Lawson clasps her hands on her lap, remains silent for a few moments, thinking. She licks her lips, admits he left her while they were on a snack break to use the restroom, gone for fifteen minutes, maybe longer. She sits up straight on the bed, brushes her hair back with her right hand. "My God," she says, and sobs.

Lopez and I make eye contact.

Chapter 22

Lopez and Magliore

We let Sandra Lawson go without the clothing she wished to retrieve. I call Captain Catebegian to request a forensic team and state troopers to secure the site.

When CSU arrives, I turn the baggies of pills over to their leader, Leona Galvin. I point out the cubbyhole behind the fake heating vent in the bedroom closet. Galvin assures me they'll test that area for prints as well as other locations. She seizes Dimick's computer to unleash the techies on it later.

Our job complete, Lopez and I are both hungry. It's four forty-five in the afternoon. We decide to try the Wahlberger's in the Hingham shipyard and grab a table for two by the windows. Green chairs are positioned around it. Green is the dominant motif at this restaurant with its signature emblem, a white swirled "W" inside a green circle on the floor, on the napkins and emblazoned on the black shirts of the wait staff.

A young waitress brings menus and takes our beverage orders; coffee, black. We peruse the menu and when the young lady returns with our coffee, Lopez selects a spinach salad and I opt for a crispy haddock sandwich. We sip our drinks in silence for a while and examine the crowds passing by outside. People watching is one of my favorite pastimes.

Lopez speaks first. "You took your time getting off the prone Mrs. Lawson after slamming her to the floor. Your eyes bulged out of your head when you peaked under her skirt."

I smile. "I got no pleasure from the contact, I assure you."

Lopez smirks and rolls her eyes, her frequent reaction to my pithy comments.

"Well. Does Mr. Arthur Lawson go to the top of our list of suspects?" she asks. "Easy to detour from his trip to the restroom to kill Dimick."

I agree. "He had the motive and opportunity, as you said earlier, but I can't see the little weasel having the guts to stab anyone. Even a man he suspects is playing hide the salami with his wife. He confronts Dimick at a party because he knows people will intervene in any physical confrontation."

"Weasel?"

"How about pompous weasel?"

"I get the message," Lopez says. "We need to interview the other chaperones on the trip."

She checks her notebook. "Mr. and Mrs. Kilgore."

"Yeah. They should be able to tell us about Lawson's whereabouts. Then again, maybe Dimick dallied with Kilgore's wife too; angered him as well. Sex is a well-known motivation for homicide."

"Ya think?"

"I do. But I also think whoever supplied Dimick with the drugs is a more likely suspect than either Lawson or Kilgore.

Or, if not the supplier, the users. Was he selling to Kids? Faculty? Street addicts? Maybe he stiffed somebody, or a parent discovered he sold stuff to his child. The possibilities are endless."

Lopez shakes her head. "You're forgetting the killer had to be someone on Georges Island that day. No parents served as chaperones. Fingerprints didn't reveal anyone arrested for drug use or distribution. The college girl had marijuana in her possession, but what college kid doesn't."

I hate it when she shoots down my theories.

I'm not ready to concede though. "Remember, Ranger Crimshaw acknowledged some visitors to Fort Warren that day moored their private boats offshore and rowed in by dinghy; were gone by the time the other people were corralled.

"And," I add, "Headmaster Watt revealed other female faculty members fawned over Dimick. Mrs. Kilgore perhaps. Watt didn't name names, but she chaperoned the field trip, had opportunity like her husband. If she discovered Dimick cheated on her with Sandra Lawson, no telling how she would react. Nothing like a woman scorned."

"Enough to commit murder?"

"Absolutely."

I shrug and lapse into silence as the waitress delivers our food. We both say yes to more coffee.

"So, where do we go from here?" Lopez asks when we're alone.

"We can't worry about who else may have been on the island that day. Let's concentrate on who was---especially the kids. Dakota Johnson and that pompous jerk Rory Belanger. If drugs are floating around the school, those two would know the source.

And if Belanger believed, as we know he did, that Dimick was messing around with his girl, he could take the man out in a heartbeat. He's a strong sucker. Could have slipped away from the class for a few minutes without Crimshaw noticing---and rejoined them later. The other students didn't notice or didn't want, or dare, to snitch."

"You really think one of the students did it?"

"Why not? They shoot up schools don't they. Kill teachers, don't they? Take and distribute drugs, don't they?"

I'm fired up. My diatribe sends Lopez reeling back in her chair. In an effort to curb my ardor, she changes the subject.

"You like the word 'pompous' don't you?"

I ignore the jab; take a bite of my fish sandwich.

Left unspoken is that kids can be victims as well as perpetrators.

Chapter 23

Miguel Chavez

The morning after doing his research on stealing guns from a major U.S. manufacturer, Miguel Chavez gathered the four top members of his organization around the dining room table in his Lynn rental house. His *El Capo*(Captain), Luis Garcia, and three *Lugartenientes* (lieutenants): Angel Herrera, Jose Renteria and Alphonso "Al" Gonzales, who handled the sale and distribution of drugs in the northeast for CJNG.

Garcia oversaw the three lieutenants who, in turn, supervised a host of soldados, enforcers and street dealers along with the *Burreros* (mules*)*, who smuggled their drugs across the border. Their operation was doing well despite recent setbacks, but Miguel hoped to solidify and expand CJNG's position and influence with his new strategy, and ensure his own upward mobility.

His team had no experience stealing weapons or transporting them. So, this meeting was designed to convince them his plan was doable and worth the gamble. Each had a steaming cup of coffee on the table in front of them and a dozen donuts to share that Chavez picked up earlier, his minor bribe to keep them relaxed and interested.

"Amigos," he began. "We have an opportunity to increase our power in the North, he pronounced it, Norte, America and become the most powerful cartel in Mexico. We must be bold and daring, take a risk none of our competitors has yet tried."

His subordinates glanced at each other, but said nothing. They waited for their leader to continue.

Miguel talked to them in English. He believed speaking Spanish while in the United States attracted unwanted attention---dangerous in the charged political situation in the country.

His *El Capo*, Luis Garcia, spoke the best English of the group, no hint of an accent. He grew up in Mexicali, Mexico, across from Calexico, California. Thousands of people in both countries crossed the border in opposite directions every day for shopping, work and school. Many Californians made doctor's appointments in Mexicali, and bought cheap prescription drugs there.

Garcia went to school in Calexico while his father toiled in the agricultural fields planting and harvesting lettuce, sugar beets and carrots among other crops. Luis used English at school, Spanish at home.

Miguel, Angel and Alphonso learned the language panhandling and acting as intermediaries for Americans looking for bargains from street vendors or seeking pleasures of the flesh. They all spoke passable English, which aided their efforts in the United States.

Miguel laid out his plan without sharing specifics. They already had a pipeline to get their products into North America. He viewed Fort Warren as a major new conduit and storage facility. With a ranger in his pocket, they could use it at least for a short time. The increased volume would justify the risk.

Establishing inside contacts at Sturm, Ruger or UPS promised to be the most difficult part of the scheme. But he found information while scouring the Internet to make that task easier.

Addiction was ravaging New England, with New Hampshire among the top five states in the country with the highest incidence of opioid deaths; more than twice the national rate per 100,000 persons. Fentanyl was the primary culprit, more potent than every other opioid. But its high is of shorter duration, leading users to inject it more often, increasing their risk of overdosing.

A crisis for authorities, an opportunity for Miguel.

He smiled. These facts increased the likelihood he would find a drug user in New Hampshire, someone who worked for Sturm, Ruger, UPS or FedEx freight or other carriers who would be willing to help in return for product or cash.

Miguel's focus turned to the Ruger plant in Newport.

Chapter 24

Lopez and Magliore

The morning after our search of Mike Dimick's condo and my tussle with the lovely Mrs. Lawson, I called ahead to the headmaster's office at Bridge Hill Academy to set up another interview with Rory Belanger and Dakota Johnson. Dr. Watt's secretary agreed to make them available at 11:30 a.m., the school's lunch hour.

At 11:15, Lopez drives our unmarked state police vehicle through the gates of Bridge Hill for a second time. As we turn into the campus, a black Chevy Suburban passes behind us, catching my attention. I think I've seen it before but shake it off as being paranoid; don't mention it to Lopez.

We approach the administration building and are confronted by the site of two Cohasset police cruisers, an ambulance and a fire rescue truck, all with flashing lights, parked in front of a red brick building adjacent to our destination. An engraved granite stone marker identifies it as Williams Hall, a student residence.

Lopez parks behind one of the patrol cars. We both exit our vehicle and flash our creds to two uniformed officers standing on the sidewalk, arms folded, chatting. Our attention is drawn to two white garbed ambulance attendants who roll a gurney down the walkway leading away from the residence. A body, covered by a white sheet, lies atop the cart.

"Who is it?" I ask.

"Student, overdose, the fifth one this month," the officer with corporal stripes on his sleeve answers. "Don't know the kid's name."

"The fifth death?" Lopez exclaims, eyebrows raised.

"No! No! The others survived. One is still hospitalized though."

"What's going on?"

"Opioids. An epidemic among high school kids. We had two overdoses at Cohasset High earlier this week."

"Who's securing the scene?" I ask.

"Two of our detectives. They requested a state forensics team. Standard procedure in circumstances like this."

His face reddens as he realizes he's lecturing two staties on proper procedures. "One of our guys is keeping everyone away from the room," he says, to cover his faux pas.

I nod and for the first-time notice Dr. Watt, the Headmaster, pacing back and forth, trance-like, on the lawn. His long legs stretch out in front of him as he moves, one hand on his chin, his suit jacket flapping in the breeze, tie askew.

Lopez and I thank the corporal for the information and move to intercept Watt.

I yell his name as we approach him.

Baffled at first, he soon dips his head in recognition. "Horrible," he says "Horrible. What will I say to her parents? They'll be devastated as am I. Devastated."

Her.

"Who is it?" Lopez asks and puts a hand on his shoulder.

Watt tears up. "Dakota Johnson. Poor girl."

* * *

We leave Watt standing transfixed and bolt for the door to Williams Hall. We're convinced, at least I am, Johnson's death, intentional or by mistake, is connected to our investigation of Mike Dimick's murder. The drugs found in his apartment clinched it for me.

I call Captain Catebegian on my cell, brief him on the situation and suggest he contact the Cohasset chief to request we take the lead on this inquiry.

In the foyer of the Williams building, a tearful student standing with two other distraught girls, tells us Dakota's room is on the second floor, number forty-two.

There is no elevator, so we climb a stairwell to our right. When we reach the floor, a Cohasset officer stands vigil outside a door halfway down the corridor. He braces as we approach and raises his hand to stop us; relaxes when we produce our ID's.

I explain why we're here and ask to speak with the detectives. We left our crime scene gloves and booties in the car, so we don't attempt to enter the room.

The officer ducks his head inside and calls out the name of one of the men who meets us at the doorway.

We shake hands.

"Detectives Lopez and Magliore, state police," I announce. "This girl's death may be connected to the murder of a teacher here."

"Charlie Rose," he says. "My partner's Phil Bengston. We've requested a state CSU team though it appears to be an OD."

Rose looks to be in his late forties, squat, wide shoulders, bull neck, miles of rough road on his face but kind eyes, warm smile. He reaches into his pocket and produces an evidence pouch containing a plastic bag filled with ten blue pills marked oxycodone with the same markings and bag found in Dimick's stash.

I nod.

"We found some white powder residue on the desk and two empty mini-Jim Beam bottles on the floor," he adds. "The kid was partying."

"Any idea with whom?"

"Nope. Evidence suggests a boy or boys. A substance that could be semen is on the sheets. A strong odor of cologne or after shave permeates the room."

Lopez sticks her head further into the room, inhales, gags, glances at me and mouths, "Belanger."

Rose's cell phone rings. He snatches it from his left breast pocket, nods several times, says "yes sir" several more before slipping the phone back into its resting place.

"Chief ordered us to turn the case over to you, assist any way we can."

He doesn't seem irritated or displeased although I sense some concern as his eyes dart to Lopez and back to me. He hands the evidence over as if parting with a prize possession.

"A hellava thing," he says, shaking his head from side to side. "The kids have graduated from marijuana, once thought to be the worst thing in the world, to coke to heroin and now to legal pain relievers like oxycodone here. I bet some doctor prescribed it for the girl."

He takes a deep breath, exhales. "Sonofabitch. I got a girl and boy of my own. I see this shit, I don't sleep at night, worrying."

"I understand Charlie. And this won't relieve your anxiety," I say, "but these tablets may contain fentanyl as well as oxy. I believe they're knock-offs."

"Why do you think that?"

"I suffered a leg wound some time ago. Used oxy. It would take quite a few pills to overdose. But combined with booze, who knows?"

"Sonofabitch. You get the supplier, call me. The bastard might have an accident on the way to lock-up."

I let that pass. The question remains: Is Mike Dimick's murder related to these overdoses on campus? Was he supplying them to his students, and if so, who supplied him?

Does it matter? As Lopez pointed out in our conversation at Wahlburger's, no known dealer or user was identified at Fort Warren at the time Dimick was killed, though the remote possibility remains the perpetrator escaped on a private boat prior to the island's lockdown.

I'm pissed. The whole idea of providing drugs to kids is abhorrent. I'm as interested in finding the drug supplier as I am Dimick's killer, even if they're not the same person.

Can't tell Big Cat or Lopez that. For now, we'll talk with Rory Belanger again. Not something I look forward to but I'm sure the kid is dialed into the dealers and drugs floating around his school. Might deal himself or even be Dimick's slayer. He's on the top of my suspect list.

I turn to Detective Rose.

"Charlie. One of your men out front, a corporal, told us this was the fifth overdose this month of a Bridge Hill student."

"That's right. One is still in a coma."

"We'll need their names and addresses."

"No problem but may I ask why?"

"I believe drugs link to our murder investigation. No evidence to support that now, but these kids may be able to shed some light on that."

"Anything to help," Rose says.

"Great. Give me your cell phone number. I'll contact you with mine. Text me the names and any info you think connect these cases and those at Cohasset High School."

"Will do," Rose says, his eyes narrowing, jaw set. "Let's catch this son-of-a-bitch."

I shake his hand again. "You bet."

* * *

The commotion outside Williams Hall attracted a group of spectators who stand across the road on one of the school's manicured lawns. Some mill around gossiping while others stand with arms folded waiting for some explanation for the convergence of police cars and emergency vehicles, as if expecting some official to come out with a bull-horn to satisfy their curiosity by providing gory details. Students comprise most of the gathering, but others include faculty, grounds-workers and visiting parents.

One observer is none of these. He's the murderer of Michael Dimick and is the individual who partied the night before with Dakota Johnson. He shoulders a backpack, wears sunglasses and a Bridge Hill baseball cap pulled low above his eyes, lest anyone recognizes him. Two students nod in his direction. He returns the gesture before averting his face.

A murmur spreads though the onlookers as two state detectives, a man and a woman unknown to most, exit the building and get into their car. The murderer turns and walks away triumphant, convinced the cops are no match for his superior intellect. They have no clue as to why he killed Dimick, and they'll be flabbergasted to learn, if they ever do, that Dakota's death was no accident.

Best of all. He's not finished. All those in Dimick's web will pay the price. He considers himself an avenging angel.

Chapter 25

We can't find Rory Belanger.

I phone Dr. Watt's secretary, Loretta, to see if he showed up at our 11:30 a.m. meeting. He didn't. She gives me his room number, 101 in Madden Hall, two buildings down from the Williams dorm.

He's not here. His roommate says he came in late the night before, left around eight to go to math. But since it's lunchtime, he might be anywhere. The kid suggests we check his social studies class at 1:00 p.m. in building 'A' across campus.

We thank the kid and exit Madden Hall when I get a call on my cell from Captain Catebegian. He wants an update in person; arranged with Dr. Watt to meet in the headmaster's office.

We intercept him on the sidewalk in front of the Administration Building as he pulls into the parking lot, and walk in together. Loretta escorts us into the conference room. Watt is on the phone trying to contact Dakota Johnson's parents; not something I relished, calling a murder victim's relatives. Too many ways for that exchange to go sideways.

Loretta leaves us with a fresh carafe of coffee and a paper plate of donuts and sweet rolls, withdraws from the room and closes the door behind her. I pour us each a cup of steaming brew, managing not to spill any on the tabletop, a spectacular feat for me.

"Okay. Where are we?" Catebegian asks, reaching for a bear claw.

Lopez nods for me to start, but before I launch into my recap of events, Catebegian puts up his hand. "Give me the Reader's Digest version, Magliore. I'll review your detailed report later." The big man's way of saying he expects such a report.

"We discovered several baggies of pills, labeled oxycodone, hidden in Dimick's condo," I say. "We turned those over to Leona Galvin of CSU for analysis. A rash of kids have overdosed at this school within the last few months culminating in Dakota Johnson's death last night. Dimick's killer could be someone in the drug supply chain, user or supplier."

Lopez glares at me, bites her tongue, doesn't want to go down that road.

Big Cat keeps silent while munching on his bear claw.

I continue. "Dimick was intimate with the wife of a colleague and possibly Dakota Johnson, though she denied it. Wouldn't surprise me if he played around with other female faculty or students. Headmaster Watt said many of the women and girls on campus found him attractive. So, a jealous husband, parent or even boyfriend could have had a motive to kill him."

Lopez is ready to strangle me, arms folded across her chest, jaw set, eyes boring into me. She's opposed to widening the suspect list beyond those on Georges Island the day of the murder.

Big Cat doesn't notice her body language, finishes his pastry and washes it down with a swig of coffee before speaking. "So, no concrete suspects, just speculation."

"Well, sir," Lopez breaks in, "some credible leads for sure, though we need to dig deeper."

"You do that," Catebegian says, pushing back from the table and standing up. "But do it fast. We don't need more bodies piling up."

Chapter 26

Eleanor Kilgore

Eleanor Kilgore was seated in the breakfast nook at her home in Marshfield. Her attempt to lift a second cup of coffee to her lips failed; hand trembling so much she put it down for fear of spilling on herself. A call from her husband Brett, a teacher at Bridge Hill Academy, unnerved her. A student died of an overdose on campus that morning and Cohasset police along with some state cops were investigating.

"Things could unravel," Brett had warned, concern evident in his voice. "We should talk with the others," he suggested. "We're all vulnerable if they connect Mike's death and the student overdoses to us. We need a plan."

A plan? We're not conspirators, she thought, as she struggled to control her emotions. Just fools.

It was fun at the beginning. Reckless, but fun.

At the faculty holiday party held at the Nantasket Beach Resort two years ago, four of the younger couples in the Social Studies Department bonded and arranged to meet once a month to maintain the connection. They gathered first at different restaurants around the South Shore before someone suggested, she forgot whom, it would be more relaxing and intimate if they met in their homes for pot lucks. Everyone concurred and as the months passed, the group drew closer.

Mike Dimick and his longtime girlfriend, Francis Brown, changed the dynamic when they brought baggies of white powder to the parties, meth and cocaine, adding drugs to the abundance of booze available. No one objected. Eleanor suspected some, or all of them, already used. After a while, everyone indulged including her strait-laced husband. Dimick upped the ante again by inserting oxycodone into the mix.

Things took another unexpected turn on one drug and alcohol fueled evening. Dimick sat next to her, stroked her thigh, kissed her neck and fondled her breasts. She didn't resist and her husband didn't intervene since he and Dimick's date pawed each other in another corner of the room.

The other two couples, the Lawson's and Wilson's, as stoned as everyone else, took their cue and also exchanged partners. The night's activities did not progress beyond kissing and caressing although Dimick's hand found its way under her skirt and reached her crotch before she stopped him.

From that night on, expectations of intimacy grew, always after much drinking and drug use. Partners switched and the evening ended with new twosomes retiring to separate bedrooms. They placed slips of pink and blue paper with numbers on them in a bowl. Those selecting a matching number and color paired up. Men selected pink; women blue. No one confessed interest in a same sex relationship although Eleanor thought at least one man might have chosen to go that way given the opportunity.

While no real problems emerged in the beginning, feelings became strained after a few months and surfaced when Arthur Lawson confronted Mike Dimick at this year's holiday party. Arthur sensed his wife and Mike catted around outside of their monthly group; a violation of their rules and a cardinal tenet of swinging--- do not swing with friends. Attachments often develop and jealousy rears its ugly head.

Mike and Sandra Lawson did not hide their feelings for each other. They crossed the line. Her own affection for Pete Wilson went beyond the initial physical attraction. Dangerous.

A cold chill enveloped her; one the coffee did not mitigate. *Did Arthur Lawson's resentment of Mike Dimick lead to murder?*

She and Brett had taken a snack break with the Lawson's on the student field trip to Fort Warren. Arthur left for fifteen or twenty minutes to go to the bathroom. They couldn't verify his whereabouts during that time and would have to tell the investigators if asked. Their lifestyle could be exposed if they revealed Arthur's rage toward Mike was based on their wife-swapping orgies.

Mortified, Eleanor could blame her conduct on an abuse of drugs and alcohol, but who would care if it led to murder? Not the police. Not parents whose children her husband supervised. The scandal would destroy their lives and the reputation of Bridge Hill.

It was rumored, though not proven, Mike supplied drugs to students and other school staff outside of their clique. Tears cascaded down Eleanor's cheeks. She feared those drugs were the source and cause of the recent overdoses ravaging the campus.

She got up from the table and walked to her bedroom. Once there, she rummaged through her underwear drawer and found the baggie of oxy she stashed; three pills remained. She took them into the kitchen and downed two with a glass of water.

A mistake.

Chapter 27

Lopez and Magliore

Rory Belanger did not show up for his one o'clock social studies class. His teacher hadn't seen him for several days and sent a note to the dean of students, Marsha Landry, reporting his absences.

Landry's office is in the administration building, so Lopez and I traipse back across campus to speak with her. She would know more about individual kids and their behavior, friends and home lives, than the more remote headmaster. His primary focus is fundraising, maintaining positive community relations and interacting with school trustees.

The dean's office, two doors down from the headmaster's, is smaller and less elaborate. Two students are sitting on a bench in the reception area under the watchful eye of a secretary. The miscreants keep their heads lowered as we approach the older gal ensconced behind a weathered oak desk.

We present our credentials and ask to see Ms. Landry. At that moment, the dean's door opens and a young man rushes out. He glances sideways at his buddies on the bench, no doubt co-conspirators in some nefarious deed. They don't speak, unwilling to incur Landry's wrath.

The secretary, or administrative assistant as her name-plate reads, Ms. Andrews, gets up and introduces us to Landry, who keeps her eyes on the boy as he flees the office, chastised.

"These two detectives, Magliore and Lopez, would like to speak with you Ma'am," Andrews says, by way of introduction. "They're investigating the murder of poor Mr. Dimick."

We didn't explain our presence. Like assistants everywhere, she has an innate intuition about such things. Much like the principal's secretary at Hull High, when I was a student, who guessed my transgression even before I showed up to answer for my sins.

Dean Landry is thirty-something, tall, slender, two or three inches shy of six feet, with auburn hair cascading to her shoulders and bright, inquisitive hazel eyes. She's dressed in school colors, blue skirt, blue flats, white blouse and gold jacket with BH embroidered in blue above the left breast pocket. To my chagrin, her skirt length does not hover around her mid thighs or butt like those worn by female students.

She greets us with a smile and firm handshake, takes us into her office and directs us to two padded straight-backed chairs in front of her desk. I flash back to my time spent facing a stern vice principal who never smiled and looked nothing like Landry. I empathize with the boy who fled the room in embarrassment. Don't share these memories, of course, and sit where instructed.

"Nasty business, Mike's murder," Landry says, opening the conversation. "Good teacher. Popular. Kids liked him. Faculty as well."

Something about the way she says this is a bit off. I let it pass and defer to Lopez who takes the lead. Woman to Woman. The dean's body language indicates she's more interested in hearing from my partner than from me. She gawks at Lopez with a look one would use when appraising a potential conquest. She might drool at any moment. Can't say as I blame her; the image of Lopez in her underwear is still implanted in my memory.

Lopez feigns disinterest, and begins. "Thank you for seeing us without an appointment. We're investigating the murder of Mike Dimick, as your assistant explained, and as part of our inquiry, we're trying to track down Rory Belanger."

Landry sits back in her chair. "Rory? Whatever for?"

"He may have been with Dakota Johnson last night; supplied her with the drugs and alcohol that led to her overdose."

Landry shakes her head. "Rory is a great athlete but struggles academically; spends more time partying than studying. He'll graduate with the slimmest of margins, though with his grandfather's connections, I won't be surprised if he gets into Harvard or Yale. That he abuses alcohol and drugs is not surprising. Many of the kids here do. Their parents do more to enable them than to discipline them or to set a proper example."

Lopez gives me a quizzical glance, turns back to Landry. "What I'm about to tell you is confidential. You must not repeat it to anyone. Okay?"

Surprised, Landry waits a moment before nodding.

"A baggie of pills in Dakota's room matches those we found in Mike Dimick's home suggesting Dimick is the source of drugs on campus."

Landry pales, her hands shake. She clasps them together on her desk to stop the trembling.

I jump in. "The opioids Mike dealt were knockoffs, tainted with other hazardous substances. That's why we must find Rory. If he uses them or passes them on to others, they're all in danger."

I don't tell her Rory's a suspect in Dimick's murder.

Landry grimaces, but understands. "How can I help?"

"Rory was not in his room, did not go to class and did not show up for a meeting with us scheduled in Dr. Watt's office. Can you think of anyplace he might hang out? To stay under the radar?"

"Yes. One. Rory's parents live in Connecticut but his grandfather resides in Cohasset. Rory sometimes visits him and might go there if he felt threatened."

"His grandfather?"

"Stan Williams, one of the school's biggest financial backers and the president of the board of trustees."

"The same man whose name is on one of the dorms."

"Yup, and he may not appreciate you interrogating his grandson."

"Well, we've already spoken with Rory since he was on the school field trip to Fort Warren. We can assure Mr. Williams it's just a follow-up if he's concerned."

"Makes sense. Ms. Andrews can give you his address."

We both stand to leave when Landry stops us. "Also," she says, gawking at my partner. "Would you give me your cell phone number should I think of something else?"

Lopez smiles.

Oblivious or knowing? I can't tell.

Lopez extracts a silver business card holder from the pocket of her slacks and hands a card to Landry. I don't know if Terry is a switch hitter when it comes to sex, or if she plays for one team, just not mine. How else to explain her rejection of a hunk like me?

Ha!

Once outside, Lopez grabs my shoulder and spins me to face her. She anticipated my evil thoughts. "Not one word, Magliore. Not one word."

I recoil, raising my hands in a surrender gesture; keep silent. I remember a sign posted in the classroom by my high school shop teacher: "Even a fish wouldn't get in trouble if he kept his mouth shut."

I should abide by those words more often. My yap is often disconnected from my brain. I can't fathom why I keep flashing back to high school. Lopez would claim I'm still a pimply faced adolescent---without the pimples, thank God.

She may be right.

The idea of her hooking up with Dean Landry is a blow to my fragile ego. Something a teenager would do. I need to get over it. They might be good for each other. But my gut is churning---an alarm or jealousy? ---can't tell.

I've got to stop obsessing over my partner. It will not lead to a positive result---either for me or Lopez.

The "Magliore Curse."

Chapter 28

Luis Garcia

Miguel Chavez dispatched his *Capo*, Luis Garcia, to Newport, New Hampshire, to reconnoiter the town and to recruit an employee of Sturm, Ruger to provide inside intelligence for their proposed gun heist--- a disgruntled laborer or someone with a drug habit looking to score some product. If he found someone who met both criteria, all the better.

Many workers at the firearms manufacturing plant ate breakfast at the local Country Kitchen before starting their shift. The diner is ten minutes away from the Ruger facility; the food tasty, affordable and plentiful.

Luis spent three consecutive days at the diner lingering over coffee, watching Ruger employees come and go. Most entered in groups of three or four, sat together and shared good-natured banter; easily identified by the clothing they sported: shirts and hats displaying the company logo, a Phoenix bird with upswept wings in red or black and white an "R" below the bird's head. One guy wore a shirt proclaiming: "I built the guns that made history."

Luis smiled. CJNG planned to add to that history, but not in the way anyone at Ruger might imagine. He didn't let that thought distract him from his mission and soon identified his target, a man who kept his head down, shunned the other employees and always ate alone in a corner table for two, a Boston Red Sox cap pulled low above his eyes.

On the fourth day of his surveillance, Garcia walked over to the man, asked to sit down but did not engage him in conversation; commented on the weather and the quality of the food, nothing more. The man grunted; didn't look up.

On the tenth day of the ritual, Luis introduced himself as Sonny Cardenas, an unemployed machinist considering applying at Ruger.

"You don't want to work in that shithole," the man said without hesitation. "Bosses are a bunch of pricks, play favorites. The pay sucks, work is dull and repetitive. Stay away."

The man's use of the term "repetitive" revealed he was educated but unhappy; the type of employee CJNG sought.

"Wow!" Garcia said, "sounds like you've had a rough time."

"Damn straight. Most of these bastards will stab you in the back to get ahead, turn you in to the boss for the slightest infraction. I trust no one. Can't leave though, need the job. The benefits are okay. Got an ex-wife and kid to support."

He dropped his eyes to the table and returned to eating.

"Notice you didn't pal around with anyone," Garcia acknowledged. "Don't think I'll apply there."

"Smart," the man said, finishing his last piece of bacon.

Garcia nodded, drained his umpteenth cup of coffee, excused himself and exited the diner. Once in his car, he used his cell phone to alert his boss, Miguel Chavez. "Found our inside guy," he said, but gave no details.

"Wrap him up as soon as you can," Chavez said, pleased.

* * *

On his next visit to the Country Kitchen, Luis Garcia finally asked his companion his name.

"Bobby Walton," the man said, and for the first time, offered his hand.

Garcia shook it with a vise-like grip and held on for longer than such a greeting might take. "You know, Bobby," he said. "I'm out of work, but I'm doing good."

"How so?"

Garcia glanced around as if to ensure privacy and leaned across the table. "I have friends."

Walton laughed. "Friends who give you money?"

Garcia smiled, eyeballed the room again. "Can I trust you?"

Walton took a sip of coffee, sat back and crossed his arms.

"Is it legal?"

"What if it's not?"

"Depends. How much money we talkin' about?"

"More than at Ruger or anywhere else for that matter."

Walton rubbed his chin, looked around. No one appeared interested in his conversation with Garcia.

"What do I gotta do?" he asked, using "street" English in an attempt to disguise his intelligence.

"Nothing dangerous. I'll tell you when the time comes."

Before he could say yes or no, Garcia slipped him a small packet filled with a white substance. "Other perks come with this as well," he said.

Walton covered the packet with his hand and stuffed it into his pocket.

"What do I gotta do," he pressed. Sweat droplets formed on his forehead, his right leg jerked up and down like a jackhammer, attracting the attention of the waitress.

Garcia, afraid he might lose him, leaned close and spoke in a soothing, even, tone. "Bobby. Like I said, nothing risky. A word is all. To me. The date and time Ruger is scheduled to send out a sizeable shipment. You call me, you're done. I give you the money. You never see me again."

Walton stopped bouncing his leg. "How much?"

Garcia tipped back, took a deep breath and exhaled. "Twenty-five."

Walton's eyes widened. "Gotta be at least three zeros with that."

Garcia repeated his deep breathing to control his anger. He nodded. But now that the man was hooked, he needed one more thing from him.

"What carrier does your company use to ship their goods?"

"FedEx freight. Same driver all-of-the-time."

"You friends?"

Walton nodded. "Kinda."

"Think he's willing to help us for the same amount of money."

Walton smiled, didn't hesitate. "Yup! He gambles. Loses a lot."

Garcia grinned, put some bills on the table to cover the tab, stood, extracted a burner phone from his pocket and placed it in front of Walton. He bent over and whispered, "Keep that with you. One number in it, mine. Call me when you have the information we need."

He walked away patting Walton on the shoulder.

Walton stiffened at the touch. Sonny, or whatever his name was, thought he could play him for a sucker. Twenty-five grand wasn't chump change, but Bobby suspected his new buddy would pay twice that. He'd push for fifty before surrendering the name of the FedEx guy. Hell! He might hold out for a hundred.

A mistake.

Chapter 29

Lopez and Magliore

Captain Catebegian assigned Lopez and me to work out of the Hingham District Court building. The Plymouth County D.A. maintains offices in Brockton, Hingham, Plymouth and Wareham. The Hingham office jurisdiction encompasses Hanover, Hingham, Hull, Norwell, Rockland and Scituate.

Except for Hanover and Rockland, the other towns border the Atlantic Ocean and lay between Boston Harbor and Cape Cod; the so-called South Shore of Massachusetts, where crime is minimal and murder virtually non-existent according to the published stats for the state. Scituate is heralded for one of the lowest crime rates in the nation. All of this explains why we're the lone detectives occupying the Hingham offices.

The red brick courthouse, built in 1936, and now sporting a new addition, lies just north of the Weir River Bridge, a boundary between Hingham and Hull. Located on George Washington Boulevard, it's a twenty to thirty-minute drive to Pemberton Pier and a short ferry ride from there to Georges Island; far better than driving in from Brockton, which could take over an hour or more bucking traffic. And best of all, close to my digs in Hull.

Our cramped office is in the basement. Our desks butt up against each other, so we can talk face to face and share documents when necessary. Their position also gives me the opportunity to sneak peeks at Lopez who continues to occupy my thoughts. I can't dismiss from my mind the image of Terri in her short robe in her condo the morning after I embarrassed myself by drinking too much. Her scent, the sight of her smooth thighs as she stood inches from me and dared me to act, are seared into my memory.

Sitting opposite her now, I marvel at her attractiveness; white blouse, clean and pressed, cropped hair combed, not a strand out of place, a hint of pink on her lips. I'm an idiot, of course, fantasizing about my partner while I should be focused on our case. My infatuation will lead to disappointment and cause a rift between us if I don't smarten up. I know it.

Lopez doesn't look up from her task, oblivious to my internal conflict. After leaving Dean Landry's office at Bridge Hill Academy, we came here to review notes and strategize our next moves. She's scrolling through a note app on her iPhone while I thumb through my pocket notebook trying to concentrate.

I'm convinced drugs played a part in Mike Dimick's murder, but our suspect list is limited to the field trip participants and other tourists on Fort Warren that day; none are documented druggies. Despite that, most of the adults are still in play.

I believe the one student with a motive is Rory Belanger. He hated Dimick, jealous of his relationship with his girlfriend, Dakota Johnson. None of the other

FRANK J. INFUSINO JR.

kids interviewed had a reason to hate their teacher. Many expressed their fondness for the man.

As I'm scouring my notepad, my cell phone rings---Park Ranger Alyce Crimshaw.

"Magliore," I answer.

"Detective, Alyce Crimshaw. Good news. The Boston police cadets found the clothes and knife used by our assailant."

"Fantastic."

"Yes sir. Do you want me to bag and tag them and send them to you at the D.A.'s office?"

I hesitate a moment before responding. "No. I'll come get them. I want to examine the crime scene again. "It's 10:00 a.m. Can I come out this afternoon?"

"That would be fine. I'll be here until five, or later, if you can't make it before then."

"No need. I'll catch a lift with the Harbor Patrol, be there by noon at the latest."

"Okay," Crimshaw says. "Around twelve."

Lopez lifts her eyebrows. "So?" she asks.

I give her the update, request she take the point on interviewing the Kilgore's, chaperones on the Bridge Hill field trip, while I return to Fort Warren.

She agrees, then her phone rings. "Yes, Yes," she repeats a couple of times and clicks off.

"That was Dean Landry. Says she has confidential, personal information, she was reluctant to share in our meeting and doesn't want to reveal over the phone. Asked to meet tonight over coffee."

I grin.

"What" Lopez says, as she stands and places her hands on her hips. A stance she takes often when challenging me.

I choose to keep the peace.

"Nothing," I say. "Landry did seem comfortable speaking to you. Could be something helpful."

Lopez drops her arms to her side and relaxes, no longer on guard. "I'll take wonderful notes," she says.

"As will I when I go back to Georges Island."

I'm eager to dispel the Fort Warren ghost stories, which hover over our investigation though Lopez and I never discuss this. Speculation runs rampant even among rational people. Perhaps, I can discover some piece of concrete evidence that points to some living person and omits the involvement of any supernatural entity.

Ghosts my ass!

90

Chapter 30

Vince Magliore

I catch a ride with the same two Harbor Patrol cops who ferried Lopez and I out to the island the first time. Georges is still closed to tourists, so just one other person in addition to Crimshaw greets me---Ranger Emiliano Santana.

Crimshaw lays the evidence out on a plastic sheet on a display table once filled with Civil War artifacts.

"The killer wore a hooded black Halloween witches cape, black mask and black gloves," she says. "He carried a five-inch serrated kitchen utility knife, blue, which he wrapped in the cape; stashed all the items on a brick ledge inside a fireplace in the "corridor of dungeons." Not visible without a careful inspection. The cadets missed them in their initial search, but one diligent young man retraced his steps and found the treasure."

I examine the clothing and the knife. "So," I say, "the killer had to bring this in with him, or her, on the day of the murder or squirreled it away at an earlier visit?"

Crimshaw and Santana nod. "A few of the adults and students toted backpacks and most of the women carried a purse or handbag," Crimshaw says. "We searched them after the fact but don't do that as a matter of policy when they arrive. The Fort is not considered a target of terrorists. We've never had a threatening incident in my ten years here...until this."

She pauses, shakes her head. "We may tighten our procedures now, though."

No point in rehashing that.

"The good news," I say, "is the lab should be able to extract DNA and even fingerprints from the clothing and the knife. If the perp is in a crime data base, we can ID our killer."

"Let's hope so," Crimshaw says. "He didn't have time to wipe everything clean. Blood residue remains on the knife blade and on the gloves. Some may be his."

"You know," I say, "these *Emeril* brand knives come with a plastic sheath. Any sign of one?"

Both rangers shake their heads no.

Long shot, but if he, or she---I keep adding the female component although Crimshaw did not---took it without the covering, it might still be in a utensil's drawer in the killer's residence. A mistake. But conceivable. Few murderers are Phi Beta Kappa's.

"I'll direct the cadets to comb the area adjacent to the fireplace again," Santana interjects. "A few are still on site."

"Thanks," I say. "I'd like to go back out to the crime scene now."

* * *

Santana escorts me back to the room where Mike Dimick was killed, excuses himself to round up a couple of cadets to re-search the area where the evidence was found. Santana acts distracted. In the visitor's center, he kept shifting his weight from one leg to the other, looked around the room often and couldn't find a place to rest his hands. Not something I wish to explore. I don't know him well enough to ask personal questions.

The CSU team left in place floodlights, powered by a gas generator. I find an on/off switch on the machine, power it up and study the interior of the murder room visually, but don't enter. The techs are always thorough. I see nothing that piques my interest.

I turn the equipment off and walk toward where the killer's apparel and knife were hidden according to Crimshaw's description of the site. As I make my way along the cavernous corridor, I envision the men who quartered here in the Civil War and in the subsequent world wars. Some were prisoners, some defenders of Boston Harbor, some trainees. Their circumstances differed, but like men in any war, thrown together in tight quarters, they shared a comradery difficult to replicate in civilian life. I can sense their presence, hear their joking and grousing.

For some reason, I'm drawn to a gloomy, narrow passageway off the central corridor. A wooden sawhorse with a "staff only" sign blocks the entrance. I squeeze around it and edge my way into total darkness.

I do that sometimes; break rules.

The killer might have hidden in this shadowy recess before slipping out to attack Mike Dimick. He emerged from somewhere if not among the identified tourists or students. Was he on the island before everyone else, hiding, waiting? Perhaps he moored a small boat at a buoy, one of several the parks department reserves for boaters; came ashore without drawing attention, left the same way. Knew Dimick would be here. A drug dealer or user Dimick stiffed or pissed off.

On the other hand, what if Dimick wasn't the intended victim. What if the attacker was prepared to play his role of ghost and assault anyone when the opportunity presented itself? And that opening came when the teacher and student crept away from the field trip?

I doubt Lopez will buy this. No evidence supports either scenario, and they'll only complicate our investigation. I'll keep them to myself for the time being.

As I stand in the dank hallway ruminating over these possibilities, my flashlight dies. I give it a couple of whacks to see if the batteries are being temperamental; doesn't work.

I'm not too deep into this side tunnel, so I turn and inch my way back to the main corridor running my hand against a wall for support and direction. As I do so, cold air envelopes me and something creases the nape of my neck—a spider or some other creature I don't want to imagine? I spin around flaying my arms to get it off me. A whisper, a hot breath on my right ear sends a shiver down my spine. A female voice says, "I will save you." I slap at it; it stops. My mind playing tricks.

My body warms and my flashlight flips back on. I shine the beam around in a one-eighty arc one way, then the other. Nothing. Blank walls. No spider webs or other crawling insects. No one. No apparition in black robes.

Am I hallucinating? I stride out of the tight hallway, through the arched corridors and into the sunlit parade ground. The strange words echoing in my mind: "I will save you."

Save me from what? Nonsense.

"Are you okay, detective?" Ranger Santana asks as he approaches me. "You look like you've seen a ghost," he adds, twisting his mouth into a broad grin.

"Just a bit claustrophobic," I lie. "Nothing open space won't cure."

We step further into the parade ground and I stop. "Where do you think it happened," I ask.

Santana regards me with a quizzical expression.

"Where what happened?" he says.

"The hanging."

He puts his hands on his waist and smiles. "You do know it's a myth?"

I hesitate a fraction of a second too long before saying, "Of course."

Santana, amused, is determined to convince me. "No one ever verified the story. No record exists of a woman being hung in Boston around the time of the alleged incident in 1862. Papers across the country would have carried the gory details, don't ya think."

"Hey! I'm convinced pal," I say, and march off toward the visitor center, Santana shuffling to catch up.

I take possession of the clothes and weapon from the killer, thank the rangers for their help and dial up the Harbor Patrol for a ride back to the mainland.

I'm not going to share with Terry Lopez my thought about Dimick being a target of opportunity; too much of a stretch and not something I believe. Our inquiry into Dimick's background revealed several individuals with possible motives to take the guy out, from disgruntled drug users to irate colleagues pissed off he might be messing around with their wives. Problem is, just a select few were here, on this island, on the day of the murder.

I also won't mention my strange encounter in the dark tunnel. Lopez and Captain Catebegian would rag on me forever. I'd never live it down.

Ghosts my ass.

Chapter 31

Vince Magliore

I reject the notion of a ghost haunting Fort Warren. My strange encounter could be attributed, as most paranormal events can, to a normal occurrence; wind blowing through the tunnels could account for a sensation of something or someone touching me; a low battery charge for the Maglite blinking on and off; the voice a figment of my imagination heightened by the gloomy setting.

Nevertheless, I'm a bit shaken and, as I often do when I need to think things through, I drive to Nantasket Beach and park my late model Rav4 in the parking lot at the bottom of Green Hill near an abandoned restaurant. I don't understand why several eateries at this location failed; prime real estate with a fantastic view. Friends tell me this is a common problem in coastal towns far off main highways. Route 3, for example, bypasses Hull and leads straight to Cape Cod.

To reach Hull, people must navigate narrow, winding roadways, treacherous in winter from snow and ice. Rather than tempt the fates, they shop and dine in their own communities without the hassle of a long, hazardous trip. Plymouth, though in a similar position, boasts historical attractions which draw visitors like the famous 'Rock,' a Mayflower replica and a model colonial Plantation. Hull once had an amusement center, Paragon Park, open in the summer, but that's long gone, scrapped in favor of bleak condos.

I shrug, not my problem. And start my trek along the concrete walkway bordering the beach; a hike I often make to clear my head. The invigorating smell of the ocean and the scenery are spectacular today, the first week of November. A frigid offshore wind carries the spray from breaking waves into my face. I lean into the gusts and march forward.

My face stings from the wet and cold, but my hooded windbreaker keeps me warm. A few people sitting in their cars, watching the whitecaps, eye me as I trudge on. No other hardy soul joins me.

I stumble past the bandstand once part of the all-wooden historic Nantasket Hotel, torn down in the sixties, and stride under a concrete overhang, an extension of a renovated bathhouse. Ahead is a more open area parallel to Hull Shore Drive. Several bars and the new Nantasket Resort Hotel stand across the road. The wind knocks me sideways a couple of times.

By the time I make the comfort station, which contains restrooms and outdoor showers, the sidewalk ends and the wind subsides, though my face still tingles from the cold. I lean over the railing facing the Atlantic and watch several boats plow through the rough seas. Don't notice the figure sitting on a bench behind me until I turn to leave; a woman, face scrunched down in her bulky jacket.

I move past her until her voice stops me: "Vince? Mags?" she asks.

I turn and gaze into her eyes. Eyes that once turned me to mush when we dated in high school.

"Angela?"

She nods, stands and we embrace.

"What are you doing here?" she asks. "Thought you went back to California after the reunion?"

"Nope. Didn't you follow the murder case of Father John?"

"No. I lived in New Hampshire until a few weeks ago; read about it. Felt bad for Johnny, but my husband was very sick. I concentrated my energy on him."

Married. Must have been her husband at our class reunion, not a boyfriend as I believed at the time. I didn't converse with her much because, once I saw Kate Maxwell, my attention never wavered from her.

"Sorry about your husband," I say. "Is he with you?"

Moisture forms at the corners of those captivating eyes.

"He didn't make it."

* * *

I wrap Angela in a hug after the news about her husband; suggest we escape the cold and grab a cup of coffee. She nods.

I grasp her hand, and we traipse over the uneven asphalt and cement sidewalk back toward the Resort Hotel and the Paragon Grill inside. The warmth and softness of her hand reminds me of days long past when we held hands navigating the halls of the high school weaving in and out of oncoming students rushing to class; imagining we'd always be together. Life has a way of smashing youthful dreams.

In the restaurant, a young hostess seats us by a window overlooking the ocean. It's cozy, so we both discard our heavy jackets. Angela wears a Red Sox sweatshirt over blue spandex workout pants and pink running shoes. Her black hair, now sporting a touch of gray, is pulled back into a ponytail. Her cheeks and nose are crimson; the result of the bitter weather. She still looks wonderful, though a tad thin.

I gawk.

"What?" she asks.

"You're still as beautiful as ever," I stammer, embarrassed.

"Thanks. I don't feel attractive. My husband's death was prolonged. I devoted myself to his care, ignored my appearance."

"Well, must be those terrific Latin genes."

She laughed and her face brightened for the first time.

"Still pushing the Italian heritage theme, eh?"

"Just speaking the truth."

We sit talking about old times for over two hours. I learn her husband, Andrew Rossi, had been a doctor in Newport, a small New Hampshire town. She served as his receptionist. No children despite trying. She's staying in Hull with her mother for a week or two, still owns a home in New Hampshire and intends to return there. At least for the foreseeable future.

I regal her with overblown tales of my college football career at San Diego State, my life as a detective in southern California and my present job with the Massachusetts State Police. I omit the reason I'm back here.

Her eyes widen when I reveal I have a room at the home of Karen Hundley, our former classmate.

"A room with Karen, huh?"

"Not a room 'with' Karen, just one at her home. Nothing's going on between us."

"Right," she says, looking away, fumbles in her purse and takes out a vial of blue pills. She pops one in her mouth without explanation; the second pill she's taken since we arrived here. She downed the other one as I returned from the restroom. I didn't comment then and say nothing now, although her actions set off alarm bells to this recovering addict.

I examine her with a practiced eye, and detect her pupils are constricted, and she speaks with a slight tremor in her voice, something I attributed to the wind and cold at the beach. Popping pills, and while not hiding it, not mentioning why, is also a red flag she might be abusing drugs.

Maybe there's a reasonable explanation. I'm in no position to question any of it. Except for a brief hello at our high school reunion, I haven't seen or talked to her in over two decades. We both have changed since our teens and have secrets. I know mine; can't worry about what Angela's might be.

* * *

I escort Angela back to her car. She drives me back to the Rav4. We ride in silence until she drops me off.

I open the door to leave and mumble, "How about dinner tonight?" like I'm back in high school asking her on a date for the first time.

She hesitates, stares out toward the Atlantic.

Before she can say no, I add, "Dinner Angela, nothing more. Loved this afternoon, but we have more to talk about. Pick you up at your mother's place at six. No commitments?"

She smiles but delivers a crushing blow to my fragile ego. "I'm not ready yet Mags. Maybe another time. Please understand."

Shot down before my plane even leaves the tarmac.

"Okay, Angela," I say. "I lost someone not long ago too; healing takes time. I'm sorry. Didn't mean to push."

She leans over and pecks my cheek; doesn't comment.

I step out of the car, close the door and watch her drive off. Shake my head. The pills she ingested at lunch resembled oxycodone. Perhaps it was a relaxant of some kind; a prescription needed to calm her nerves.

I'm fooling myself; I know better. She's in trouble, feel it in my bones. But what can I do?

Hope I won't regret doing nothing; sense that I will.

Chapter 32

Lopez and Magliore

Still reeling from Angela's rejection, and my suspicion about her drug abuse, I receive a phone call from my partner requesting to meet at South Shore Hospital. She skips the details; assures me it's related to our investigation of Mike Dimick's murder. I smile. I'm such a regular at the hospital, I should request a private room.

The young female receptionist directs me to the third floor. When I step off the elevator, four people are standing outside a room midway down the hall. One is Terry Lopez. The others include a woman EMT, a uniformed Marshfield officer and a man I don't recognize. He turns out to be Brett Kilgore, a teacher at Bridge Hill Academy and one of the chaperones on the ill-fated school field trip to Fort Warren.

"Fill me in," I ask, directing my question to Lopez.

"Eleanor Kilgore overdosed on these," she says, and holds up a baggie containing a blue tablet labeled oxycodone similar to those we found at Mike Dimick's condo and in Dakota Johnson's dorm room.

Counterfeit. Dangerous.

I study Brett Kilgore who hasn't moved or spoken since I arrived. His face is ashen, head bowed, hands clasped in front.

I place a hand on his shoulder. "Mr. Kilgore. I'm Lieutenant Magliore, state police. You've met my partner here. We'd like to speak with you."

Kilgore tilts his head toward me, in shock, his eyes expressionless. He doesn't move or acknowledge me.

"We need to talk with you sir," I stress.

His head snaps back, eyes shift to my hand on his shoulder.

"Yes. Yes. I'm sorry. Eleanor? Is she okay?" he asks.

Lopez cuts in. "She had a close call, but the doctors are confident she will recover. She's resting now."

"Let's find some coffee sir," I suggest. "There's a visitor's lounge at the end of the hall."

The lounge is hospital basic; tiled counter with a coffee pot, couch with aluminum legs and multicolored cushions, three straight backed gray plastic chairs, a wooden rack on the floor in one corner holding outdated magazines.

Kilgore sits on the couch. Lopez and I pull up two chairs facing him.

"I'm sorry about Eleanor, Mr. Kilgore," I say. "We suspect her overdose is connected to Mike Dimick's murder."

"What? How?" He stammers, swaying backward as if punched.

"We believe Mike Dimick provided the pills your wife took. We think he was dealing drugs at Bridge Hill; to kids as well as faculty."

"Kids. My God."

"We don't have time to be sensitive or diplomatic, Mr. Kilgore. Lives are at risk. Please tell us what you know."

He leans forward, placing his arms on his thighs, keeps his voice low, rubbing moisture from his eyes. He tells a shocking story. One that would be a terrible blow to the reputation of Bridge Hill Academy if it became public; reminiscent of "Peyton Place," if you're old enough to remember the book, movie, and TV drama depicting a sexually depraved community.

Chapter 33

Brett Kilgore

Brett Kilgore relates how the gathering of four couples from the social studies department at Bridge Hill, teachers and spouses, started innocently enough with monthly dinners at restaurants. These get-togethers later morphed into pot lucks at the homes of the participants and spiraled into drug fueled wife-swapping parties initiated by Mike Dimick, who provided the drugs.

He named the members of the group.

"How long has this been going on," Lopez asks.

"Thirteen or fourteen months," Kilgore replies. "Things unraveled when that weasel Arthur Lawson provoked a row at the last faculty Christmas party. He suspected Mike and Sandra Lawson had become romantically involved, something we all promised to avoid."

Lopez and I lock eyes when Kilgore calls Lawson a weasel.

"You were on the field trip to Fort Warren," Lopez says. "Did the chaperones, you and the Lawsons, remain together?"

"Yes. But Arthur went to the bathroom while we grabbed something to eat. He was gone for twenty-minutes or so."

This syncs with what Sandra Lawson told us.

"So, he had the chance to kill Dimick?" I ask.

Kilgore nods, a quick dip of his head. "Ordinarily, I would say he didn't have it in him. But the thought of Mike and Sandra sneaking around behind his back infuriated him. He worried the gals in our group had sex with him as an obligation rather than a desire. He was right. The men lusted after Sandra. The women tolerated Arthur."

* * *

Arthur Lawson's a weasel, but jealousy can drive even mild-mannered people to commit crimes of passion. His restroom hiatus gave him the opportunity. Once alone, he kills Dimick, strolls back to the other chaperones. He's known to the park rangers and students; a respected teacher. No one would give him a second look.

I'll discuss this with Lopez later. Now I pursue the drug angle. "What types of drugs did Dimick bring to the parties?"

"Coke, meth, heroin, oxy."

"Can you identify his supplier?"

Kilgore squirms, laces his fingers behind his head, turns away. Keeps silent.

"Mr. Kilgore, Brett, this isn't a game. Lives depend on your cooperation."

Kilgore exhales and brings his hands down to his lap. "He asked me to go with him one day, to New Hampshire. Mike worked in a small town there for a while before coming to Bridge Hill. He injured himself playing softball. The doctor who treated him continued to prescribe opioids for his pain long after they were necessary. Any time Mike wanted a refill, he could get it. Mike later discovered this dude had access to illegal drugs."

"Do you remember the name of the town and the physician?"

"Yeah, Newport. The doctor's name is Andrew Rossi. I never went into the clinic; saw his name on a signpost outside."

"Are you sure about this Brett?"

"Yeah! I took two trips with Mike. He wanted the company. It's a three-hour drive from here. Both times we stopped at the same doctor's office. You might find one of those prescription bottles in Mike's condo or in his room at school, though he's been getting baggies of the stuff the last month or two. Coke and pills."

I fight to keep my composure, but Lopez senses a change in my body language; blood draining from my face, posture stiff. She stares at me with a quizzical expression.

She's not aware Andrew Rossi is, or was, my former sweetheart's husband unless by some quirk of fate two doctors with the same name practice in the same town.

Fat chance.

And now I suspect Angela's dependent on opioids herself, furnished by him, legally or from his stash of counterfeit stuff?

The bastard.

We thank Brett Kilgore for the information and leave the room. Lopez touches my arm when we're in the corridor. "What happened in there?"

I hesitate a beat before responding. "The doctor who supplied the drugs to Dimick. I think he was Angela's husband."

"Was?"

"He died of cancer."

"We should update the captain," she says, "now."

I nod.

Shit. How do I tell Angela her husband pushed illegal narcotics? Yet, how could she not know? She worked with him, knew his clients, both respectable and shady. He hooked her for Christ's sake. If we tell Big Cat of my former relationship with her, even if it was as far back as high school, he might take us, me, off the case; conflict of interest. I need to convince him I can remain professional despite the consequences and my link to an individual involved.

I also must persuade Lopez to pursue this. She's not swayed a drug dealer or user killed Mike Dimick since none was among those detained on the island after the murder. If I'm right, that raises the possibility, again, that an unknown person fled before lock down. A hard sell without any concrete evidence. Going out of state in pursuit of a drug connection or phantom drug crazed killer will be a distraction in Lopez's mind, prevent us from honing in on the real murderer.

I fear she's right, but can't let it go.

Chapter 34

Lopez and Magliore

We drive from South Shore Hospital to the Plymouth County District Attorney's central office in Brockton in silence, a thirty-minute trip, give or take, depending on traffic. Captain Catebegian waives us inside when he sees our approach through his glass walled office. We sit in plastic straight backed chairs facing his department issue metal desk, clear except for a white phone on the right, an in/out box on the left and a manila folder in front of him.

He taps it with his finger. "This is the autopsy report on Dakota Johnson. Interesting results."

We wait for the shoe to drop.

"M.E. reports asphyxiation as cause of death, not a drug overdose; fibers from her pillow were found in her mouth and nose. Someone smothered her."

My partner and I share questioning glances.

"Oh, she took pills, alright," Catebegian says. "Counterfeit oxycodone spiked with a lethal combination of fentanyl and heroin. Probably, would have died from that, but the killer chose not to wait."

We're stunned. Another murder.

Big Cat isn't finished though. "Most of the fingerprints taken in the girl's room were smudged; kids coming and going. One was identified as Dakota's roommate and another as a girl living in the dorm. These were in the school's database, not AFIS. (The Automated Fingerprint Identification System used by the FBI and other law enforcement organizations).

"Bridge Hill fingerprints faculty, students, support staff, grounds-people and anyone else who might come in contact with kids who, for the most part, come from wealthy families. Ideal targets of a kidnapping for ransom. The staff prints go through state and national criminal databases to check for sex offenders, wanted persons, gang members, the whole nine yards. Student fingerprints, because of privacy laws, stay within the school's system."

Catebegian's on a roll, yet he gets up and pours himself a cup of coffee from a pot resting on a counter behind his desk; doesn't offer any to us.

He sits down, takes a sip of the hot brew and continues. "Two clear prints were also discovered on the wall above Johnson's pillow. One belonged to student Rory Belanger and the other to a man named, Stan Williams."

I jump in. "Belanger was Dakota Johnson's boyfriend. Williams is a member of the Board of Trustees and Belanger's grandfather, an influential financial backer of the school. Terry and I suspect Belanger and Dakota partied in her room the night she died. The kid doesn't understand less is more when it comes to cologne. A strong scent of the stuff lingered in the room when we investigated. Not conclusive though. It could be from an earlier visit.

"Not sure why the grandfather's print would be above the bed in a girl's dorm room, although as a trustee, he could visit classrooms and residence halls from time to time as part of his oversight of school conditions. Certainly, the building that bears his name."

"Talk to the boy and his grandfather," Cat orders.

He doesn't ask us to report on our investigation and I choose to keep silent about the drug situation involving Dimick and Angela Rossi.

Lopez doesn't rat me out, but her silence will come back to bite me in the butt, I'm sure.

Chapter 35

Theresa Lopez

After the conference with Captain Catebegian, Theresa Lopez went home to shower and change before meeting Dean Marsha Landry at **The Fours**, a sports bar and grill in Norwell, a couple of miles from her condo. She selected a short gray skirt, blue blouse, flats and a matching purse to conceal her badge and Glock. She assessed her image in the full-length mirror behind the bathroom door and nodded her satisfaction.

Changing clothes for an appointment connected to a case was not her usual procedure, but she picked up on the vibes from the dean in her office while appearing to be oblivious; a ploy to keep Magliore from breaking her balls. Perhaps she could use those vibes to get information from the dean. She would be walking a delicate tightrope though, exploiting the sexual feelings of another. Her love-life was screwed up enough without complicating it more.

She had little time for romance. Work came first; the hours long and often depressing. Smiling and feigning interest in some guy's lament about his "rough day at the office" didn't fly. Not to mention that female cops intimidated many men. Guys questioned their femininity and feared getting their ass kicked if they tried anything.

Lopez had experimented with online dating for six months, omitting her occupation in her profile. The men often vanished when it surfaced. One junior attorney in a Boston law firm survived three dates before ghosting her. Didn't break her heart. No sparks flew.

She did have a same sex relationship in high school with a close friend, a cheerleader as it happened, and another with a secretary at the police academy. Both were experiments of a sort. Neither endured. The experiences were awkward, not awful, but taught her she was not a lesbian or even bi-sexual. She preferred men, as fickle as they could be. Babies. Like Magliore.

Marsha Landry was charismatic, intelligent and knew Lopez's occupation. That she requested to meet after work, to disclose confidential information, piqued Lopez's curiosity and fear. She worried the dean would make a move on her; not sure how to fend it off. To lead her on would be deceitful and unkind and Lopez was neither. Yet, she had no choice. Landry might have crucial information to help them solve two murders. Lopez couldn't let her concern for the woman jeopardize getting to the truth and finding the killer or killers.

The Fours touted itself as a neighborhood restaurant catering to families, sports fans and all residents of the town. Flat screen TVs covered the ceiling from every angle. A long circular bar dominated the main room with tables scattered throughout and booths lining the perimeter. When Lopez entered, she glimpsed Marsha Landry sitting at a side booth under a wall-sized photo of Fenway Park, iconic home of the Boston Red Sox. Lopez pointed to Landry as the hostess approached and mouthed she would be joining her.

Landry sat tall, back arched. She wore a short blue skirt, heels and a white blouse with a blue and gold scarf; her smile radiant, her complexion scrubbed. Her eyes wide, inquisitive.

As Lopez scooted onto the bench seat opposite the dean, a waitress appeared to take her drink order. She requested a California Cabernet, something Magliore might choose when not guzzling draft beer.

"Thank you for coming," Landry said when they were alone. "I don't know if the information I have is pertinent to Mike's murder. It's personal and something I didn't want to reveal in front of the other detective."

Lopez reached across the table and put her hand over Landry's which rested next to her glass of white wine. "Anything you say to me or my partner will stay confidential, Marsha."

Landry shivered at the contact and smiled, her white teeth setting off a face that belonged on the cover of a fashion magazine.

She placed her other hand over Theresa's. "I felt I could trust you from the start," she said, a breathless quality to her voice.

Lopez returned the smile, but her stomach churned. Taking Landry's hand was an intimate act, not that of an objective detective questioning a member of the public seeking information. She was manipulating the dean; leading her on. She reminded herself that she was a cop doing her job.

Didn't make it any easier.

* * *

Landry paused when the waitress returned with the Cabernet for Lopez. Glancing across the table for confirmation, she advised the young server they would stick to drinks for now, order food later.

Landry raised her glass to toast, hesitated, unsure what to say or even if such an action was appropriate under the circumstances.

Lopez got her off the hook by clinking glasses. "Why don't you tell me what's on your mind, Marsha."

The Bridge Hill dean nodded, relieved. "Earlier this year," she said, "Mike Dimick came to my office and informed me that a small group of social studies teachers and their wives, four couples, met once a month to socialize and bond professionally. His longtime girlfriend was out of town on business. He asked me to accompany him, not as a date, but to even the number of men and woman and as a way for me to get to know the staff better."

Lopez nodded, took a sip of wine, kept silent.

Landry continued. "The group gathered at the Kilgore's for a pot luck. I brought a tuna casserole."

Lopez smiled at this small detail and Landry shook her head. "Pretty naïve of me. Everyone drank quite a bit and Mike dispensed baggies of white powder to each couple, saved one for himself and me. I knew the substance was a drug of some kind. Frightened, I got up to leave and reached the door before Mike caught up to me. He assured me it was just something to help us relax and promised I needn't take anything. Stupidly, I agreed to stay.

"Not long after, the other couples paired up, not with their spouses, and left the room to go to other parts of the house, bedrooms I assumed."

Landry inhaled and exhaled a couple of times, took a sip of wine and studied Lopez for a reaction. She got a pat on her hand in understanding and encouragement.

"Mike and I stayed in the dining room drinking and talking until I passed out."

Her eyes watered as she pressed on. "I woke up in bed with Brett Kilgore. Mike convinced Brett that I agreed to join in on the fun. The bastard."

Tears cascaded down her cheeks, she choked out several guttural sobs and her body quivered. Lopez passed her a tissue, got up and slid in beside the dean placing an arm around her.

Reassured, Landry spit out the rest of the story.

"Mortified and terrified, I leaped out of bed, put on my clothes and bolted for the front door again. I got outside and down the street before Mike, alerted by Brett, chased me down. He wrapped his arms around me, and we struggled until I gave up. I threatened to expose the whole sordid mess.

"Mike spoke to me when I calmed down. His voice otherworldly. His eyes burned into me. He threatened that everyone at the party would swear nothing happened. I hallucinated after taking drugs, which I brought with me. My reputation would be destroyed. I would lose my job and never get another, not in a school anyway.

"I went back to the house sobbing. Arthur Lawson and Brett Kilgore confronted Mike, and they got into a shouting match. Mike had turned me over to Brett, who was with Sandra Lawson, so he could be with Sandra. That infuriated Arthur and angered Brett because Mike deceived him into thinking I willingly participated."

Landry stopped talking and rested her head on Lopez's shoulder.

The story intrigued Lopez. Arthur Lawson and Brett Kilgore, both upset with Dimick, chaperoned the high school field trip to Fort Warren. Both had motive and opportunity to kill their colleague. Sex and money always topped the list as reasons for murder.

The waitress approached their table. Lopez waived her off and signaled for the check, moving back to her own seat. She settled the bill when it came, left a generous tip and the two women exited the restaurant.

"Where are you parked?" Lopez asked and Landry pointed to a white Toyota Camry in the back of the lot under a light.

They made their way to the car arm and arm. Landry opened the driver's side door with a remote and turned to face Lopez.

"Thank you for listening and not judging. I'm sorry I couldn't keep it together. I've been suppressing these feelings for a long time."

Lopez nodded. "I understand. Being violated by someone you trusted is not an easy thing to deal with. You may want to seek professional help."

Landry offered a lopsided smile that resembled a grimace. Her eyes reflected indecision, disappointment. She embraced the detective and pecked her on the cheek. She stepped back, made eye contact, moved in to kiss Lopez on the lips.

Lopez placed both hands on Landry's chest. "No Marsha," she said. "I didn't mean to mislead you. You are an attractive, intelligent woman, but I'm not drawn to you in that way. Our relationship must remain professional. You may be called as a witness if this case goes to trial and either Brett or Arthur killed Mike. Defense lawyers would destroy your credibility and attack my professional conduct with any hint of a personal involvement between us. I'm sorry."

Landry teared up again, her body shuddered. She grabbed the car door for support. "I understand," she said. "I would never compromise your integrity."

She slid into the Camry, closed the door, backed out of her parking space and drove off, tires squealing.

Motionless, Lopez kept her eyes riveted on Landry's car long after it disappeared from view. She would report the dean's information to Magliore, emphasizing the actions of Arthur Lawson and Brett Kilgore, whose anger with Dimick at the party could be a motive for murder.

She would paint Marsha as the victim, as she was, but omit Landry's awkward advances toward her, lest Magliore torture her with sexually charged jokes and innuendo.

Asshole.

Magliore had feelings for her. She sensed it in the not so discreet glances he stole toward her when he thought she was unaware and the obvious lust he displayed in her condo the morning after their booze filled trip to a pub the night before. His constant sexual inuendo directed toward her, which he disguised as humor.

She couldn't go there. Just as she couldn't allow her empathy for Marsha to cloud her judgement and endanger the investigation.

She'd go back to her condo, sink into a hot bath, brew some green tea and concentrate her thoughts and energy on the case. Or just go to bed.

Chapter 36

The Murderer

He waited inside Landry's home using a key she slipped to him after the day in her office when she flashed him.

He waited, listening, shuffling his weight from one leg to the other, folding and unfolding his arms, flexing his fingers.

He waited with her scarf wrapped around his right hand, raising it to his nose, inhaling her scent.

He heard the car pull into the driveway, the engine shut down, the driver's side door open and close, her heels clacking on the stone walkway, the key inserted into the lock.

She opened the door and stepped inside. He slammed it closed with his foot, pulled her to his chest, wrapped the scarf around her neck and twisted.

Startled, she thrust her hands up, attempting to twist away to free herself, eyes bulging, breathing difficult. Near collapse, she relaxed, stopped resisting, recognized the cologne of her attacker. They played this game many times.

Being choked during sex heightened her sensation of being ravished; gave her power over her assailant. He was a slave to anything she wanted. She reached back and tapped him on the thigh, their signal to stop.

He ignored the warning and instead, increased the pressure with his strong hands as she thrashed around gasping, struggling to break away, eyes wide with fear.

Her movements aroused him to the point of release, but he continued twisting the scarf.

Landry, no match for youth and strength, went limp, slumped to the floor as he released his grip and guided her down.

He scooped her up, carried her upstairs to the master bedroom, dropped her on the bed, removed her skirt, blouse, panties and bra and arranged her legs six inches apart.

He was street smart, or so he imagined. Knew from watching cop shows on TV that fingerprints and DNA would link him to Marsha's murder. He swept through the house earlier, wiping down surfaces he may have touched. He would do so again before he left, including rubbing her body down with moist towelettes from the bathroom. He considered setting the house on fire to destroy evidence, but rejected that as extreme and unnecessary. He did decide to take her cell phone and laptop computer; no telling what she kept on those. He didn't want to risk taking time to try to access them. He'd drop them in a commercial dumpster in the next town.

He smiled.

Even if they found his fingerprints in the house, it meant nothing. He was the victim of an older predator who took advantage of her position to seduce him.

He had been a junior in high school when it started. No doubt other boys, maybe some girls, would confess, under interrogation, that she did the same thing to them. She was toast; he an innocent lamb.

He would allege she succumbed during a sex game she taught him. He freaked out when she died; the reason he moved her body to the bed.

He cleaned up as best he could, left the house by the back door and walked two blocks to his car, which he never parked in front of her residence. Exhilarated, he skipped twice while walking away like a child who had just received a treat from his parents.

He wouldn't admit it, although he suspected it from his reading. He was a psychopath. He snickered when he recalled the definition describing such a person, which he memorized: antisocial personality disorder, characterized by aggressive, perverted, criminal or amoral behavior without empathy or remorse.

He did feel bad about some things he had done, but not for long. He wasn't responsible. How could he be? He had a personality disorder.

His laughter echoed throughout the quiet neighborhood.

Chapter 37

Willie Wilkins

William "Willie" Wilkins drove for FedEx freight; the pay decent with a matching 401K savings plan. Willie had a wife, two children and a small house inherited from his parents. Life should have been good. Unfortunately, he gambled---a lot. On sports teams, didn't matter what sport or team, Willie bet--- on over/under, final score, score by quarter or period, yardage gained in football, goals scored in hockey or soccer. Sometimes he won, more often he lost.

He owed money to his bookie, not a patient man, who might or might not be connected. The guy implied he was. And flexed his muscle; put the squeeze on Willie. No more wagers until he coughed up the *vig*, in gambling parlance, the bookie's cut for placing a bet. He threatened Willie. Hinted he wouldn't be pleased with the consequences if he didn't come through.

Willie's wife worked as a minimum wage checker at a local grocery store. Her salary kept the family afloat but the daily struggle to put food on the table and a roof over their heads stressed the marriage. She kicked Willie out of the house more than once promising to make it permanent if he ran up more debts. She banished him to sleep on a couch in their cramped living room. Wouldn't let him touch her.

Willie needed dough bad. So, when his buddy at Sturm, Ruger, approached him with a proposition, one that promised to pay Willie a ton of cash, he listened.

He was a gambler after all.

Chapter 38

Miguel Chavez

Miguel Chavez, on the I-95 driving north to Portsmouth, New Hampshire, took a cell call from Luis Garcia who notified him they had their man at the Ruger plant. Chavez smiled. Money and/or drugs never failed to seduce vulnerable individuals into doing your bidding. And once hooked on either, they could not refuse anything you asked. Women, politicians, police, generals, didn't matter. Their man at Ruger was theirs for as long as he proved useful.

Chavez intended to rent a fishing boat in Portsmouth and recruit its crew for the second phase of his gun heist scheme. He chose Portsmouth instead of Gloucester or any other nearby coastal community for three reasons: First, it was less than two hours from the Ruger facility in Newport. Second, a local vessel would not attract attention. And third, from his research, the declining availability of fish and shellfish in the area forced many small boats out of business; those remaining were struggling, their captains more inclined to jump at a lucrative proposition. Chavez would not reveal the cargo he expected them to transport. It would be labeled farm equipment or something else innocuous. Garcia would handle that.

Not long after arriving in Portsmouth, Chavez found a captain keen to rent his boat for an undisclosed outing when offered a thousand dollars cash up front. He located his man at the "Goat," a bar with big screen TVs and live country music, a hangout for locals as well as tourists, young and old.

Chavez sat drinking with his new associate until the bar closed, spinning phony stories about his interest in deep sea fishing and his dream of one day buying a cabin cruiser to sail around the world. He babbled on, his newfound friend captivated or feigning enthusiasm because of his upcoming payday. Chavez didn't care which. His plan was coming together. He envisioned himself as a cartel legend, surpassing even the notorious "El Chapo" Guzman.

Again, blinded by his chance at fame, he ignored the old adage that the best laid plans often go astray.

It would cost him everything.

Chapter 39

Luis Garcia

Luis Garcia was meeting with Miguel Chavez at Chavez' house in Lynn on a sunny afternoon when he received a call on his burner phone from Bobby Walton, their Sturm, Ruger, contact.

"Bobby. Good news, I hope," Garcia answered.

"Monday, nine in the morning. Twelve hundred rifles, shotguns, pistols, revolvers. The whole shootin' match."

Bobby laughed at his own pun, but Garcia missed the humor, so he continued. "Going to Manchester airport to be shipped around the country to different stores like Bass Pro Shops, Cabela's and Walmart. The merchandise will not be packaged as weapons. Supposed to keep guys like you from knowing what's inside."

Again, his wit met with silence.

"Driver with us?" Garcia asked.

"Yeah."

"Carrying other packages?"

"No. Direct from Ruger to the airport. No stops."

Walton paused, fidgeted, but pressed, "When do I see the money?"

"Tomorrow at the Kitchen. Five in the afternoon. Parking lot."

Garcia dipped his head toward Chavez before finishing. "I'll have another phone for the driver. Make sure he gets it."

"Okay."

"And Bobby."

"Yeah."

"Dump your phone now. Don't want to find out you didn't. Understand amigo?"

"Yeah. Sure. No problema," Walton answered after a brief pause, a tremor in his voice.

The hesitation on Walton's part and his attitude troubled Garcia. A loose end. They couldn't afford loose ends.

* * *

Bobby Walton leaned against the driver's side door of his car and smiled when Luis Garcia rolled into the Country Kitchen parking lot in Newport, New Hampshire, and pulled up beside him.

Bobby knew Garcia as Sonny Cardenas and acknowledged him as such. "Good to see you, Sonny."

Garcia returned the smile, exited his vehicle and stood facing Bobby. "Glad you came through, amigo, real glad." He pulled a burner phone from his pocket. "For your friend," he said.

Bobby took the device, appeared anxious, shifted his gaze left and right, anticipating cops swooping in on them; worried he might be being played. Set up. Cops did that.

When the police didn't charge in, lights blazing, sirens wailing, he grinned, and stuffed the phone into his jeans pocket.

"Got something else for me?" he demanded.

Garcia nodded, opened his trunk and zipped open a black duffel bag, which he tilted in Walton's direction. "Twenty-five grand. Yours once the guns are ours. We don't contact you again."

Bobby's eyes bulged; the money more cash than he had seen at one time in his life. Nevertheless, he pressed for an even bigger score.

"About that," he said, shifting his weight from one leg to another. "I'm taking a big risk here. There will be an investigation when that many guns go missing. Might force me to take off, leave the state, find another job."

He stopped talking, stared into Garcia's eyes for a moment, glanced away, right eye twitching.

"What are you saying Bobby? We got a deal here."

"I know. I know," Walton stammered. "But got to look out for myself, my family. Another twenty-five is fair."

Garcia anticipated the ploy, not the first time some player tried to extort him; drug dealers, users, gangsters from other cartels offering to sell out their compadres for a huge payday.

Didn't end well for them.

So, Garcia played along. "Sure, Bobby. Fifty-grand. Same conditions. We take possession of the guns; you get the money. Everybody's happy."

Bobby exhaled, surprised and relieved his con worked. "Okay man. I'll come through. You can count on me."

Garcia grinned. "We do, Bobby. We do. I'll expect to hear from your friend, the driver, before Monday. I'll have some instructions for him."

Walton nodded, got into his car and drove off, unaware that one of Garcia's men followed him home from work two days before and passed his address on to his boss. Someone would pay him a visit after their successful heist from Storm, Ruger. Business was business.

Bobby Walton was a dead man walking.

Chapter 40

Lopez and Magliore

Lopez and I meet in our office in the Hingham courthouse. I'm eager to get a recap of her conversation with Marsha Landry the night before and to diss her about the dean's obvious infatuation with her.

Lopez is at her desk when I arrive around 8:00 a.m., not an unusual occurrence, except her face is drawn, hair unkempt, no lipstick, eyes bloodshot. May have been crying. Not a time for any ribbing or my lame jokes. We exchange greetings and I plunge ahead.

"How did it go last night?"

"Marsha confirmed Brett Kilgore's story about the wife swapping bash and Arthur Lawson's confrontation with Dimick?"

"Great."

"And she offered a new twist?"

"Oh?"

"Dimick invited her to substitute for his girlfriend who was out of town. Didn't tell her the true nature of the gathering."

"Yikes."

"Yeah. She wound up in bed with Kilgore; roofied, she suspects, by Dimick. Kilgore acted unaware that she was not a willing participant. The night ended with both Kilgore and Lawson in a shouting match with Dimick who had pulled the switcheroo, so he could diddle Sandra Lawson."

"So," I say, "Lawson and Kilgore, both on the field trip, had an ax to grind with Dimick."

She nods.

"What about Dakota Johnson?"

"I didn't reveal the kid was murdered."

"Good. Best to keep that quiet for now, I think."

We stow a white board on wheels in our office, jammed into a corner. I jump up and grab one of the colored markers in the attached tray, write in blue, the word <u>Suspects</u> and put it at the top middle of the board.

With a red marker, I place Dimick on the left and Dakota on the right under that. Beneath Dimick, I list Lawson, Kilgore and Belanger.

Lopez balks at Belanger, but we hash it out for a couple of minutes, and she agrees to leave him up there.

We struggle to come up with suspects for Dakota's murder. Again, I suggest Belanger with the same motive for killing Dimick---jealousy. He couldn't abide by the thought of his girl banging his teacher. Resented her.

Lopez shrugs, shakes her head, but without other alternatives, concurs.

No drug dealers or users are listed as suspects. We can't identify anyone in those categories at this point.

I turn the white board around and face it toward a wall away from the prying eyes of those passing by the office.

As I sit down, my cell phone sounds with a text message from Detective Charlie Rose of the Cohasset PD. He texts me the names of the five Bridge Hill students who OD'd within the last few months.

I remove a yellow notepad from the middle drawer of my desk, write the names down and turn the pad so Lopez can read them. One is familiar, Emma Paulson, the girl in a coma, but I can't place the name. I'll check my notes later.

Lopez draws a blank on her as well as the others. Stymied, we decide to contact Brett Kilgore, meet with him to compare his story with Marsha Landry's.

I call him and Kilgore agrees, but he's just driven his wife home from the hospital and asks to talk there. He's taken a couple of sick days to care for his wife. They live in Marshfield and he gives me the address.

* * *

It takes us thirty minutes on Route 3A to reach the Kilgore's house on Springfield Road not far from Marshfield High School. Back in the day, our football team played there, so I'm familiar with the area. I also know the town of Marshfield is named for several coastal salt marshes present within its geographical area, a nugget gleaned in my eighth-grade geography class. I don't share this with Lopez, who appears distracted.

Kilgore welcomes us into a family room with an L-shaped leather sectional oriented toward a flat screen TV. He sits on the bottom of the L facing us while Lopez and I sit next to each other on the long section. Kilgore holds a cup of coffee in his hand, but places it on a table between the couch and the TV to keep from spilling it.

He leans back and asks, "How can I help you detectives. Thought I answered all of your questions at the hospital."

Lopez, resting both hands on her knees, is poised to pounce. She confronts Kilgore with Landry's version of the events that occurred at the wife swapping party.

Kilgore laughs, shaking his head from side to side.

"She's lying her ass off," he says. "She knew full well what to expect."

"How can you be so sure?" Lopez challenges.

"Dimick told me. He supplied Marsha with cocaine for more than a year. Banged her as payment."

Lopez pales, balls her fists. "If you're bullshitting us," she threatens, "We'll arrest you for obstructing justice."

"I'm telling the truth. Marsha was high that night, slept with both Mike and me. Thought she might jump my wife's bone's too, the way she ogled her. Ask Eleanor? She'll confirm my story."

He exhales, reaches for his coffee and takes a sip before continuing. "There are also rumors about the good dean. Not flattering ones."

"What rumors?" I ask.

Kilgore turns away as if measuring his next words, the truth or some fiction perhaps, to keep us chasing our tails?

He turns back. "Stories about the dean and boys, athletes. Word was she enjoyed the young muscular studs."

"Any proof?"

"No. You'd have to ask the boys."

"You'd assassinate someone's character on hearsay," Lopez says, raising halfway off the sectional.

Kilgore shrugs, sits back, putting more distance between him and my partner.

Lopez asks permission to verify his story with his wife. He nods and leads her into the master bedroom where the woman is awake and resting on their bed. She confirms her husband's version of events at the wife swapping gig.

We leave the house; Lopez fuming.

We walk back to the car in silence. Lopez slips behind the wheel as usual but doesn't punch the ignition button. She drapes her forearms on the steering wheel, bows her head, eyes closed, digesting Kilgore's revelations.

She remains in that position until I shift in my seat making enough commotion to break her trance.

Frowning at me, she asks, "Do we believe them or Landry?"

"Got to follow up either way," I say, placing a hand on her shoulder.

She doesn't pull away, sits back in thought for a moment or two, then says, "Let's go see Landry."

She grimaces, lips pressed together, eyes narrowed, as if swallowing a bitter pill. I say nothing. I'm like that fish keeping his mouth shut to stay out of trouble. My glib tongue has gotten me into more problems than I care to admit, particularly with my partner. I don't want to alienate her, but in the brief time we have worked together, I know she will follow the truth no matter where it leads. Doesn't mean she won't be hurt by what we find. Favorable impressions of people can evaporate once their façade is penetrated. We all harbor secrets, as I know first-hand. Landry's may devastate Lopez. Nothing I can do to protect her, much as I yearn to do so.

Chapter 41

Lopez and Magliore

On the way to Landry's house in Hanover, a twenty-five-minute drive from our location in Marshfield, Lopez drops a bomb.

"I saw you," she says, keeping her eyes glued to the road.

"What are you talking about?"

"You snatched one of those baggies of pills we discovered in Dimick's condo."

Caught by surprise, I consider stonewalling, but that would make matters worse considering Lopez's current state of mind.

So, I confess with a weak caveat, "I haven't used any."

Lopez glances at me out of the corner of her eye. "What are you a little kid? Doesn't matter. You took them. Tampered with evidence. Why?"

"I don't know."

"Lame, Magliore. Pretty damn lame."

I try dazzling her with the findings on opioid use which I researched. "Opioids can change brain chemistry, overwhelm normal circuitry and form others that drive compulsive behavior. Your brain believes you can't live without drugs. I fight it every day. I'm human. What do you want from me?"

She shakes her head from side to side, unimpressed by my argument. "The truth or I turn your ass into Catebegian. You'll be finished in law enforcement."

"You'd do that?"

"In a nano second."

She's sincere, so I play the sympathy card. "I still experience pain in my leg, real or imagined, I'm not sure. For a minute or two, I considered taking a pill to dull the pain."

Lopez comes unglued. "Are you crazy? Those pills are counterfeit, might contain fentanyl, heroin, anything? They could kill you."

"You do care about me?"

"Don't push it, asshole."

I drop my head to my chest, eyes riveted on the floor mats of the car, chastised, awaiting my fate. Lopez holds my future in her hands.

"Where are the pills?" she demands.

"At my room, in Hull."

"Okay," she says. "We're going to get them now and you're going to make an appointment with your shrink."

"She's not a shrink," I mumble.

"Whatever! I'm serious, Magliore. Pills now or you're going down. I'm not having an addict as a partner; one I can't trust or count on. May not be able to work with you anymore as it is."

I open my mouth to speak.

She cuts off my response. "And call your shrink now."

"She's not a shrink," I repeat, with not much conviction.

Lopez turns and glares at me.

Defeated, I take my cell phone out and punch in Mavis Fisher's number from my contact list, arrange an appointment through her secretary.

"When can she see you?"

"Later this afternoon."

"Perfect," Lopez says and executes a U-turn which elicits some angry honking of horns from two cars behind us. She ignores them.

Our detour and my lapse in judgement puts off our visit to Marsha Landry's. No rush.

Chapter 42

Lopez and Magliore

We ride in silence all the way to the Hingham courthouse to pick up my car. Lopez follows close behind, afraid, I suspect, I might lose my nerve and hide the pills for future use.

In twenty minutes, we pull up in front of the house on Sunset Point in Hull where I've had a room ever since we thought Karen Hundley, my former classmate and wife of the murdered Hull police chief, was in danger from a Mexican cartel. Hundley launched a personal investigation into the group he suspected of construction fraud. Turns out he was the one at risk. I stayed on even though he died almost a year ago.

Lopez thinks I'm sleeping with Karen. I'm not, though we came close once during a night of binge drinking after Randy was killed.

I exit my car, walk back toward Lopez who rolls down her window. I lean in to make a last attempt to gain sympathy.

"She suspects I suffer from PTSD."

"Who? Your lover?"

"Karen's not my lover. No! My psychologist."

"You served," she says, astonished. "Iraq or Afghanistan?"

"Neither. I wasn't a soldier. It's related to the incident when I received my first leg wound."

Lopez raises her eyebrows as if to say, 'tell me.'

Lopez is unaware of the story behind my injury. Only Captain Catebegian and my therapist know the details. I decide to confess everything in the hope she'll understand and not hate me.

Takes me ten minutes to set the stage for my encounter with the rogue LA cop in the San Bernardino Mountains; another ten to describe how I killed him.

I finish by saying, "the drugs I took were as much for the pain as for an attempt to forget what I did. They worked for a time. But my conscience won't let me forget. Sometimes the guy's face appears in my room at night or looms in the halls of the courthouse. Fisher thinks the torment will stop when, and if, I go back to California and take responsibility for my actions."

Lopez smiles. "Good to know you have a conscience."

I shrug.

"Get the pills."

"We still partners?"

"Maybe," she says. "No more secrets."

"Understood," I reply, walk around her car and trudge up the stairs of the house as if facing a date with the hangman.

To me, staying off drugs and confessing my deed to my former boss in California is worse than death. It will mean relinquishing my badge, possibly going to jail.

I'll put that off as long as possible.

Chapter 43

Magliore

I sit in Mavis Fisher's reception area for over thirty minutes before the door to her office opens. The same women I saw leave on my first visit strides across the room and out the door, a tissue pressed to her right eye. Fisher's face is etched in sadness watching the gal exit.

She invites me in; her expression changing to one of amusement as she notes my puppy dog look. I jump up as if expecting a bone, and walk past the doctor into her inner sanctum. She follows me in, and we take our usual seats; Fisher behind her desk, me in an overstuffed chair facing her.

"So, what's so urgent, Vince?" she asks. "Your next appointment isn't until next week, if I'm not mistaken."

"Right doc, but I'm under orders."

Fisher chafes at my use of the term "doc" to address her. Her back stiffens; lips curl down. She stares at me.

My signal to speak.

"My partner caught me taking a packet of pills from a stash we found at a murder victim's residence. Threatened to turn me in unless I promised to come here."

Fisher raises her eyebrows. "What do you expect me to do Vince?

"Fix me."

She laughs, a full-throated guffaw reverberating through the room.

"Not how it works," she says, after gaining control. "Our sessions are only effective if you buy into this process, understand the underlying cause of your addiction, and do something about it."

I lean forward, elbows on my knees, hands clasped together, head bowed.

"And there is just one way for you to expunge your demons," she continues.

I keep my head down and whisper the mantra Fisher drums into me each time we meet: "Go back to California; talk to my chief. Confess. Face the consequences: possible jail time, the loss of my badge, my reputation."

I lift my head, and Fisher nods.

"You can keep coming here, and we can work out some ways to lesson your guilt, but that's papering over the problem. The root cause will continue to eat at you. It's the reason you persist in seeking refuge in drugs."

"I didn't take any of the pills I snatched from the drug dealer."

"Commendable, Vince, but in your job, you can't avoid being exposed to them. It will happen again; a time when you may not be as strong."

I dip my head, depressed. I feel like a bobble-head doll raising and dropping my head continually.

Fisher grins, gives me hope. "From what you told me about the circumstances leading up to your problem, I'm not sure you committed a crime."

That jolts me upright in my chair.

"How can that be?" I ask. "I killed a man in cold blood."

"Well, maybe not. When you approached the cabin, the killer had been firing at the officers surrounding the building, including you, right?"

"Yes."

"And when you went inside, you didn't know if he was aware of your approach and waiting to ambush you, correct?"

"True."

"You were afraid for your life?"

"Yes, I suppose so."

"No doubt he would shoot you if he got the opportunity?"

"No doubt at all."

"I'm not an expert on the law, of course, but in doing some research, I found that an officer who believes he or she is in imminent danger of injury or death, may shoot first and ask questions later."

Sounds like the old west, but I'm buying it. Fisher is laying the groundwork for me to legally justify what I did.

Her next statement clinches it.

"The courts have ruled," she says, "in cases where a suspect believed to have killed someone is fleeing, and can only be halted by deadly force, an officer may fire first."

"Fits my situation." I say, eyes wide, hopeful.

"Yes, perhaps. The Supreme Court set what is called an "objectively reasonable standard," back in 1989. If an officer has an "objectively reasonable fear" for his life, deadly force is justified."

I'm heartened. In my view, my actions meet those guidelines. The law may vindicate me.

I've heard enough, and stand.

"Thanks Mavis. I appreciate your guidance and support. What you found is thought-provoking; gives me some peace of mind. If I return to California to talk this out with my former boss, I'll discuss this with him; make the case for the "reasonable fear" you outline as a justification."

Fisher smiles, pleased she helped me take a step forward.

"I understand my recovery is on me," I add. "I need to reconcile, in my own mind, if what I did was defensible under the circumstances and not a revenge killing as payback for my partner's murder. At any rate, using drugs to dull the pain or ease my conscience won't provide the answer."

Fisher nods, gets up, and comes around her desk to escort me to the door.

Her last words to me are, "You're strong, Vince. You can do it."

Hope she's right.

Chapter 44

Magliore and Lopez

My cell phone rings as I leave Mavis Fisher's office in Hingham---Theresa Lopez. No doubt making sure I made it to therapy.

"Magliore," I say, in my official detective voice.

"I'm at Dean Landry's in Hanover," Lopez says. "House is locked up tight. Car in the driveway. No response to the bell or loud knocks."

"You sure it's her car?"

"Yeah. We walked to it at **The Fours** after dinner the other night."

"I assume you made a visual check of the outside of the house, looked in windows, tried the back door, etc.?"

She pauses. I expect a wise-ass remark, but she answers with no hint of sarcasm. "Yeah. The blinds are drawn on all lower floor windows, side door locked. I wrapped on a window adjacent to the front door. Nothing. No movement inside."

"She could be in the shower or taking a nap."

"Been ringing the bell and knocking for at least forty-five minutes. I'm concerned."

A tremor in her voice reveals her anxiety. Not like Lopez.

"Okay," I say. "Give me the address. I'm in Hingham near Queen Anne's Corner. Should be there in ten or fifteen minutes."

"Bring your lock picking gear," she says and disconnects.

I always carry these tools in the glove compartment of my car. I've been known to enter a suspect's residence without knocking and without a warrant; a practice I will deny if ever challenged about it.

* * *

I roll up to Landry's residence twenty minutes after the call from Lopez. Got snarled in traffic on Route 3A. Lopez stands on the sidewalk, and waves me to the curb.

I push myself up and out of my Rav4, and approach my partner. Her face is ashen. For the second time, I consider putting my arms around her, and for the second time, hold back.

"Still no response?" I ask.

She nods. "Break out your tools."

Picking a lock is easy with the right equipment. A small tension wrench and metal pick work magic. I insert the wrench into the bottom of the keyhole on the front door lock, and use slight pressure. I slip the pick into the top of the lock, apply torque to the wrench, and wiggle the pick back and forth until all the pins set.

Presto. Access.

Lopez storms through the door ahead of me and shouts Landry's name one last time. Nothing.

I grab her arm before she goes too far into the house. "As a precaution," I say---just a precaution---we should get our crime scene gear."

Lopez doesn't argue. I retrieve vests, two pairs of latex gloves and blue booties from my car to slip over our shoes. We put them on before moving inside.

The first floor of the two-story house contains a family room directly in front of us, with a couch and two matching chairs arranged facing a wall mounted flat screen TV. A kitchen and bathroom are off to the left along with a tiny bedroom.

We visually inspect the rooms, move forward and check them out, each in turn. Find no one and nothing suspicious. No clutter anywhere. No dishes in the sink, no coffee cup on the counter, no trash in any wastebasket.

We climb the stairs on our right to the second floor. I take the lead, draw my weapon, as does Lopez, following three steps behind. Like in the military, soldiers on patrol maintain several feet distance to make it difficult for a sniper or IED to take out multiple people at one time. SWAT teams do the same when approaching armed suspects. I hope this maneuver will be unnecessary.

On the top step, I again eyeball the area. A small bedroom, set up as an office, lays before us. A bathroom is situated between that room and another bedroom, to allow access to both.

All doors are open. No one visible.

One closed door is at the far end of the hall. The master bedroom?

Lopez and I inch down the hall, weapons at the ready, and take up positions on either side of the closed door. I turn the knob; shove the door open. We dart through shouting police and taking stances opposite each other.

Silence.

Bursting into a room, and sweeping it with weapons, is always traumatic. You're exposed and an easy target for a cool gunman hiding inside. No other way to do it. You hope the shooter is taken by surprise, is shook up, shoots wildly or the shot hits your vest. Not great, but better than a round to the head.

We needn't have worried. The lone person in the room is Marsha Landry, dead, lying naked on her bed, a scarf around her neck, legs flexed open.

I glance sideways at Lopez who is shaking, moisture forming at the corners of her eyes. Again, I'm tempted to hug her. Again, I hold back, afraid she'd feel disrespected as a professional. Probably slug me.

I back out of the room and call the crime scene unit office, catch one of the techs working late, ask him to send a team over ASAP. Give him the address and duck back into the room.

Lopez, now composed, stands with arms folded across her chest viewing Landry with sad, resigned eyes, back in detective mode, personal feelings pushed aside.

She turns her attention to me. "Smell that?" she asks.

I inhale deeply; a familiar aroma permeates the room. The same scent we encountered in our interrogations of Bridge Hill students, and in Dakota Johnson's dorm room after her overdose or murder as it turns out.

Rory Belanger. The jock. Egotist.

"We have to find that bastard," Lopez says, as she marches out of the room, down the stairs and out through the front door to catch some fresh air.

I join her in the driveway to wait for the CSU. We'll let them do their work first, go over the house again later to search for anything they missed. Not likely, but necessary.

Now though, what meager evidence we have, points to one suspect---student Rory Belanger.

Lopez may now be willing to accept my contention that Belanger is also a prime suspect in Mike Dimick's murder.

Chapter 45

Magliore and Lopez

The CSU team arrives at Dean Landry's house at 9:30 p.m. The lead tech, Jonathon Crowle, does not look happy to be rousted out at this time of night.

"We'll do our best, but may need to return tomorrow in daylight," he says, as he approaches us.

He leads his team of four into the house; doesn't stop to chat. "I'll post a trooper at the door when we leave," he shouts over his shoulder and disappears inside.

"We should go home. Rest. We can come back in the morning," I tell Lopez as she turns to watch Crowle.

"Let's go for a drink first," she answers. "Couldn't sleep if I tried."

"I've got a long ride back to Hull," I protest. "Last thing I need is a drink."

"I don't want to look like a desperate woman drinking alone," she complains. "Guys will descend on me like locust."

I'd be one of them.

"We can go to **The Fours,** and you can sleep at my place tonight. It's not far from there," she says. "I'll even give you sheets and a pillow for your favorite couch."

"Okay, if I can change in the morning," I say, reminding her of the last time I spent at her condo when she rebuffed my pleas to put on unwrinkled clothes before we went to Fort Warren.

She nods.

My little soldier stirs. I'd be alone with Lopez again. Maybe things would be different this time.

Or not.

* * *

The Fours bar and grill is in Norwell. Landry's home is in Hanover, but the two towns border each other. It takes fifteen minutes to drive there from the crime scene.

Lopez requests to sit in the booth she and Marsha Landry shared; a bit over the top, I think, but don't intervene. Never get cross-wise with a woman who has her mind made up or is grieving. Especially if you're hoping to knock-knees with her later.

An animated young waitress in a Patriot's jersey takes our drink orders; a Martini for my partner, a house Cabernet for me. Hungry, I also order from their "Starting Lineup" of appetizers; it's a sports bar motif after all. I select the "Triple Play," a delicious array of Buffalo fingers, potato skins, and steak and cheese egg roll, served with celery sticks, sour cream, blue cheese and caramelized onion

BBQ mayonnaise. My mouth waters ordering those goodies. Lopez smiles at my obvious anticipation.

When our drinks come, Lopez takes a long swig of hers. I sip my wine; wait for her to initiate conversation.

"Why Marsha?" she asks, then guzzles more of the Martini. At this rate, she'll be on the floor in five minutes.

"I feel responsible," she continues. "She was vulnerable, needy. I exploited that. Should have known she was in danger; protected her."

"How?" I ask, trying not to sound sarcastic.

She shakes her head.

"Look, I offer, "we have three victims from Bridge Hill---Dimick, Dakota Johnson and now Landry. The common denominator is the school. And our primary suspect is student Rory Belanger. He dated Dakota, attended the field trip with Dimick, and interacted with Landry."

Lopez finishes off her Martini, signals for another, and glares my way, daring me to object. Wisely, or not so wisely, I keep my mouth shut.

Our waitress returns with another glass for Lopez, my "Triple Play" and two dishes for sharing. I take some Buffalo fingers, potato skins and celery sticks. Lopez ignores the food, content to nurse her drink while gazing off into the bar.

I break the silence; try to bring her thoughts back to our murder investigation. "Sex would seem like a possible motive. We know from our interview with him that Rory suspected Dimick abused Dakota."

Lopez turns back to me, blinks several times, focusing and asks, "Why kill his girlfriend?"

"Because he's a kid. Jealous she would fuck---excuse the language---a teacher he despised."

Lopez swallows more of her booze, crosses her arms. "Where does Marsha come in? She didn't molest Dakota."

As soon as the words escape her lips, she blanches. I don't know what occurred between she and Landry; suspect the dean made a move on her, and Lopez fears she may have done the same with female students, too, like Dakota. Belanger could have found out. Resented both Dimick and Landry. Who knows what goes through a teenager's mind? Studies have shown their brains are not yet completely formed. They do stupid things; spontaneous things, often hurtful or destructive things.

I don't express this to Lopez. She's still fragile. Her guilt palpable.

She drifts off again in her own world, finishes her Martini and signals for another. This time I reach out and place my hand on hers.

She recoils, snatches it away. "Don't monitor me, Magliore, you're my partner not my father."

"Because I'm your partner, and I hope a friend, I'm concerned. This isn't like you."

"You don't know what I'm like. So, fuck off."

Wow! This is the first time either of us has used the f-word. Are we bonding?

Lopez persists. She demands that drink.

I give in and the waitress brings her another Martini, which she finishes in short order.

Unwilling to risk another rebuke, I excuse myself to go to the little boy's room; settle the bill on the way back.

I find Lopez with her head on the table, her glass empty. She doesn't argue when I help her out of the restaurant and into my car.

I drive her home, fish her keys out of her purse, and carry her into the condo. She's out cold. No problem; I'm a buff dude, and she weighs next to nothing.

I ease her down on the bed, unclip the weapon from her belt and debate my next move---undress her or let her be. She appears small and vulnerable lying there. I sit next to her, brush the hair away from her face, caress her cheek. I lean forward to kiss her forehead; pull back. She'll be pissed if she questions me about this evening, and I'm forced to admit I kissed her when she was helpless. If she awakes in bra and panties, I'm toast.

I faced a similar dilemma after my high school reunion when Kate Maxwell passed out in my hotel room. I did remove her expensive dress, so that it wouldn't be wrinkled in the morning, at least that's what I told myself. Didn't matter. Kate and I wound up showering together, and later became lovers.

Different circumstance now. I pull the sheets and blankets back, ensure Lopez is tucked in, clothed except for shoes. Satisfied, I retreat to the family room to sleep on the couch, again with no sheets, though I snag a pillow from the bedroom.

Examining the motive for the three murders of Bridge Hill employees will be put off for another time. As will my report to Lopez of my therapy session with Mavis Fisher.

And I remain celibate for another night. The "Magliore Curse" holds, but I'm not discouraged. If anything does develop between me and Lopez, I want her to be awake, sure of her feelings.

I continue to hold out hope despite a gut feeling such a melding of our souls, physical and mental, would be catastrophic for both of our careers; hers more than mine. I'm an established detective with a reputation as a rebel; she's an up-and-comer destined for advancement.

Being a "wise guy" and letch is part of my persona. So, despite the gamble, and perhaps because of it, I doubt I'll back off in my pursuit of Lopez. Nevertheless, I'm not certain of my reaction if she ever succumbs to my charms.

Ha!

Chapter 46

Magliore and Lopez

I slept fitfully on the couch in the living room of Terry Lopez's condo. My back aches and my neck is jammed in an awkward position when I awake the morning after our ill-fated trip to **The Fours**. Lopez downed three Martinis in rapid succession and the result was not pretty.

I check my watch, which I hadn't taken off my left wrist; 7:38 a.m. Unlike my last visit, the aroma of bacon does not permeate the room. I sit up and twist my neck from side to side to get the kinks out.

I'm going through my contortions, when Lopez strolls into the room in a bathrobe, white towel wrapped around her head, fresh from the shower. Her brown skin glows; her eyes dart around the room, alert, mischievous.

"This is the second time you've spent the night in my condo, Magliore. I should charge you rent," she jokes.

I ignore the jab, and launch one of my own. "Yeah! And you look better than last night when I carried you in here."

She dips her head. "Sorry about that. Landry's death hurt. More than I realized. Being a cop sometimes sucks."

I grimace as an electric shock shoots through my neck and into my shoulder.

"Are you okay, Vince?" Lopez asks.

She uses my first name. A sign I'm back in her good graces. "I'd be better if I smelled bacon sizzling like last time."

"Meals don't come with the couch. We'll catch breakfast at **Stars** in Hingham on the way to the courthouse."

"You promised I could change before work, remember."

She smiles. "I do; after breakfast."

"No morning kiss?"

She flips me a middle finger, pivots and retreats to her bedroom to dress for the day.

I get no respect, like that old-time comic, Rodney something.

Chapter 47

Magliore and Lopez

We pick up Lopez's car at **The Fours** parking lot where we left it the night before; drive separately, Lopez in front, to the **Stars** in Hingham Harbor. We take Route 53 to Queen Anne's Corner and turn right onto Route 228(Main Street) in Hingham, a road Eleanor Roosevelt once called the most scenic in America. Doubt she knew the Corner got its name from Anne Whiton, a local tavern owner who along with her daughters ran a "house of ill-repute." The archaic meaning of *quean* is prostitute.

I Googled it once. Can't remember why.

At **Stars**, I order coffee, eggs, bacon, hash browns and wheat toast. Lopez, no doubt feeling queasy from her martini marathon, sticks with black coffee.

While we wait for my food, I remind Lopez of our chat last night regarding Rory Belanger and his possible motive for killing Dimick, Dakota Johnson and Marsha Landry--- sex and jealousy.

Lopez is more open to the argument in the light of day and absent the mind-numbing booze that addled her brain.

"Makes sense," she admits. "I just can't imagine Marsha could be involved with her students."

"A few years ago, I held the same belief. Male teachers yeah. Women no. But the headlines nowadays reveal many instances where female teachers have bedded students of both genders. Equal opportunity abusers."

My droll comment doesn't draw a smile out of Lopez. Instead, she blushes, sips her coffee, segues into another topic. "What about drugs as a motive? You seem obsessed that they're at the heart of our case."

Before I can respond, the waitress drops off my breakfast and my cell phone rings. Caller ID reveals Detective Rose of the Cohasset PD. I answer, as much as I hate it when someone in a restaurant carries on a loud conversation on their phones while I'm trying to eat or talk with a friend or colleague---like now.

"Magliore," I say in a hushed tone, so as not to upset other diners.

"We found Belanger," Rose announces without preamble.

"What? Where?" I ask as Lopez raises her eyebrows.

"At his grandfather's house in Cohasset on Jerusalem Road."

"Is he in custody."

"Not exactly."

"What do you mean, not exactly?"

"The kid has access to guns. At least one high-powered rifle. He fired at our officer when he pulled up in the driveway."

"Jesus."

"Yeah. We've contacted his grandfather at Bridge Hill. He's on his way. We hope he can talk the boy down. Nothing to be gained by storming the place."

I stand up. "Right. We're on our way. Message me the address."

Lopez stares at me with a quizzical expression.

I explain what's going down. She stands, drops a twenty on the table, and we bolt for the exit. I love it when the lady pays the bill.

Once in the parking lot, I motion Lopez to my car. I grew up in this area and know the fastest way to Jerusalem Road from our location. Two roads branch off from a traffic circle just south of us; one to Hull the other to Cohasset. The Hull route is more direct if we stay straight and don't turn onto Washington Boulevard.

We get into my car, and I glance at Lopez, shake my head.

First ghosts. Now a kid with a rifle.

Does this prove Belanger's guilt?

* * *

I hate rotaries, the name for traffic circles in Massachusetts, at least by many locals. Research shows they reduce accidents, but I find entering one a game of chicken. I forget who has the right-of-way. I cut off one car and nick the rear end of another as I careen around the circle. The driver flips me off and shouts something. Lopez hangs on to the overhead safety handle by her door, her knuckles white.

I stay on Rockland Street past the George Washington Boulevard turn-off to Nantasket Beach and roar into West Corner, a unique junction bordering the towns of Hingham, Hull and Cohasset. I roll through a stop sign, California style, pick up Jerusalem Road to my right, and push the pedal to the floor until we encounter a police roadblock at the intersection of Atlantic Ave and Jerusalem Road. Two uniformed cops stand next to their cruiser, which straddles the road.

I pull up to the officers, roll down my window; flash my creds. "Detective Rose is expecting us," I say, as one of the blue suits leans in to inspect my ID. He gives a thumbs up sign to his partner, who waves me around their car and onto the dirt shoulder.

A mile down the road, we locate the home of Stan Williams. Not hard to spot; a massive wood shingled home perched on a hill, set at least thirty-yards back from the highway. A Cohasset police cruiser rests on the circular drive in front, back window blown out. Three other Cohasset squad cars and two from Hull are parked on the shoulder. Officers, guns drawn, hunker down behind the cars, using them as shields.

I spot Detectives Charlie Rose and Phil Bengtson, whom we met at Bridge Hill Academy during their investigation of Dakota Johnson's death. They crouch behind their unmarked vehicle a few yards ahead of a caravan of police cars. Rose holds a bullhorn in his hand.

Lopez and I spill out of my Rav4 and scamper, hunched over, toward the two detectives.

Rose nods as we approach. "What's the situation?" I ask.

"One of our guys staking out the place spotted the kid. He notified us and drove up to the house. As he stepped out of his car, two shots fired from the third-floor blew out his right front tire and shattered his rear window. He took cover and called for back-up.

"I used the bullhorn to try to coax the boy out. Told him he wouldn't be hurt. He answered by firing another round over our heads into the Atlantic. There are homes on the ocean side of the street behind us, thankfully no one was hit."

Reckless! What was the kid thinking? Or was he just scared?

Rose continues. "I contacted Bridge Hill. His grandfather was there for a meeting. I briefed him on our situation; requested his help. He's on his way."

"Any idea how Rory got access to weapons?"

"A gun safe. He has the combination. Williams says they go to a rifle range once or twice a week. Tells me the kid is an excellent shot."

"Wonderful."

"Yeah."

As we talk, a police cruiser inches its way up to our position and a tall, silver haired man steps out of the passenger side. The grandfather. He stands erect not fearful his grandson might shoot at him.

Stan Williams is pushing eighty, but is trim and fit. He has blue eyes, a firm chin and a wrinkle free neck; skin taught. A dark spot on the left side of his forehead the one mark that betrays his age.

He wears a pinstripe gray suit that cost more than my Rav4. His starched white shirt gleams in the sun. He's the picture of a successful businessman and school benefactor.

"I want to see my grandson," he demands, in an authoritative voice; he's comfortable giving orders. "You don't need to cower behind your vehicles," he says. "If he wanted to hurt you, he would have done so."

Glad he's so confident.

"Do you know his cell phone number," Rose asks.

"Of course," Williams replies, fixing the detective with a withering glare. He doesn't suffer fools.

Rose ignores the disdain in the grandfather's voice, and his dismissive body language. He's also a professional with a job to do.

"Please call him," he asks, "and tell him you and I want to come in and talk."

"I go alone," is the response.

"I can't let you do that," Rose cautions.

"You don't have a choice, detective. Either I go in alone or I leave now."

The man is used to being in charge. Money will do that.

Asshole!

* * *

Charlie Rose and Stan Williams are nose to nose arguing over who will enter the house to try to coax Rory Belanger to surrender, when another unmarked police car rolls to a stop behind us. The door opens, and a man resembling a fire plug climbs out. His neck muscles bulge like ropes. His chest and biceps stretch the fabric of his short-sleeve white shirt; black slacks adhere to his thighs as if ironed on.

Almost as buff as me.

Rose breaks eye contact with Williams and introduces Lopez and me to Lieutenant Hank Jacoby, CPD.

We all shake. He grasps my hand in a viselike grip. I grin and stare him down, my face a mask of calm despite the pain.

I catch Lopez's smirk out of the corner of my eye. She's aware of our mano-a-mano face off. She'd love to see me humbled.

Fat chance.

Stan Williams interrupts our posturing with a throat clearing sound, irritated he's been ignored.

Jacoby disengages and smiles at the older man. Rose, humiliated by his mistake, introduces the two men; explains to the lieutenant that Williams seeks to enter the house alone to talk to his grandson.

"Your call, sir," Rose says, deferring to his superior, content to let him make the decision, and take the flack if things go sideways.

"You think the boy will listen to you sir?" Jacoby asks, stepping closer to the older man, perhaps attempting to intimidate him with his bulk.

Undeterred, Williams replies, "Of course," in a tone and manner expressing his displeasure with the whole scenario and with the officers he considers inferior.

Jacoby locks eyes with his sergeant before glancing toward Lopez and me. Neither of us makes a move to intervene. We're in charge of the murder investigation that got us here, but Cohasset PD is responsible for handling the standoff.

"Very well sir," Jacoby says, "you may go in unaccompanied, but I'd like you to wear a vest."

The older man's face reddens; his eyes bulge. He leans forward bouncing up and down on his tiptoes. "Absolutely not. My flesh and blood won't hurt me."

Jacoby sighs, gives in, no other choice but a prolonged standoff, potential media circus. "All right. Please contact the young man. Alert him you're going in."

Williams nods, makes the call on his cell phone and climbs the steep driveway to his home. He takes measured steps, stops twice to look back before covering the remaining distance and disappearing through the front door to his massive edifice.

None of us speak as the minutes tick away, each of us grappling with our own thoughts and concerns until a shot from inside the house shatters the group reverie and sends everyone scrambling for cover. Lopez and I dive behind a rock formation, while others crawl under and behind vehicles.

No outgoing fire follows. Everyone is safe until the door of the mansion is flung open and Rory Belanger, waving a rifle in the air, stumbles onto the driveway, a splash of red on his shirt.

"I shot my grandad," he shouts. "He's hurt bad."

Not listening to the words, seeing the weapon as a threat, the cops around us raise up and a volley of bullets strikes Belanger, knocking him backward. The rifle flies out of his hands.

"Cease fire, cease fire," Lieutenant Jacoby bellows, too late; the youngster is down, hit multiple times. Unlikely to rise again anytime soon.

Lopez and I charge up the hill, past the boy's crumpled form and into the house.

Stan Williams writhes on the carpet in the expansive entryway pressing his hands to his stomach trying to stanch the bleeding from an ugly wound.

Lopez, sizing up the situation, dashes back outside and yells to the officers surrounding the fallen teenager to dial 911.

They had already done so.

In the meantime, I scan the room and pull a protective covering from an antique chair to aid Williams.

"Take it easy," I whisper. "Help is on the way. You'll be okay."

Williams searches my eyes to see if I'm spewing bullshit.

"It wasn't his fault, detective," he rasps, blood seeping from the corner of his mouth. "I tried to grab the gun. It went off. An accident. He ran because he assumed you guys blamed him for Dakota's murder. He swore to me he didn't do it."

I nod, press the chair covering, now saturated with blood, tighter to his body.

"He didn't mean to harm me," Williams repeats, gasping and doubling over on his side with pain. "He didn't kill Dakota. I know my grandson," he chokes, holding back tears. His eyes roll back, and he loses consciousness.

Lopez stands over us, concern etched on her face.

"The arrogant bastard deserved it," I say, referring to Williams who insisted he get his own way.

Lopez recoils, shocked by my callousness. She crosses her arms on her chest and stares down at me in disbelief.

"What about Rory?" she says. "Did he deserve it? He's just a kid."

"He killed three people, Terry. He's a murderer. No sympathy from me."

"You're an asshole, Magliore. His grandfather might be right. The boy took off afraid we'd accuse him of murdering Dakota, which we---you--- planned to do. He panicked. Hell, anyone in his place might do the same."

"Why shoot at the police?"

"Same reason. Fear."

"I don't buy it, Terry. He did all three vics. Case closed."

Lopez shakes her head, turns away, and storms out the door uttering her favorite expletive to describe me. Doesn't help my chances of getting in her pants.

Ha!

Chapter 48

Magliore and Lopez

Rory Belanger died at the scene.

His grandfather, Stan Williams, suffered egregious injuries from the rifle bullet discharged into his gut, his liver and spleen perforated, spinal column nicked; paralyzed from the waist down. Doctors hope the paralysis is temporary, but can't make a definitive determination.

The day after the bizarre scene at the Williams mansion, Lopez and I sit behind our desks in our office at the Hingham courthouse providing an update to our boss, Captain Ed Catebegian.

Big Cat, all two-hundred and sixty-five pounds of him, is ensconced in an unsteady plastic chair against one wall in our cramped room. We turned our chairs to face him.

"So, are we ready to close the case?" Catebegian asks, swishing a wad of gum around in his mouth---a substitute for his former habit of chewing tobacco.

I nod and start.

"Rory Belanger had the motive and opportunity to kill all three victims. Evidence is circumstantial but, in my view, compelling. He attended the field trip to Fort Warren. According to his own statement to us, he hated the teacher, believed the guy was screwing his girlfriend."

Catebegian continues to chomp on his gum, says nothing, so I continue.

"We're convinced Rory and Dakota Johnson partied in her dorm room the night she died based on the strong odor of the kind of cologne he uses. Drugs and alcohol littered the place. Rory was an arrogant narcissist. Not a stretch to believe that fueled by cocaine and whisky, he flew into a rage when he realized he wasn't alone in sampling Dakota's charms. Either intentionally or unintentionally----perhaps part of a sex game----he smothered the girl."

Lopez lets me carry the ball as Catebegian listens without interrupting. "The stench of Belanger's cologne also permeated Dean Landry's bedroom. He may have complained to Landry about his suspicion that Dimick was abusing his girlfriend. Nothing suggests she investigated or took any action. Belanger might have held her responsible for what he assumed was ongoing abuse."

I pause to catch my breath.

"Anything else?" Big Cat says, stroking his chin.

"Marsha Landry lay nude on her bed, strangled by a scarf around her neck. Position of the body suggests, like Dakota, she died during sex. According to teacher Brett Kilgore, rumors circulated around campus about the dean's involvement with students. Her death may have been accidental also. Belanger was a muscular athlete and hot headed. Not difficult to think he lost control. His obnoxious cologne leaves no doubt of his presence at both scenes. The cologne is like the kid's signature."

Catebegian sits back in his chair, laces his fingers together behind his head, facial expression a mix of anger and frustration. He suppresses his irritation, pushes his wad of gum against his right cheek and speaks in a measured, even tone. "I'm not convinced. The aroma of cologne and speculation about motives doesn't cut it. We'll be laughed out of the D.A.'s office."

Lopez smirks, shoots me a "told you stare," and jumps in. "I agree," she says. "The knife and cape used by Dimick's killer haven't been analyzed for fingerprints and DNA. Same with the crime scenes at Johnson's dorm room and Landry's house---no DNA or fingerprint matches yet. If Belanger's prints and DNA are on the cape and knife, that would nail him for Dimick's slaying. All it would prove in the cases of Johnson and Landry was that he was there, and had sex with them, not that he killed them."

She takes a deep breath and continues. "Belanger's cell phone is now in our possession as is Landry's office computer. We'll check them for contact between the two. The devices may reveal threatening texts or emails from the kid."

"But there are other possible suspects," she adds. "The wife-swapping group of Bridge Hill faculty and spouses unraveled to some extent. Two members of the clique quarreled with Dimick. One jealous husband pushed him at a staff party."

Lopez doesn't stop there. "A long shot possibility is somebody in the drug supply chain---user or supplier. Dimick was the man to see for opioids and other narcotics. Some private boats were moored off Georges Island on the day of Dimick's murder, and departed before the lockdown. The killer could have been on one of them."

Lopez finishes and crosses her arms, content to shoot down my indictment of Belanger.

Catebegian leans forward, rests his elbows on his knees, cradles his chin in his hands, closes his eyes and, for the moment, ceases his incessant gum chewing. He remains in that position for a minute or two, then stands up.

Looking at me he says, "I concur that Belanger is the most viable candidate for all three murders. A jealous husband or drug supplier doesn't account for the girl or the dean. Yet, what you have on the kid is weak. Keep digging. Wait for the DNA and fingerprint analysis and scour the electronic devices for any connections. I'm not confident we have enough to inform the D.A. we've got our killer. Not going to hang her out with the press if your circumstantial stuff unravels."

Lopez interrupts before I can protest. "Of course, we'll continue to investigate, sir. Too many loose ends. The grandfather swears Rory ran because he feared we'd pin Dakota's murder on him."

"Williams would say anything to help his grandson," I interject, glaring at Theresa.

"Maybe," Lopez says, ignoring my challenging stare. "I still would like more hard evidence."

Catebegian holds up his hand. "If even one of you expresses doubt, the case will remain open. The D.A. will be crucified publicly if word leaks that we're not a hundred percent convinced the boy is our perp. Reporters badger her for updates. She's not happy with nothing to say except 'we're exploring all possibilities.' And if she's not happy, I'm not happy. Capisce?"

Ha! He's a closet Italian. I know it.

"I'm still confident Rory is our guy," I tell Terry Lopez, after Cat leaves, trying to melt the ice in the room. "None of the other suspects has a reason to kill Dakota or Marsha. Arthur Lawson is a wimp. Brett Kilgore chaffed at Dimick diddling his wife, but he surrendered that right by participating in the group orgies. Doubt he'd be angry enough to kill.

"So," I challenge Lopez, "if not Rory, who?"

"The drug dealer who supplied Dimick?"

"You didn't buy that idea when I proposed it. No evidence supports that theory, and still does not account for Marsha and Dakota. Dealers don't off their clients."

Lopez reddens---I struck home---but she now introduces something to blow us out of the water.

"What if we can't connect them because they're not related. There's more than one killer?"

I sit back in my chair, understand her frustration, but also adhere to the old cop philosophy---there are no coincidences. Three people connected to Bridge Hill Academy, part of the school community, for Christ's sake, killed within days of each other, cannot be a coincidence or not be connected somehow, someway. If it's not Rory Belanger, we're missing something or someone. I don't believe that and can't let go. I remain calm, but my blood is boiling. Lopez is smart, perceptive. Why is she defending this punk kid?

"There is a link, Terry, and Rory is that link," I insist. "We'll prove it. We can't go off on a tangent now."

Mollified for the time being, she nods, shrugs.

I won this round.

Certain Rory is our guy, I ignore a quote from Voltaire, the famous French writer: "Doubt is not a pleasant condition, but certainty is absurd."

Hey! I studied world history and the Enlightenment. Some might even say I'm an 'enlightened' man.

Not Catebegian or Lopez though.

I get no respect.

Chapter 49

The Murderer

The media skewered the Cohasset police for the "execution" of a high school boy. The Boston Globe and the local paper, the Patriot Ledger, among others, carried front page stories decrying "trigger happy cops."

Lieutenant Hank Jacoby, in charge of the standoff, who permitted a civilian into the house with an armed teenager, became the public fall guy, placed on administrative leave, his law enforcement career derailed.

The official news release naming Belanger a "person of interest" in multiple murders is overshadowed by his grandfather's assertion that his grandson swore to him his innocence. The fact the grandfather is paralyzed by a bullet from his grandson's gun, lends credence to his contention.

Reporters, rebuffed in efforts to talk with the state police detectives investigating the murders of three people affiliated with Bridge Hill Academy, speculated on why. Conspiracy theories abounded as to police motives; a possible cover-up implied.

From his room, the young man smiled as he watched the talking heads on the local NBC affiliate dissect the short life of Rory Belanger. His grandfather spoke in glowing terms of his grandson's academic potential, while his lacrosse coach extoled his prowess on the field. Several teachers believed he was bound for an Ivy League school.

His parents, on their way to Cohasset to claim his body, could not be reached, but put out a statement declaring how devastated they were to lose such a beautiful, loving son.

What bullshit, the killer mused. Belanger, an arrogant asshole, helped distribute drugs at Bridge Hill; got what he deserved. So did Mike Dimick, Dakota Johnson and Dean Landry, all responsible for the drug overdoses at the school. Belanger, Dimick and Johnson because they were part of the pipeline and Landry because she knew and did nothing to intervene.

Dimick and Landry, also sexual predators, exploited their positions to win the confidence of students, took advantage of them. He didn't see himself as a victim, though. Sharing a bed with Landry, sex in her office behind locked doors, thrilled him. But her indecisiveness in the face of the drugs being distributed at school overshadowed his pleasure. He had to take action. Felt no remorse; glad he snuffed her.

And...he hadn't restricted himself to exacting revenge on the Bridge Hill culprits. The source of the drugs, the doctor in cahoots with a Mexican cartel, also paid the price. No one was beyond his reach.

He got up from the couch, turned off the TV and fist pumped as if he had just scored a touchdown.

PART III

The Heist

Government reports suggest thousands of firearms have vanished from interstate shipments over the last two decades.

Brian Frescos
Reporter

CJNG is like no other cartel the world has ever seen before in terms of its reach, its financial, military and organizational power.

Todd Bensman,
National security expert

Chapter 50

Luis Garcia

On a Saturday afternoon, Luis Garcia received a call on a burner phone from the FedEx driver who would pick up the shipment of guns from Sturm, Ruger on Monday morning.

"Sonny, here," he answered using his pseudonym.

"Ah, this is Willie. My friend told me to contact you."

"Yes Willie. Did Mr. Walton explain the job?"

"Ah, I think so."

Garcia shook his head. Either this guy was a moron or he wanted the mission spelled out for him. He opted to give few details, but enough information to ensure the plan's success.

"You are delivering the merchandise to the regional airport in Manchester, right?"

"Yeah"

"You will take Interstate 89?"

"Yeah."

Garcia smiled. At least the man was smart enough not to reveal too much even on a burner.

"Take the Kings Hill Road exit to the right. You will pass an auto body shop on your right-hand side."

"Lauridson Auto. I know it."

"Yeah. A mile beyond that is a small road leading to a barn. Pull in. We'll meet you with a U-Haul van."

"But I think someone lives there."

"Not anymore. The building is abandoned. Follow directions."

"Okay," Willie said, after a moment or two of hesitation.

"How many containers will there be?" Garcia queried.

"Not sure. But as I 'unnerstan' over twelve hundred pieces of equipment are being sent out to different stores around the country. It will be a lot."

"Not a problem."

"Another thing," Willie added. "FedEx monitors how much time it should take and the number of miles I should travel to get from Newport to Manchester. They check our routes and schedule to figure out if we're goofing off on the way, costing them money. You'll have to be quick in transferring the cargo. The short detour shouldn't raise suspicion, though. Sometimes we take bathroom breaks at a truck stop or gas station. They don't like it, but we got it in our contract."

Garcia anticipated the shipments would be tracked. He'd round up enough men to make sure the stop he planned would be brief.

"Don't worry, Willie. We'll move fast."

"Good. Good."

FRANK J. INFUSINO JR.

"Okay, Willie. See you on Monday."

Willie, not ready to hang up, wanted to confirm his payoff.

"Will you have something for me?"

Garcia raised his eyebrows expecting the same type of stiff- arm tactic his buddy tried.

"The payment agreed upon," he said.

Willie didn't protest or push for more. "Okay. Monday it is."

Luis Garcia disconnected, and gave a thumbs up sign to his boss, Miguel Chavez, who sat nearby listening to the conversation.

Miguel smiled. Another step forward. He expected success; not familiar with the Robert Burns poem warning "The best laid schemes of mice and men, often go astray."

Miguel did understand sometimes things didn't go as intended, and usually had a back-up plan.

Not this time; the pay-off was too great. Had to take the risk.

He was all in on this scheme.

Ben Franklin could have told him, as he often advised, "Failing to plan is planning to fail."

Of course, Miguel didn't know Ben Franklin any more than Robert Burns.

Too bad.

Lives might have been saved.

Chapter 51

Willie Wilkins

At 8:00 a.m. on a Monday, Willie Wilkins maneuvered his ten-wheeler up to an open, roll-up aluminum door at a loading dock at the Sturm, Ruger, firearms plant in Newport, New Hampshire. He exited his truck, opened the lock on his own roll-up door and shoved it aloft.

Six Ruger employees appeared and began stocking fifty crates in the truck's cargo bay. The rifle boxes were longer and heavier than those containing compact pistols and revolvers, but the task took less than twenty minutes to complete.

The foreman presented Wilkins with a manifest detailing the number of weapons being shipped and their destinations; gun stores and shops in Illinois, Missouri and Michigan and retailers like Cabela's, Bass Pro Shops, Fred-Meyer and Walmart in the far west.

Wilkins glanced at the document and signed his name at the bottom indicating he accepted and received the shipment. His eye twitched, and his hand trembled as he did so. The foreman didn't pick up on Wilkins' discomfort, concerned only that he and his men completed their task. Nor was he troubled that the FedEx man did not physically inspect the name and destination on each box and match it to the bill of lading. Most drivers didn't. They assumed everything was in order.

Wilkins shook hands with the foreman, closed and locked the rear door on his vehicle, hopped up on his seat and drove five miles per hour out of the plant. He turned on to Sunapee Street heading east to I-89, and ultimately to Manchester-Boston Regional Airport---with a critical stop in between.

Not more than two miles on his route, Willie spotted a New Hampshire State Police car fall in behind him. His left leg shook, his hands ached as he gripped the wheel with white knuckle force. He checked his speedometer to verify he was driving within the speed limit.

He was.

Next, he inspected his rearview mirrors to determine if anything out of the ordinary was clinging to his truck.

Nothing.

Shaking his head, he held firm to the steering wheel and stared straight ahead. He could not turn off on Kings Hill Road if the cops continued on his tail.

But why were they shadowing him? What had he done wrong? Did the company ask the state police to shepherd the load because it contained so many weapons? Would Sonny understand?

He had to pee. For real.

* * *

Luis Garcia, and one of his *soldatos*, picked up the FedEx van two miles after it departed the Ruger facility to ensure Wilkins took the designated exit. They rode in a tan colored older model Toyota Camry. Luis left three car lengths between the two vehicles so as not to attract attention should the highway patrol notice a car too close to the freight carrier, and stop it for a moving violation. But the opening gave the police cruiser room to swing in behind Wilkins.

The move startled Garcia. He saw nothing to prompt such an action by the authorities unless Wilkins or his buddy Walton, the Ruger employee, had revealed what was about to go down. He doubted either man would have done that given their thirst for a big payday, but he, like Willie, wondered what concerned the police.

As Luis considered his next move, the flashing lights of the police cruiser flipped on, signaling the FedEx truck to pull over.

Luis slowed. He and his companion possessed enough firepower to overcome the two officers riding in the cruiser, but a firefight on a well-traveled New Hampshire highway would not be wise. It would ignite a statewide manhunt for the perpetrators. The barn, their destination, would conceal them for a time, but not forever. And then they would be outgunned, destroying the plan and their whole operation in the Northeast. Miguel would lose his command, even his life. And if Luis survived, he too faced death. The CJNG leader, "El Mencho," did not tolerate failure.

Luis opted to pass the traffic stop and pull off at the next exit to await a call from Wilkins. If the call didn't come, he would abort. He had money stashed away to disappear if necessary. Miguel would blame him for the screw-up. They were friends, but he held no illusions. If the operation failed, he would be made the fall guy. Miguel aspired to reach the top of their organization and would sacrifice anyone to achieve his goal.

Luis and his companion sat without speaking at the first exit beyond where the FedEx truck had been detained by the cops. The *soldato* fingered his Ruger 10/22 semi-automatic rifle, anticipating action.

"Get that out of site," Luis commanded, in Spanish. "We don't fight state police."

The man nodded and placed the weapon on the floor near his feet.

Luis kept his eyes riveted on the highway. Waiting.

* * *

Willie Wilkins sat in the cab of his truck also, awaiting the arrival of the officers who signaled him to pull over. He looked in his rearview mirror and observed three men in the police car. One emerged from the backseat with a dog on a leash.

A drug sniffer? Did they think he was transporting drugs along with his cargo? He took a deep breath and exhaled.

Willie always stowed a gun beneath his seat to protect himself from hijackers. He reached for the weapon now and laid it by his thigh, finger on the trigger. Stressed; his body shook. He'd never shot anyone in his life. He doubted he could, or even should, do it now. Cops for Christ's sake. He jammed the gun under his seat as one of the staties came up to the driver's side of the cab and gestured him to lower the window.

Wilkins complied.

"Please step down and lift the cargo door sir," the trooper ordered.

"What's the trouble, officer?" Wilkins asked, as he jumped down.

"Routine inspection."

Willie smiled, relieved. "Yes sir," he said.

When the door was open, the canine handler unleashed his charge and the animal leaped into the truck, sniffing the crates, moving from one to the other, nostrils flaring. Willie folded his arms across his chest and studied the canine's every move, hoping one of his co-workers hadn't slipped drugs inside without his knowledge. Willie smoked pot, but didn't take any on this trip. He'd score once his load was delivered.

The dog took his time, but found nothing. After thirty minutes, the cops called off the search and the "sniffer-dog" and his trainer returned to the police cruiser.

"Sorry for the inconvenience," the lead trooper said as he shook Willie's hand. "You know we have a huge opioid epidemic in this state. The stuff is shipped many different ways. Sometimes the dealers send contraband through the mail or ship it through legitimate carriers. You understand?"

Willie nodded. "Yes sir. I appreciate your hard work. My brother died of an overdose. I hate drugs," he lied.

The cop gave him a card with a number to call in case their intervention caused a problem with FedEx management. He knew all delivery drivers were on tight time schedules, and might be docked pay or fired for tardiness.

Willie kept his eyes on the troopers as they drove off, shuffled to his cab and called Garcia. "It was a drug stop. They're gone. I'll get on my way, and now have an excuse for any delay that shows up on my records."

"You're a lucky man, Willie, a lucky man," Garcia said.

That comment, and the way it was said, sent a chill down Willie's spine.

Chapter 52

Willie Wilkins

Willie Wilkins, shaken by the traffic stop, drove five miles an hour below the speed limit to his rendezvous with Luis Garcia, though the promise of a cash windfall relieved some of his anxiety.

He veered off on to Kings Hill Road checking his rear-view mirror for anyone tailing him. He passed the auto body shop, less than two-hundred yards beyond the exit road, and found the dirt path leading to the abandoned barn "Sonny" described. The massive sliding door was ajar, and an individual he didn't recognize stood in the opening. Another bout of panic gripped Willie, but eased when the man stepped aside and "Sonny" appeared, smiling.

Two men pushed the barn door open enough for Willie to drive straight in. He pulled parallel to a U-Haul van and cut his engine. As he did so, six men jumped down from the back of the van, poised to make the cargo exchange.

Willie slipped out of his cab and joined the men. The rickety barn door was rolled shut, darkening the interior, which remained dimly lit by the rays of the sun streaming through cracks in the walls and roof.

Luis Garcia strode up to the group of men and extended his hand to Willie. "Good job back there on the highway. You didn't panic."

Willie, stomach queasy, stifled a nervous twitch, and acted as if it had been no big deal. "No problem man. No problem."

"Take a break," Garcia said, "while we go to work."

"Remember," Willie responded, an edgy lilt to his voice. "We got to do this fast."

Garcia, annoyed by Willie's statement, let it pass. No time for that. At a dip of his head, two men climbed into the bed of the FedEx truck and passed down the wooden crates containing the guns. The boxes had hand holes at both ends, making them easier to grip. Other wooden, unmarked crates, resting on a sprawling blue tarpaulin, lay stacked behind the U-Haul van. Willie's eyes widened, marveling at Garcia's planning.

Fortunately, the crates from Kruger were drop style boxes allowing the tops to be "dropped" into the bottom. Unfortunately, wrap-around metal bands secured each one.

Garcia anticipated this, and brought along bolt cutters. He also purchased, from a Staples store, a deluxe steel stripping dispenser to replace the cut-off strips after the guns had been transferred.

"We're going to leave a few weapons and packing in each of the boxes from Ruger," Garcia explained to Willie. "They'll be lighter but I doubt your compadres at FedEx will notice or care."

Willie smirked. "Great idea. Once they're shipped, and opened at a Walmart or wherever, no one will have a clue how or where the rest went missing."

"That's the idea, amigo," Garcia said and slapped Willie on the shoulder. "It will be difficult, if not impossible, to trace the loss back to you. And if past history is any indication, according to my boss, the theft may not even be reported."

Willie perked up after hearing that, though he would feel much better when his bank account overflowed with cash.

Chapter 53

Wilkins and Garcia

Luis Garcia's crew transferred the fifty crates of guns from the FedEx truck to their U-Haul van in thirty-minutes. Garcia sent Willie Wilkins on his way with the original, though lighter boxes, stacked in his cargo bed. The delivery to the FedEx facility at the Manchester-Boston Regional Airport would be accomplished within management's expected time of arrival.

Once at the airport, Willie helped unload his shipment, which would be ferried by carts to several aircraft waiting to deliver it to stores around the country. None of the workers commented on the weight of the boxes. They did their job. That's all that mattered. Any investigation would show the consignment intact at the time of transfer.

* * *

Luis Garcia and his men remained in the barn off Kings Hill Road until dusk, then trekked to Portsmouth, New Hampshire, where Miguel Chavez waited with a fishing trawler to relocate their haul to Georges Island, to be stored there until safe. Later, another vessel would ferry the cache, by way of Florida, to Mexico.

This would be the most weapons any cartel in Mexico had ever received at one time. It would solidify CJNG as the most powerful gang in Latin America and boost Miguel's standing in the eyes of their leader, "El Mencho."

With Fort Warren closed to tourists until May, Miguel also intended to set up a pill lab in one of its tunnels. He could increase his volume of product and distribute it from the island to the American northeast. He felt confident in his plan's success as long as Emeliano Santana was in his pocket.

* * *

Alerted by Chavez that they would need him that evening, Santana stood alone on the dock at Georges Island waiting for the boat to arrive. He arranged to be the ranger on duty at the otherwise deserted fortress complex.

The sixty-foot trawler with Miguel and a crew of four arrived five minutes before eleven in the evening. Offloading began at once.

The original plan had been to store the cargo---Emeliano did not know the contents---in one of the myriad rooms of the fort, but hauling them from the pier the long distance required proved impractical. Since no other accessible point to dock and unload a boat in proximity to the tunnels existed, Emeliano suggested they hide them under a tarpaulin in an unused maintenance shed a few yards from the red brick visitor's center.

Emeliano led the men to the outbuilding where they stacked the boxes. They finished their work in less than an hour and hopped back aboard the boat.

Emeliano covered the crates with an old tarp and locked the door. The building sat vacant for some time, but it paid to be cautious.

"You have done well, my friend," Miguel Chavez said, as he prepared to shove off from the pier. "The equipment will not be here long. We will be gone in two or three days, our business complete. Your family will be protected from anyone who may threaten them."

Emeliano nodded, shivering, although the night was warm for this time of year. His family faced peril from Chavez and his henchmen, no one else.

Chapter 54

Emeliano Santana

The night after Miguel Chavez and his men deposited their contraband on Georges Island, and no other rangers or workers were around, Emeliano Santana, to satisfy his curiosity, went to the shed to inspect the stored crates. He rolled back the tarp and discovered the boxes marked as "farm equipment;" all sealed with metal bands, except for one small box. Emeliano pried off the cover, removed some packing and stood dumbfounded by the sight of stacked handguns. He feared as much, and now suspected the larger containers stored rifles and assault style weapons.

Emeliano resealed the opened box, replaced the tarpaulin and exited the shed, locking it before he left. He ambled to one of the covered picnic shelters provided for tourists, sat down, placed his elbows on a table, and held his head in his hands, devastated, afraid.

After several minutes of self-reflection, he realized he must act, overcome his fear. But Miguel and his contingent of thugs were dangerous---killers. They wouldn't hesitate to massacre Emeliano and his family or his fellow rangers. His weakness put everyone at risk.

He needed advice, but couldn't discuss the situation with any of his colleagues. He had no real friends. His wife ran off. He held her responsible for this mess; if only she hadn't deserted him.

He got up from the picnic table and walked, heavy footed, toward the shore. As he did so, his attention drifted back to the dark silhouette of the fort, to thoughts of the soldiers and prisoners who served or were incarcerated within its walls. Many times, he sensed their presence or imagined their conversations. Sometimes he swore he could hear their banter, some with distinct southern accents.

Of course, he never shared this with anyone, afraid of being viewed as a crackpot. Now though, he rubbed his eyes, and for a brief moment believed he glimpsed a shadowy figure suspended over the northern parapet---not the first time such a vision appeared to him at night. He attributed these sightings to an active imagination. He rejected the notion that a lady in black, or any other ghostly spirit for that matter, haunted the fort. Yet?

He turned away and moved closer to the ocean, stood on some rocks and let waves lap against his shoes. The salt air was invigorating and the skyline of Boston in the distance uplifted his spirits. He shook off crazy notions of voices from the past and ghosts flying around the island; screwed up his courage, took out his cell phone and dialed the office of Mavis Fisher, his therapist, hoping to catch her before she left for the day. He would seek her advice on how to deal with Miguel and his men.

He suspected his call would set in motion a series of events that would either end his career or strike a blow against the incursion of cartels into the United States. Emeliano might yet become a modern Mexican folk-hero like Zapata, his namesake.

He didn't dwell on, or remember, Zapata had been ambushed and killed by the government forces he opposed. Instead, he buttressed his resolve by something Zapata allegedly said: "Better to die on your feet, than live on your knees."

He was prepared to die if I came to that.

Part IV

The Killer Unmasked
&
The Lady Returns

The police shall never catch me,
because I have been too clever for them.

The Zodiac Killer
1969

Do not stand at my grave and weep,
I am not there; I do not sleep....

Mary Elizabeth Fry

Chapter 55

Lopez and Magliore

I plan to take a few days off since our primary suspect in the multiple murders of teacher Mike Dimick, student Dakota Johnson, and Dean Marsha Landry is dead, killed by a fusillade of police bullets outside of his grandfather's mansion in the town of Cohasset. In my judgement, Rory Belanger, a student at Bridge Hill Academy, was the one person with the motive and opportunity to have committed the crimes.

My partner disagrees. So does our boss, Captain Ed Catebegian, who has directed us to keep the investigation open. In his words, "keep digging."

Despite their concerns, at 9:00 a.m., I exit my office at the Hingham courthouse to prepare for my getaway, perhaps to Cape Cod. I make it as far as the parking lot when my cell phone rings. The caller is Marilyn Torrelli, the mother of my former high school sweetheart, Angela.

Marilyn Torrelli is a striking lady, tall and slender, olive skin, prominent cheekbones, Romanesque nose, reminds me of Sophia Loren; intimidated the hell out of me in High School. I hadn't seen or talked to her since I went off to college in California.

Why is she calling me? And how did she find my phone number?

Confused, I answer tentatively.

"Vincent," Mrs. Torrelli shouts. She always called me Vincent. "Angela's gone."

Shocked, I'm ready to offer my condolences, thinking "gone" means her daughter died.

Good thing I didn't.

Torrelli explains. "She's not well Vincent, takes too many pills, doesn't listen to me. She needs help. Your help. Please find her. Please, Vincent. Please."

I don't want to get involved. I like Angela, but our fleeting encounter at the beach was strained. I suspect she's an addict. I'm a recovering one. The prognosis for success in any renewed relationship with her is not great. Can't risk it.

"Mrs. Torrelli—Marilyn---Angela's an adult. Unless she's broken some law, there's nothing I can do."

"I don't give a shit about laws, Vincent," Marilyn responds, the anger in her voice palpable---a mama bear protecting her fragile cub.

"My daughter's in trouble. You're her friend. I need your help," she pleads. "I'm worried about her Vincent, terribly worried."

Arguing with a distraught mother is pointless. My vacation plans are evaporating, but past friendships should count for something.

I concede. "Okay, Mrs. Torrelli, I'll check into it. Do you think she went back to New Hampshire?"

"Yes. To her home."

"Okay. Text me her address. I'll ask the local police to follow up."

"Thank you, Vincent. I knew I could rely on you. Please call me as soon as you find out anything."

She breaks the connection and my heart sinks. I immediately regret my decision. I bemoan it even more when her text arrives reminding me Angela lives in Newport, New Hampshire.

* * *

Newport is the town Mike Dimick's fellow teacher, Brett Kilgore, claimed they had gone together to pick up drugs. Worse, he said they got them from a doctor Rossi, Angela's husband's name. Unless two doctors with that name operate out of Newport, which I doubt, Angela's husband is the source of counterfeit drugs flooding Bridge Hill Academy.

Shit.

As I stand in the parking lot of the Hingham courthouse, I'm mesmerized by cars flying by on George Washington Boulevard, some heading into Hull, others toward Hingham; none abiding by the posted speed limit. That offends me, but I can't explain why. Where are the traffic cops when you need one?

"Hey," Theresa Lopez says, walking up behind me, and jolting me out of my brief reverie. "Why aren't you on your way to the Cape."

"Something came up."

She tilts her head sideways in her questioning manner.

I know enough now not to hold anything back from my partner. She senses things. Women's intuition. A sixth sense. A cop's insight. Doesn't matter. I can't bullshit her.

I spill my guts. Tell her what's going down, although even I'm not sure. What am I going to do if and when I find Angela, beg her to go home to her mother?

How crazy is that?

Instead of going on vacation, I'm going north to New Hampshire and, no doubt, to trouble.

"Want company?" Lopez asks.

I hesitate, reluctant to drag her into my personal problems, although I can make a case the trip ties into our investigation of Dimick given the possible drug link.

I shrug.

Lopez takes that as a yes and says, "Let's clear it with the captain, so if we talk to the local constabulary, we can say our interest relates to our murder inquiry, which it does, right?"

"Local constabulary?"

She smiles. "Learned a lot in my two years of college."

I smile, but my stomach tightens. A confrontation with Angela will not go well. Accusing her husband of dealing illegal substances won't convince her to return to Hull.

Chapter 56

Lopez and Magliore

Captain Catebegian approves the trip to Newport, New Hampshire, but not without reservations. "Explain what you hope to find there?" he asks.

"The source of the drugs inundating Bridge Hill Academy," I answer.

"This is a murder investigation, Magliore. Our drug enforcement unit can trace that. It's within their baily-wick."

Baily-wick; willy-nilly. Love those expressions.

"I'll keep them in the loop, sir," I say, "but don't want to take the time to bring them up to speed. Something always gets lost in translation. And a squabble over drugs could have sparked our murders."

"So, are you looking at someone other than the kid?"

"Just dotting the "i's" and crossing the "t's." Digging deeper as you suggested."

Doesn't hurt to stroke his ego. I omit any reference to Angela Rossi or her husband, the doctor.

After a moment or two of hesitation, Catebegian relents. "Take forty-eight hours. If you can't turn up anything useful in that time, get your ass back here."

I stifle a laugh. Big Cat must like my ass. He refers to it often; like get your ass in here, or dumb ass, when ordering me into his office. I don't mention this, of course. I tease him a lot, but don't push the envelope. As a college quarterback, defensive lineman often threw me around like a rag doll; Big Cat could yank the stuffing out of the doll and scatter it over the field.

So, I thank him profusely and wiggle my eyebrows to signal Lopez we have a green light. I punch the off button on my cell, ask her to follow me to Hull where I can put some clothes in a duffel bag for an overnight stay if needed. She can leave her car in front of the Hundley's where I'm staying. After that, we can go to her condo in Hanover and grab some of her stuff. Her place is close to Route 3, which we will take us to 93 and three-fourths of the way to Newport.

"So, you're planning an overnight?" Lopez asks, crossing her arms across her chest.

She thinks I'm harboring ulterior motives, but I'm focused on the case at this point, although my horns can emerge at any time.

I explain my reasoning. "It will take at least three hours to drive to Newport and who knows how long to convince Angela to return to her mother's. And we can't pass on the opportunity to look into her husband's background. Brett Kilgore pegged him as the source of drugs at Bridge Hill. I don't want to rush and overlook something significant."

Lopez meets my eyes with hers. A mini-smile creases her lips.

"You're not getting in my pants, Magliore. Don't even think about it. We reserve separate rooms if it comes to that; and you pay."

"Of course," I answer, trying not to look like a cat about to pounce on a canary.

I promise myself nothing will interfere with our murder probe, not even the prospect of an intimate interlude with my sensuous partner, though my little soldier doesn't always abide by my promises.

I am Italian, you know.

Chapter 57

Lopez and Magliore

I use the time parked outside Theresa Lopez's apartment in Hanover, waiting for her to throw some clothes in a carry case for our trip, to phone Special Agent, Phillip Murray, at the DEA Office in Boston. I recall Murray's name from a newspaper article chronicling a huge cartel drug bust in Maine, Massachusetts and New Hampshire, and hope he might share some intel on Dr. Rossi.

A receptionist patches me through to his office after I identify myself and the reason for my call.

"Murray," he answers.

"Agent Murray. Vince Magliore, a detective lieutenant with the Plymouth County, D.A.'s office. I'm seeking some information on the recent raid involving CJNG in New Hampshire. Specifically, if a Doctor Rossi was implicated."

After a pregnant pause, Murray requests my badge number, and an office phone, so he can verify my identity. I give it to him, and he promises to call me right back.

As I wait, Lopez comes out of her condo with a small travel suitcase and throws it in the back-cargo space of my Rav4. She slides into the shotgun seat, and as she does, I catch a whiff of her perfume. She smells great. She's dressed in jeans, white blouse and pink Nike's, hair pulled back in a pony-tail of sorts. She carries a blue blazer with a New England Patriot's logo on the breast pocket to later conceal her gun if necessary. She looks at me in her sideways questioning manner.

"What are we waiting for? Let's move," she orders.

"Expecting a call back from a DEA agent about a raid they conducted in New Hampshire, hoping he has info on Angela's husband."

At that moment, my cell phone rings. I put it on speaker and alert Murray my partner is listening.

"How can I help you, Lieutenant?" Murray asks, raising no objection to Lopez overhearing the conversation.

"As I said, I'm interested in a doctor Rossi in Newport. We suspect he supplied drugs to some of our suspects and victims in a murder case in Cohasset."

Murray laughs. "Wouldn't doubt it. The man ran a clinic from which he prescribed hundreds of opioids---ninety-percent of his inventory was obtained legally, though questionably, from a local pharmacy. When his clientele multiplied, to keep up with demand, he scored counterfeit pills from CJNG, some cut with fentanyl."

Murray's anger is real. He raises his voice. "The bastard worked the system. Fraudulently represented to insurers that his patients had cancer, an approved use of fentanyl---handed the stuff out like candy. Once he tapped into the illegal pipeline, his practice skyrocketed, and so did overdoses. He was one of the major reasons we staged our raids in New Hampshire."

"Jesus," I respond. "But he died of cancer, right?"

Murray laughs again. "Who gave you that information?"

"A source during an investigation," I lie, keeping Angela out of it.

"He's dead all right," Murray confirms. "Murdered. M.E. initially concluded overdose. He had a small apartment attached to his office, and was discovered sprawled on his bed. But the autopsy revealed fibers in his throat. Somebody smothered him, ransacked the clinic. Possibly killed by an addict needing a fix, and no money to pay. Good riddance."

I glance at Lopez who shrugs.

"Thanks Phil," I say. "My partner and I are going up to Newport to see if we can find anything that ties into our case. Can you clear us to access Rossi's place?"

"I'll make some calls," he says.

Before he breaks the connection, I ask for another favor. "I assume you have copies of his phone records and text messages. Can you send those to us? I want to see if any people here were in contact with him."

He hesitates. "You understand these documents are still part of our ongoing investigation?"

"I do, but we're talking homicide on our end. At least one child murdered."

"Okay. Give me a secure site where I can email it."

"Thanks Phil. I'll owe you one."

I give him our work email at the Hingham courthouse, tap off, lean back in my seat, shake my head. "Something's not right," I say.

"What?" Lopez responds. "Rossi dealt drugs to some scary, unstable people. Occupational hazard."

"Doesn't it raise a red flag he was killed in the same way as Dakota?"

"Nope. The doc sampled his own product; passed out. A customer, short on cash, desperate, finds him, sees an opportunity to score and grabs the first thing handy, a pillow, takes him out."

"Why kill him? He's unconscious. Won't know what you did or who you are. He's your golden goose, you need him."

"Addicts don't behave rationally, Magliore. You of all people know that."

My face flushes.

Lopez pales, regretting the barb.

"Sorry man," she says, and reaches out to touch my shoulder.

I turn away, mumble again, "something's not right."

Dakota Johnson and Doctor Rossi were smothered; not an unusual way to be killed, but for two of our victims to die in the same way, in my view, not a coincidence either.

You know what I think of coincidences.

Chapter 58

Angela Rossi

Our three-hour trip to Newport takes over four since we stopped for lunch near Manchester. At two in the afternoon, we arrive at Angela Rossi's on the edge of downtown. The house is a stately three-story mansion with a gabled roof and turret like structure on the left front. A black Ford Escape, with New Hampshire plates, is parked in the circular driveway.

I park by the curb on the street. Lopez and I step out of my Rav4, walk up the cement steps to the entryway of the house and ring the doorbell. We wait three or four minutes with no response. I pound on the door.

Still, no answer.

I peer through a side window; see no one and no movement. Frustrated, I try the door. It's open. Not a good sign to cops. We draw our weapons and burst inside, sweeping the area with our eyes.

We encounter no one.

We're in a spacious living room filled with antique furniture and walls decorated with landscape paintings. Lopez clears the kitchen, and a small bedroom off to our left, while I climb a spiral stairwell to the second floor calling out Angela's name as I ascend.

A noise off to my right and behind a closed door grabs my attention. I call out again. No answer. Lopez joins me as we position ourselves on either side of the door. She reaches for the doorknob as I raise one, two, three fingers. At three, she pushes the door open and I rush through, weapon at the ready.

The master bedroom.

A man, in the process of pulling up his pants, cries out as we storm in. He stumbles backwards and falls as his legs become tangled in his trousers.

"Don't hurt me, don't hurt me," he yells, his eyes like saucers, his face contorted in panic.

Angela Rossi lay unconscious on a king-size bed, naked from the waist down, her blouse and bra pushed up exposing her breasts. Her skin is bluish-purple, as are her fingernails and lips; signs of an opioid overdose. A bottle of Jim Beam, along with two empty pill vials, rests on a bedside table.

I shake my head, grasp her left wrist, check for a pulse; there, but faint. I punch 911 into my cell phone, identify myself as a police officer, and call for the paramedics.

"We were partying," the man on the floor croaks as Lopez stands over him. "Just partying," he repeats.

His eyes are red and his hands tremble as he holds them in front of his face. I seize him by the shirt collar.

"Where did she get the pills?" I say, tugging the collar around his neck.

"Angie always has 'em. She likes to party."

I raise my fist to punch him, but Lopez grasps my arm.

"No, Vince," she says. "No."

I straighten up and walk over to a window in the room, move the curtains aside and look out, don't really focus on anything out there. Rather, my high school days with Angela flash through my mind; the after-game football bashes, drives along the Cohasset coast, Angela clinging to me; running down Nantasket Avenue during the summers, snatching salt water taffy from the outdoor counters of the hot dog and ice cream joints. No worries, just fun, our futures yet to be determined.

A deep sadness engulfs me. I shake my head, sigh and cross my arms; continue to stare outside.

Lopez, sensing my mood, comes up beside me and places an arm around my shoulders. I'm touched, turn from the window, and give her a chaste hug; still focused on the past, on what might have been.

After a brief embrace, Lopez steps away, stares into my eyes, and says, "Not your fault. Nothing you could have done."

I nod. She's right. Too much time has passed for me to have had any real influence on Angela, despite what her mother may think. Whether Angela survives or not, our youthful, carefree relationship will never be recaptured.

The "Magliore Curse" or the normal passage of time?

As Lopez and I stand facing each other, once distant sirens pierce the air outside the house. I turn away, ready to assume my professional demeanor as a homicide detective.

A flurry of noise and the pounding of boots resonates as the paramedics rush up the stairs, hurry in, acknowledge us without speaking and take Angela's vital signs. One blasts her with a nasal spray of Narcan, but when she doesn't respond within two or three minutes, they snap a breathing apparatus over her nose and mouth, maneuver her on to a gurney and dash out.

The guy, surprised when we charged into the room, guns drawn, managed to tug his pants on and sits in a chair, overwhelmed by the commotion. Tears roll down his cheeks and a wet spot appears between his legs.

Angela will have to clean that chair.

Chapter 59

Lopez and Magliore

Angela Rossi's luck ran out.

She won't be able to clean her soiled chair or anything else. She tempted the beast once too often and was swallowed, died on route to the hospital without regaining consciousness. Her companion, who Lopez and I drove to the emergency intake area, said they had been popping oxycodone and drinking whiskey most of the afternoon. He was so blitzed he didn't realize she was unresponsive as he pounded into her. I still feel like punching him, but inside know Angela was responsible for her own actions. She was, after all, the source of the pills that killed her.

I give hospital staff Angela's mother's phone number and her home address, which I still remember from our high school days. I decline a suggestion that, because I'm a family friend, I contact her mother.

As the drama unfolded with Angela, afternoon slipped into evening. We make the decision to spend the night in the Newport area and get an early start in the morning. We'll search Angela's house, later visit the clinic where her husband plied his trade. I clear it with the local PD who control access to the building. The DEA already swept through the place and confiscated whatever material they thought relevant. Special Agent Phillip Murray promised to send me the clinic's phone records and any text messages on Doctor Rossi's office and cell phones. Nevertheless, a second look by Lopez and I can't hurt.

Both of us are hungry, so I google restaurants nearby and settle on the Salt Hill Pub on main street in Newport. Few patrons are in the restaurant when we arrive. We choose a corner table for two and order bottled Miller Lite. Lopez asks for a glass. We scan the menu, and when the young waitress returns with our beer, Lopez orders a spinach salad and I select a teriyaki chicken wrap with a side of potato chips.

When we're alone, Lopez reaches across the table and clasps my hands "Are you all right, Vince?" she asks, her voice soft, caring.

I pull back. "Stop treating me like a child," I snarl. "I've had worse days. You're not my mother."

Lopez recoils as if slapped. She arches her back as her eyes bore into me. "I know who you are, Vince," she says. "You're a man who suffered a terrible personal loss and are struggling. I'm your partner and, I hope, your friend. I'm offering you support, not sympathy, understanding, not pity, respect not criticism."

Those words cut into me like a knife, but she isn't finished.

"You don't see a colleague, a partner. Your macho brain just views me as a woman, a maternal being who wants to mother you, take care of you."

She pushes her chair back, stands and points a finger at me, her voice rising several octaves. "You're an asshole."

A recurring theme in our relationship.

She storms off, brushing past the startled waitress bringing our food. I grin and tell the shaken girl my friend needs some air and will be right back, though I'm not sure.

I order another beer and sit waiting, perhaps willing, Lopez to return, hoping my "foot-in-mouth" disease hasn't permanently fractured our relationship.

The bar fills up and an older couple is seated at a table a few feet away. I offer one of my best shit-eating grins and tilt my head in their direction, happy they didn't witness the exchange between Lopez and me.

I suppress a smile, and my heart skips a beat, when Lopez wends her way through a line of patrons waiting for a table and again sits opposite me. She doesn't speak, attacks her salad, stabbing the lettuce with her fork, perhaps pretending it's my back.

I break the uncomfortable silence to apologize. "Sorry Theresa. Took my frustrations out on you. I'd confess my sins to a priest, if I wasn't a lapsed Catholic."

She keeps her head down, but her lips betray the hint of a smile.

"An apology doesn't make you any less of an asshole," she says, raising her eyes to mine.

I counter with a typical Magliore retort. "Can we kiss and make up?"

Her belly laugh catches the attention of several couples nearby. The older lady in the next table beams; her husband looks on with a puzzled expression.

I think all is right with the world again, but whenever I feel good about things, shit happens.

I should know better.

Chapter 60

Lopez and Magliore

Before we leave the Salt Hill Pub, I make an overnight reservation, two rooms, at the Common Man Inn and Restaurant twenty minutes away off the John Stark Highway, Route 103. I passed up a couple of bed and breakfast places and lodges suspecting Lopez would view them as too intimate.

At 9:00 p.m., we exit the pub and walk down the sidewalk to my Rav4 parked at the end of the block. With sparse traffic, I notice a black Chevrolet Suburban crawling past us. Tinted windows obscure the driver and passengers. I have an uneasy feeling, but shake it off as paranoia.

I don't mention my concern to Lopez when we slide into the Rav4 and drive out of town. We clear some commercial buildings and pick up the poorly lighted highway dwarfed by trees on both sides. Traffic is light to nonexistent.

We travel in silence preoccupied by our own thoughts until a vehicle with high-beams storms up behind us and crashes into my rear bumper. The impact shoots us forward, our bodies whip backward, necks slapping against the headrests.

"What the hell?" Lopez shouts, and cranes her neck to look back. As she does, the car behind speeds up and rams us a second time. We're swerving all over the road, and ricochet off the dirt shoulder scraping tree branches hanging over the right lane.

I'm sure the attacking car is the Suburban I spied in town. If so, this contest of chicken is like a heavyweight boxer pummeling a bantamweight fighter. The smaller man's one hope is to bob and weave and stay out of the big man's killer punches. Unfortunately, we can't outrun the massive automobile behind us; the narrow highway limits our escape options. The bobbing and weaving we're doing is the result of being rammed.

The sedan darts toward us again and this collision hurls me into the oncoming lane which, thankfully, is devoid of traffic. Sparks fly when the rear of the Rav4 crumples and scrapes the asphalt. I wrestle the car back to the proper lane as the giant trees recede, revealing an open field to our right with a gravel road leading to a farmhouse and two out-buildings. I grip the wheel with as much strength as I can muster and veer onto the stony road. Sand and rocks shoot upward and sideways. The Suburban sails by, caught off guard by my evasive maneuver.

The Rav4 wobbles and vibrates as I brake hard and steer behind one of the red painted barns. Lopez and I bale out, draw our weapons and seek cover behind the building and my vehicle. Tires squeal as our tormentor executes a U-turn and stops perpendicular to the road we took. Two men with automatic rifles spill out, take up firing positions and spray multiple rounds in our direction. Shards of wood from the barn splinter off and shower down on us as other bullets ping off the ass end of my Rav4, which sticks out a foot from the corner of the barn.

Shit. I love that car.

We hold fire, waiting for our assailants to advance, giving us a better chance to take them out with our handguns. The driver shouts something in Spanish and the gunmen move toward us. They march forward, weapons at hip level, when two halogen spotlights mounted on the roof of the farmhouse, spring to life. Curtains are pulled aside, faces peer outside.

Our two attackers fire a couple of additional bursts, but spooked by the lights which silhouette them for us, retreat to the Suburban. They jump in and speed off if in the direction of Newport while sirens blare in the distance.

The good-guys are on the way.

Lopez and I raise up and holster our guns, not having fired a shot. The farmhouse door opens and a man and a boy of about ten or twelve, I guess, emerge, both wielding shotguns. We hold up our badges, which I doubt can be seen from where they stand, and shout in unison, "Massachusetts State Police."

The farmer squints trying to decipher our IDs, when two police cruisers roll up and careen down the rutted driveway fifteen or twenty yards from us. The cars squeal to a stop and officers exit, guns drawn. We thrust our badges and hands high and repeat our state police mantra.

The wary cops order us to our knees, hands on heads. We comply, and they approach close enough to read the insignia on our shields.

"What's going on?" one of the men asks, and signals us to stand.

"That's what I'd like to know," Lopez whispers.

For the benefit of everyone, including the farmer and his son who now join our little group, I explain.

"We're in Newport investigating the death of Doctor Rossi and his possible link to two homicides in our jurisdiction. We believe he supplied drugs to our victims and obtained at least some of those illegally from a Mexican cartel operating in New England. I suspect our attacker's tonight are cartel thugs who object to our snooping around."

"Are you talking about CJNG?" one of the officers asks.

"Yes," I respond. "They also may have a hit out on me. I helped throw a wrench into a fraud and human trafficking conspiracy they operated in the Boston area last year."

"You sure get around pal," the officer says, breaking into an expansive grin.

"He sure does," Lopez chimes in, her mouth twisted into a frown.

What can I say?

Chapter 61

Lopez and Magliore

One of the Newport officers, taking stock of the situation, strides over to inspect my vehicle. The back end, including the iconic tire attached to the rear door, is crumpled. The cover hangs by a thread and falls to the ground when the officer touches it. He jumps back to avoid gashing his foot.

After the close call, he continues his inspection to determine if any part of the chassis cut into the tires. When finished, he saunters back to us.

"You can drive it for now," he says, "but the insurance guys will total it out. The parts are worth more than attempting a repair. I recommend Spikes Auto Body in Newport. Ask them what they can do in the short term to help you return home."

The news my car will be totaled is depressing, but not surprising.

I love that car.

"Will do," I say. "I made reservations at the Common Man Inn and Restaurant tonight. Tomorrow we're going to check out Rossi's clinic for anything related to our case."

The officer raises his eyes at my mention of the Inn.

"Nice place," he says. "Expensive though."

I glance at Lopez and shrug. "I'll put it on our expense account."

Both Newport officers' laugh. One says, "That wouldn't fly in our department."

"And not in ours either," Lopez adds.

I roll my eyes, thank the officers for responding to our crisis and apologize to the farmer for the damage to his barn.

"Think you can add that to your expenses?" he asks.

Everyone laughs.

We again thank everybody for their help and return to the Rav4. To my surprise, it starts.

Lopez, opening the back door, throws the damaged tire cover into the cargo area on top of our luggage and slides in.

I back out from behind the barn and exit the farm on the gravel road which adds to the cacophony of sound serenading us. Lots of parts shimmy and shudder, but the engine purrs. We're on our way to the Common Man Inn to spend a restful night, I hope.

The attack on us is disconcerting and proves to me the cartel does not let bygones be bygones. They want my ass on a platter, and as long as we pursue the source of drugs pervading Bridge Hill Academy, we're going to be targets. I'm still convinced drugs somehow motivated the killings---can't let go despite not having a suspect.

But Lopez didn't sign up for this. I'll try to convince Captain Catebegian to let me work the case alone to protect her. She'll protest, and the Cat may not buy into the suggestion. Threats and danger come with the territory. Give in, and criminals have an easy avenue to commit crimes without consequences. Maybe I can seek the protection of a supernatural being?

Hah!

Chapter 62

Lopez and Magliore

The Common Man Inn and Restaurant, I read online, once a textile mill on the banks of the Sugar River in Claremont, New Hampshire, now has thirty unique rooms and stone-walled suites according to its promotional info. I reserved two standard rooms.

I'm impressed by the intimate quality of the lobby which is furnished with comfortable looking couches, a fireplace and bookshelves. Less impressed when the clerk behind the reservation desk informs me that because of plumbing issues, many of the rooms are unavailable, including the two I reserved.

The young woman catches the look of displeasure on my face, and the distraught demeanor of Lopez. She jumps in with an option.

"One suite is available with a king-size bed and pull-out trundle. I can let you have it for the price of one of our standards."

She smiles expecting we will leap at this opportunity. She doesn't know cost isn't the obstacle, but rather the tenuous personal relationship between me and my partner.

I twist away from the woman to muffle the sound of my voice and whisper to Lopez, "You take the room. I'll sleep in the car."

Lopez folds her arms across her chest and moves two steps closer to me. "You're not sleeping in the Rav. You ARE taking the trundle."

I turn back to the clerk before Lopez changes her mind. "We'll take it."

The young woman beams and requests a driver's license and credit card.

After entering the information in her register, she slips me a small card holder with two room keys. Ours is on the first floor not far from the lobby.

I hand the packet to Lopez and trudge outside to retrieve our luggage. The back of the Rav4 is trashed; the rear swing-out door inoperable. But this model has no real trunk. The two back seats fold down permitting access to the cargo area where our bags are stored. I yank both out with no problem, and return to the lobby where Lopez awaits, arms still crossed.

We walk the short distance to our room. Lopez slides one of the key cards through the door slot and we enter a huge room dominated by a king-size bed, a fireplace with a fire raging, a couch concealing the hide-a-bed, a writing desk and a stuffed chair. The window drapes are pulled back revealing a spectacular view of the Sugar River. Under different circumstances, a very romantic get-away, though romance is verboten on this trip.

Lopez snatches her bag and heads for the over-size bathroom.

"I need a shower," she says, closing and locking the door.

I raise the sofa bed, find some pillows and a blanket in a long walk-in closet, and fall onto the bed without removing my clothes.

I don't wake up until the next morning.

* * *

I'm not a ball of fire when waking under normal circumstances; experience trouble focusing. Having slept in my clothes doesn't help, a circumstance that happens on occasion, often after a night of boozing.

As I lift my head from the pillow and wipe gunk from my eyes, I see Lopez in her pink pajamas sitting in the middle of the king-size bed, gazing straight ahead, arms folded, rocking back and forth. Her face wet from crying. The clock on the bedside table reads 7:45 a.m.

I need a shower and smell bad, but can't leave Lopez so distraught. I push myself off the sofa bed, stand facing her, and ask what's wrong.

She keeps rocking and staring into space.

"Theresa," I repeat, raising my voice.

She blinks several times, faces me as if just becoming aware of my presence.

"Never been shot at before," she says, her voice distant. "We both could have been killed."

Pain and guilt overcome me. I put my partner in harm's way. I warned Captain Catebegian this could happen. He ignored my concern. The latest attack proved me right again. Cartel hit men tried to take me out at the cemetery where Kate Maxwell was buried, and made a second attempt last night. They will try again unless we can nail the bastards at the top of their food chain. That's why I'm intent on tracing the origin of the drugs floating around Bridge Hill Academy. If we can prove Dr. Rossi got his supply from CJNG, and passed those on to Dimick, we can shut them down.

But my partner is hurting. I hope she won't misinterpret my attempt to console her. I sit on the edge of the bed; reach out to take her hand. She gazes at me with sad eyes, tears flow and she buries her head in my chest, shoulders shaking.

I wrap my arms around her, stroke her hair, but say nothing. We remain clinging to each other for ten minutes, or so, until I realize the trembling stopped. Her eyes are closed. I lay her head back on a pillow and cover her with the blanket from my roll-out.

I stand looking down at her for a few seconds, grab my bag and head for the shower, not sure how this episode will affect our relationship. One thing is clear. I should work alone on this case. I'm determined to convince Big Cat of that when we get back to Massachusetts. After her brush with death, I don't expect Lopez to object. Mr. macho will ride into the valley of death perched on a white steed and brandishing a long lance to vanquish our foes.

Hah!

Chapter 63

Lopez and Magliore

Lopez sleeps until check-out time. Once awake, she staggers to the bathroom, washes her face, dresses and returns. We pack our bags in silence, check out and find my car in the lot. I scan the damage in the light of day, grimace, shake my head in disbelief. My pride and joy is now destined for the scrap heap to be carved up for its parts.

Lopez anticipates my thoughts. "Think of it this way, Magliore," she says. "The Rav will be like an organ donor, dying so others may live."

I can't stifle my laugh. "Great analogy, Lopez."

She smirks. "Analogy. I'm impressed college boy. You didn't sleep in English class."

My cell phone rings before I can snap off one of my famous come-backs; it's Big Cat.

"Yes, your highness," I answer as Lopez rolls her eyes.

"Get back here ASAP," Catebegian says, without preamble.

"We're not finished here, Cap," I protest.

"Yeah, you are. Come back now, Lieutenant. The Newport chief called and told me about the attack on you and Lopez."

"But."

"No buts. I want you two back here now wrapping up our murder case instead of galivanting around New Hampshire chasing shadows or phantom drug dealers."

At least he didn't say ghosts, but the determination in his voice tells me not to offer a challenge.

"On our way, Cap," I say, hoping the beat-up Rav can make it.

* * *

As we make our way back to Massachusetts, the Rav4 shake-rattle and rolling every anxious mile, another idea dawns on me. I give Lopez my cell phone and ask her to dial DEA agent Murray's number, which I stored in my contacts. I ask her to put us on speaker.

Murray answers on the third ring.

"Agent Murray, this is Lieutenant Magliore again. You're on speaker with me and my partner, Theresa Lopez."

"No problem. What's up?"

"I assume your agents and the Newport police dusted Doctor Rossi's office for prints."

"Yup."

"Any interesting hits?"

"The usual suspects. Rossi's clientele consisted of many good citizens as well as some shady characters on our watch list. We eliminated most from consideration as Rossi's killer."

"Any not identified?"

"Sure. Not everyone's in the criminal database."

"Understood. Our murder victims include a teacher, administrator and student at a private academy here. They keep the fingerprints of both students and staff on an internal system. If I alert the headmaster to open his files to you, will you submit your prints to them?"

"Looking for anyone in particular?"

"Yeah. A Michael Dimick, Brett Kilgore or Rory Belanger."

"Okay. Give me the contact info for the headmaster."

He punches off.

"Why Brett Kilgore?" Lopez asks.

"He claimed he didn't go into Rossi's office. If his prints are found, he lied to us. Could be lying about other things too."

"So, you think he's a suspect?"

"Worth a shot," I say. "My money's still on Belanger. His prints in the clinic will seal the deal for me."

"And if they don't turn up?"

"Won't change my mind."

Lopez frowns, gives me her customary scowl of displeasure and is about to admonish me with her infamous epithet.

I cut her off. "I know. I know. I'm an a-hole."

She smiles, but asks, "Will you ever let go of Belanger?"

I shrug.

Chapter 64

Lopez and Magliore

When we get back to our office, lurking by our door with two laptop computers under each arm is B.A. Duffy, a computer forensics specialist and state police legend. His given name was Brendan Aiden Duffy, anglicized from the Irish, (Breandan) and (Aedon), he would explain to anyone who listened, or couldn't find an excuse to depart for an important meeting elsewhere. In Ireland, Breandon was the patron saint of seafarers, while Aedon meant, "born of fire."

No one would mistake Duffy for a firebrand or any kind of expert. Under six feet tall and overweight, he resembles a walking unmade bed. His long, graying hair caresses his neck, envelopes his ears and endangers his eyesight. He might be mistaken for a homeless person except his clothes, despite their wrinkles, are spotless, his teeth gleaming and his celery green eyes clear and penetrating. He's flashing a dazzling smile as we approach.

"Good news, detectives," he says, as I unlock our door and usher him in.

He places the laptops on my desk; one labeled Landry, the other Dimick.

"Found hidden folders on both devices," he says, looking from Lopez to me expecting praise, I assume, but neither of us takes the bait.

"What they did won't hide files from an expert, like me," he says, tooting his own horn, "but they will be invisible to the prying eye. The casual user wouldn't stumble across them by mistake."

We both nod and I realize he's going to launch into an elaborate explanation of his discovery. "Just give us the Reader's Digest version of how they did it, please B.A.," I say, stealing one of Captain Catabegian's favorite lines.

Duffy drops his head as if scolded, but a mere rebuke can't curb his enthusiasm. He lifts his head, eyes twinkling. "They both used Mac computers, which under 'system preferences' contains a folder identified as 'Security and Privacy.' Within that is a subfolder called 'File Vault" that automatically encrypts its contents.

He takes a breath and continues; "You need a login password or recovery key to access the data. Neither Landry nor Dimick was very creative. I uncovered their keys after a few hours of trial and error; a combination of their initials and the word Bridge Hill in caps.

He smiles and crosses his arms on his chest, savoring his digital victory.

"Fantastic B.A.," I say, stroking his ego. "What did you find?"

"Hey," he says, "I accessed the files. Up to you to decipher how they relate to your case---if they do."

He pauses before giving us the bad news. "There are threatening emails to both Dimick and Landry from someone who calls himself "The Wood."

"Problem is," he admits, "this person used an app called 'Burner Mail' that creates random, unique and anonymous email addresses, and once sent, the sender can delete the burner address, which this individual did. To compound this, he used a disposable phone. Can't trace it unless he reactivates it, which is doubtful. This joker definitely wanted to conceal his identity."

"Ya think," I say.

Duffy shrugs, gives us a perfunctory wave like a member of the British Royal Family, and strides out of the office leaving Lopez and me to search the data for anything relevant to our investigation and to ascertain if we can identify this "Wood" character. I'm sure if Dimick and Landry went to the trouble of hiding the stuff, it must be useful to us and dangerous to them.

* * *

I suggest Lopez take Dimick's computer while I inspect Landry's. She gives me a sharp glance, but doesn't protest. We both know her connection to the dean is problematic; could cloud her judgment or cause her pain.

There are two folders in Landry's **File Vault**, one for photos, the other emails. I open the photo's first and am glad Lopez deferred to my suggestion. The first image is of the dean on her bed, in the nude, with a young boy. In another, she's in an intimate embrace with two other lads---a ménage-a-trois.

These were incriminating enough, but the next one shocked the hell out of me: Landry in her office with an arm around Dakota Johnson, her hand inside the girl's sweater, confirming the rumors she batted from both sides of the plate.

I've seen enough. I exit the photos and transfer to the emails. There are only five, but these are also unsettling. The first is from Brett Kilgore telling her how much he enjoyed the get together at his house and asking to see her again. Why would she keep that one if she was drugged and not happy about it?

Curious.

The next four emails are from "The Wood," accusing her of not doing enough to prevent Dimick from distributing opioids on campus and blaming the dean for his sister's overdose; the language is abusive and threatening. In one, he warned, "I trusted you and you betrayed me. I won't forget or forgive."

I'm digesting this when Lopez says, "Hey! Listen to this." 'You prick. You're a cancer on the school. You and your sycophants, Rory and Dakota, are responsible for all the overdoses on campus. You'll pay for that.'

"Wow! Let me guess. From the "Wood?"

"Yup. There are a couple more in a similar vein from him. The other messages are from Sandra Lawson professing her love and describing in intimate detail what she'd like to do to him."

"Yikes."

"Yeah. And three more, from different women, recounting sexual trysts with Dimick."

"The man got around," I say, and tell her about the email from "The Wood" threatening Landry for not protecting his sister. Sounds like a motive for murder to me.

"And he blames Rory and Dakota, too, for helping spread the drugs around. He didn't kill Rory---the Cohasset cops beat him to it---but it's possible he murdered Dakota, though I'm still locked on the fact of Rory's dreadful aroma in Dakota's dorm room and Landry's house."

"He's not the only boy who uses that brand," Lopez challenges.

"Do all of them douse themselves with a whole bottle?"

"Maybe," Lopez says. "I'm not an expert on teenage boys use of deodorant to mask their body odor, and neither are you."

I'm offended, lift my arm and sniff my armpit. "Old Spice Swagger," I say.

Lopez shakes her head. "You never cease to amaze me, Magliore."

"Aw shucks."

"Didn't mean it as a compliment. Someone who wanted to throw suspicion on Rory had a perfect way of doing so. And make us chase our tails like frisky dogs."

The only dog I've been compared to in the past is a dirty one, as in "you dirty dog" describing my lecherous behavior.

I don't mention this to Lopez.

She's right. The cologne would be a perfect deception to incriminate Belanger. This "Wood" person is rising to the top of the suspect list. He gave us a clue to his identity by complaining to Landry about his sister falling victim to the drugs on campus.

Got to follow up on that.

Chapter 65

Magliore and Lopez

I wrack my brain trying to make sense of the clue left by "The Wood" when it comes to me. Should have followed it up earlier. My head has been in another universe inhabited by Angela Rossi, drugs and the Jalisco cartel. I let the killer lead me around by the nose with false, too obvious clues designed to incriminate an innocent kid.

I check my phone for the names of the students who overdosed at Bridge Hill, the ones texted by Detective Charlie Rose. There are five: Sylvia Redding, Billy Malone, Yolanda Gutierrez, Walter Camp and Emma Paulson.

Paulson is the name I thought I recognized before because I had seen it on another form. I pull the folder given to us by Ranger Crimshaw out of my middle desk drawer; the list of the tourists on Georges Island the day of Dimick's murder; find what I'm looking for half-way down the page. Hayward Paulson, the college kid from BU supposedly writing an article to debunk the Lady in Black legend. Instead, he pranked the high school kids by pretending to be a "dark spirit." Emma and Hayward, brother and sister?

"Bingo," I say aloud and smile as Lopez fixes me with a quizzical stare.

"Hang on," I tell her and punch in the number for Dean Landry's office at Bridge Hill Academy. Her secretary, Ms. Andrews, picks up on the fourth ring. I identify myself and ask her to answer a few questions that might help us find the killer of her former boss.

"I'd be happy to," she says.

I get to the point. "Did Emma Paulson's brother, Hayward, attend Bridge Hill?"

"Why yes! Yes! He did," she says, offering an editorial on the young man. "Pompous ass, if you ask me. Brilliant student. Let everyone know it. Played lacrosse. Started calling himself, 'The Wood' as in "I really put the wood to that guy" after cross-checking an opposing player with his stick, which is illegal, by the way. And sticks aren't made of wood anymore either. Arrogant jerk."

"Wow! You know the sport of lacrosse," I say, ignoring her jabs at Hayward.

"Yes. My son plays at Cohasset High. He's co-captain."

I congratulate her on her son's success, but avoid being side-tracked. "When did Hayward graduate?" I ask.

"Three years ago. Valedictorian." She spits out the word "valedictorian" as if it's a disease. "He attends Boston University now," she adds.

I thank her for the help and prepare to punch off when she offers more insight. "Poor Emma is still in a coma. Hayward came in a day or two after it happened, got into a shouting match with Marsha in her office. Couldn't make out what they said, but Hayward bolted out of the office, red-faced and slammed the door."

She lowers her voice and sighs. "You don't think Hayward had anything to do with Marsha's murder, do you?"

I deflect the question. "We're following up on some leads, is all. Thanks again for your help."

I cut off before she can ask anything else.

* * *

I hand the Crimshaw report and my iPhone to Lopez. "Check for the name "Paulson" on each of those," I say. "Landry's secretary says Hayward referred to himself as "The Wood" in school."

Lopez raises her eyebrows in recognition, understands we may have discovered our multiple murderer, and it wasn't Rory Belanger. Paulson's emails clinch it for me.

Of course, I've been jumping to conclusions a lot lately. So, I realize, I must take it slow. "Let's pay a visit to Paulson's family," I say. "Their address is included in Rose's text. They can offer some background on their son before we confront him at BU."

"If that bastard killed Marsha, I'll rip his heart out," Lopez says, not holding back her guilt for the death of the deceased dean. She holds herself responsible for reasons that escape me.

I raise my hands in surrender mode.

Lopez stomps out of the office ahead of me. We take a state police unmarked vehicle since my Rav4 is headed to the scrap heap and my partner's car is still in Hull, where we left it before going to New Hampshire.

Lopez drives along Route 3A and takes First Parish Road toward Scituate Harbor. The Paulson's live in a three-story New England style gray clapboard home bordering the coast with a spectacular view of the Atlantic and the nearby Scituate Lighthouse. The house is set back from the beach, perched atop some huge boulders, no doubt to protect it from the ravages of Nor'easters which plague coastal communities from Hull to Plymouth.

We leave our car on the side of the two-lane road that fronts the home and ascend a flight of wooden stairs to the front door. Lopez rings the bell which is answered within two or three minutes by a fifty-something women wearing a multi-colored apron and carrying a dishcloth. We flash our badges and ask for Mrs. Paulson.

"I'm Jeanette Paulson," the woman says, smiling at our obvious surprise.

"Our housekeeper has the day off," she explains, "and I enjoy baking on such blustery days. How can I help you?"

"We're investigating the death of teacher Michael Dimick at Bridge Hill Academy," Lopez says, "and the wave of drug related incidents at the school."

The woman's smile disappears, her shoulders slump forward, and she clutches the cloth held in both hands. Near tears, she remains silent for a minute or two before inviting us to come in.

We enter a spacious room dominated by a stone fireplace and filled with two couches and several stuffed chairs. Ornate rugs cover the wood floors in front of the furniture and a log burns in the fireplace. The image is that of a comfortable, welcoming environment.

"Would you like some coffee," Mrs. Paulson asks. "Just brewed a fresh pot."

Lopez and I nod in the affirmative as we sit on one of the couches.

The picturesque vista seen through the double glass doors to the right of the fireplace of churning waves crashing against the rocks outside contributes to our desire to sample the hot brew.

Mrs. Paulson returns with two steaming mugs of coffee, hands one to each of us, and sits in a chair facing us. She settles in with her hands folded on her lap, knees together, back straight, eyes glued to us in anticipation of our questions.

I give Lopez a sideways glance, signaling her to begin.

She takes my cue. "We're very sorry to learn your daughter is in the hospital, Mrs. Paulson, but that's one reason we're here. We think drugs had something to do with Mr. Dimick's murder."

"I'm appalled at what's happening in this country today, in our schools. No one is doing anything about it," Paulson responds.

"We intend to do something, Mrs. Paulson. And you might be able to help. Any idea who supplied the drugs to your daughter?"

Paulson retrieves the towel beside her and twists it. "My son Hayward holds Mr. Dimick responsible. Two of Hayward's friends had to separate them before they came to blows after school on the day Emma overdosed."

She leans back and sighs. "I can tell you; Hayward wasn't saddened when Mr. Dimick was killed; said he deserved it. My husband and I were appalled, tried to calm him down. He would have none of it. He's still upset especially after he visits Emma."

I see an opening. "You don't think Hayward hurt mister Dimick, do you."

"My lord no," Mrs. Paulson shouts and stands up. "Is that why you're here, to accuse my son?"

Furious, she doesn't wait for an answer, demands we leave the house and stomps out of the room leaving Lopez and me sitting there. We look at each other, stand, place our mugs on an end table and exit the home.

We don't speak until we get into our department vehicle.

"First time we've heard about a scuffle between Dimick and a student," Lopez says.

"And Hayward is still mad. Based on his threatening emails and this information, the more I like the kid for the murders."

"Yeah. Like you were convinced of Rory Belanger's guilt," she says, cutting me to the quick.

My mouth falls open. I'm speechless for one of the few times I can remember. Our partnership is fraying and I fear it might not be mended anytime soon.

If ever.

Chapter 66

Hayward Paulson

Before Lopez engages the car's ignition, a white Mercedes SL350 pulls to the side of the road in front of us and two men exit, father and son, mirror images of each other. Mr. Paulson and Hayward, who I now recognize from the photos on Landry's computer. The older man wears a blue sport coat, striped maroon tie, gray slacks; the younger, a Boston University letterman's jacket and jeans.

The family has bucks. A Mercedes, three story home on the coast, two kids in a private academy costing upwards of sixty-grand a year. A comfortable life devastated by drugs.

Lopez and I scramble out of our vehicle, hold up our credentials as we approach the men.

"Lieutenant Magliore and Sergeant Lopez, state police," I announce.

Mr. Paulson's face registers surprise; Hayward's mouth the slightest uptick, a smile or smirk, take your pick.

"Does this have something to do with my daughter?" Paulson asks.

"Yes sir, in a way," I answer. "We're investigating the murder of teacher Mike Dimick from Bridge Hill Academy. We suspect your daughter's condition is connected."

Hayward's smirk widens. "Everyone knows Dimick was dealing drugs on campus. The headmaster's head is up his ass. I told Dean Landry and the Cohasset cops; nobody listened."

Mr. Paulson's head jerks sideways at his son's language, but he doesn't admonish him.

"That's why we're here," I say, "you may be able to help us in our investigation, Hayward."

* * *

Despite his father's protests, Hayward Paulson agrees to accompany us to our office in Hingham. He's eager to spin his web of lies and demonstrate his superior intellect. I can read it in his smug demeanor and mischievous eyes.

I catch myself. Reading guilt or jumping to rash conclusions based on a suspect's body language can be chancy and misleading. A recent study of how strangers relate to one another concluded that many detectives, FBI agents and even CIA professionals, often misread the mannerisms of suspects or colleagues with disastrous results. Spies and moles in top security posts skated undetected for years. Their friends and associates picked up no tell-tale vibes from these people. They looked and behaved as expected.

On the other hand, Amanda Knox, the American college student convicted of murder in Italy was railroaded because Italian police concluded that her strange behavior---like donning pink booties at a crime scene and spinning around and saying 'Ta Da'-made her a criminal capable of murder, despite a total lack of evidence.

So, while my gut tells me that Hayward Paulson is a cunning, arrogant bastard who killed three people without remorse. I vow to nail him based on proof and his own lies, not conjecture.

We interview Paulson in a small conference room three doors down from our office. Not designed as an interrogation room, there is no two-way mirror to observe or monitor our interaction. I give him a cup of water before we begin hoping to extract his fingerprints and DNA from it later and match them to one of the crime scenes.

"Thank you for agreeing to talk with us, Hayward," I say.

"I'm not under arrest, am I?" he asks.

"No, of course not. We think you may be able to help us with your knowledge of Bridge Hill Academy, the students and teachers."

He nods, takes a sip of water and leans back in his chair.

Someone who can kill multiple individuals is a psychopath in my book. I've encountered them before. They can be charming but feel no empathy for others and lie with ease. Hayward will be difficult to break---but perhaps easy to catch in a falsehood. He murdered three people because he held them responsible for his sister's overdose. Killed them, if I'm right, not because he loved his younger sister, but because by hurting her, they offended him.

That's my logic anyway. We can play to his ego, his feeling of superiority, get him to brag about what he did; take credit for being a masterful killer outwitting inept cops.

"Tell us about the drug dealing at Bridge Hill, please Hayward," I ask.

"Like I said, any idiot could tell you about that," he responds. "Everybody knew."

"Why don't you tell us?"

"Very well," he says, shaking his head as if we belonged in the idiot category. "Dimick was the dealer. He got kids anything they wanted—cocaine, meth, opioids."

"Including your sister?"

"Not directly. She got them from Dakota Johnson and Rory Belanger. Big shots on campus; super jock, head cheerleader."

He spits out the names as if expectorating phlegm.

"Emma idolized Dakota," he continues. "Wanted to be like her, a puppy following her master around; made me sick."

His face flushes and his hand trembles as he works himself up. "Dakota and Rory were Dimick's sycophants. He gave them the stuff, they passed it on to their friends. Big shots" he repeats. "They didn't know who they were fooling with."

"Meaning you?" I press.

Most people would fire back, protest when confronted. Paulson stifles his anger, takes another sip of water and exhales. "They got what they deserved," his singular response.

I continue my line of questioning. "Did you ever tell Dimick to back off? Threaten him?"

A curt "no."

First lie?

"You also held Dean Landry responsible for the spread of drugs on the Bridge Hill Campus, right?"

"I did," he says, without hesitation.

"Did you kill her?"

"Of course not."

"We found your DNA in her bedroom," I lie. We had the nude photo of both Landry and him, no DNA.

"I screwed her? So what? Doesn't mean I killed her. Nice piece of ass."

He eyes Lopez with a hint of a smile creasing his lips. No remorse; no apology for embarrassing or offending a woman.

"I bet you smelled traces of Belanger's cologne in Landry's room also," he adds. "The guy used half a spray can of the stuff, obnoxious twit."

He let that sink in, reverses direction, like a trick play in football. "And he and I weren't alone in screwing the good dean. Half the boys in school got into her pants, some girls too."

The kid is a superlative liar and master manipulator. Planting the cologne in Dakota Johnson's dorm room and Landry's bedroom. Offering up Belanger as a suspect. Could we prove it?

I glance at Lopez. She raises halfway out of her chair, her knuckles white from gripping the edge of the table to control her anger. Silent to this point, she challenges him.

"You killed Mr. Dimick, Dean Landry and Dakota Johnson, Hayward. You're a cold-blooded killer."

Paulson leans back arms crossed. "Prove it," he says, returning her challenge. He exudes confidence, matching his superior intelligence against two lesser beings, lowly police detectives. That pisses me off as much as knowing he's a murderer.

Our circumstantial evidence is sufficient to hold him and perhaps enough to convince the D.A. to charge him, so I end the charade and place him under arrest.

He remains unflappable, arrogant. "You've got nothing, detective, nothing. I'll walk out of here as soon as my lawyer shows up."

I fear he's right. We need more, something irrefutable; a smoking gun as they say in the movies and on TV. The threatening emails to Landry and Dimick help. Landry's secretary can testify he called himself "The Wood" while in school. Others can verify that, I'm sure. We can prove he's the author of the emails, but not the murderer.

I do feel vindicated in some respect. Drugs were the central reason for Dimick's murder and those of Dakota Johnson and Marsha Landry. Paulson blamed them for his sister's access to the opioids that resulted in her condition, and he sought revenge.

Chapter 67

Lopez and Magliore

Lopez and I place Hayward Paulson in a holding cell until he can be transferred to a more secure lockup, the Plymouth County Correctional Facility. Paulson's father and his attorney, William Wallace, confront us in the parking lot as we exit the building. He's furious when we notify him of his son's arrest; fumes and threatens us with a defamation lawsuit; balls his fists, juts out his jaw, poised to strike me until Wallace steps in, puts a hand on his chest, and backs him off. After a tense moment or two, Wallace is able to steer the irate father toward the courthouse entrance. The man continues to mumble expletives as he's led away.

"Hayward did it," Lopez whispers to me.

"I concur," I say, "I'm convinced a jury will convict him on what we have. But additional evidence can't hurt."

As if on cue, my phone rings; DEA Agent Phillip Murray.

"Yes sir," I answer.

"Got some news," he says. "May or may not be helpful?"

"You're on speaker," I say. "Shoot."

"The fingerprints you asked me to run through the Academy database came back. No Brett Kilgore or Rory Belanger. We got hits on a Mike Dimick and a former student, Hayward Paulson."

Bingo. The "smoking gun.".

Somehow, Paulson learned Rossi was the man behind the opioid drug pipeline to Bridge Hill, tracked him down. Killed him. Smothered him like he did Dakota.

I thank Murray and punch off.

Another nail in Paulson's coffin.

I'm prepared to declare total victory, when Lopez rains on my one-man parade.

"How did he identify Rossi?" she asks. "Landry didn't know. Dakota and Rory had no clue."

After a moment or two of thought, we both spout a name: Brett Kilgore.

He drove Dimick to the doctor's office more than once; the one person other than Dimick who knew.

But why would he tell Paulson?

We can't come up with a god reason, so I decide to abide by the K.I.S.S. philosophy; keep it simple stupid.

Kilgore didn't need to tell Paulson. The simplest answer is that the kid followed the two teachers to New Hampshire on their trip to restock, waits until he's sure no more patients are in the office, goes in to confront the doctor and discovers Rossi unconscious. Takes him out.

Revenge complete.

We've got the son-of-a-bitch. No way, in my view, can Paulson explain his fingerprints in Rossi's clinic. He had no reason to go that distance, in that town, to seek medical help. Doesn't matter how he found out or got to the clinic; irrefutable evidence puts him there.

The D.A. and a future jury should agree.

I lower my eyes, grovel, admit to Lopez that blaming Rory Belanger was premature.

"We got the son-of-a-bitch," I say, repeating my earlier thought aloud. I hold my hand up in a high five gesture. Lopez arches her eyebrows, but slaps my hand.

Like my rush to judgment on Rory, my celebration proves premature. Another situation arises that pushes our murder investigation to the back burner and puts our lives at risk.

Chapter 68

Emeliano Santana

Still standing in the courthouse parking lot digesting Agent Murray's news about finding Hayward Paulson's fingerprint at the Rossi clinic in Newport, my phone rings. I'm ready to chuck the damn thing into the bushes until I see the caller ID: Mavis Fisher.

I punch the accept button.

"Yes, Mavis. What can I do for you?" I say, before she speaks.

She doesn't hesitate. "One of my patients, Emeliano Santana, a park ranger on Georges Island, wants to share some information you'll want to hear. Can you come to my office in an hour?"

"Not about ghosts, I hope."

"You may wish it was," Fisher says, and breaks the connection.

Lopez spreads her arms in a "what?" gesture.

"More intrigue about Georges Island."

"I hope it's not about ghosts," she says, breaking into a broad grin.

I double over with laughter but wonder why Mavis Fisher sounded so concerned.

Ghosts may be the least of our worries.

* * *

Lopez and I meet Santana in Mavis Fisher's office. He knows me but balks at Theresa's presence. Fisher convinces him we both can be trusted.

Santana, shaken and pacing back and forth, tells us about his involvement with three so-called businessmen and their hold on him. He explains how he discovered the cache of guns stashed on Georges Island and that several workers, hiding in the tunnels of Fort Warren, are even now stamping out bogus oxycodone tablets on hand cranked machines.

He keeps running his hand through his hair as he speaks. When finished, he slumps, exhausted, on the couch.

"Why are you telling us, Emeliano, and not your superiors?" I ask.

"Two reasons," he says, after sitting two-or three-minutes staring at the floor. "First, Ms. Fisher persuaded me you can help."

He raises his eyes, stares straight ahead, and drops the bomb. "Second, not enough time; too much red tape. They ordered me to be on duty tonight. They're going to move the guns and pills after dark. I don't want to be responsible for supporting the killing of innocent people by gangsters using those weapons."

I shake my head. Nightfall is a few hours away.

"Emeliano," I say. "I need to alert my captain and organize a force to intercept these guys. Any idea how many men they'll have?"

"No. Four men unloaded the guns, but I don't know how many will be there tonight; a boat crew along with some others to carry the boxes, I suppose."

"What kind of boat?"

"Don't know. I'm sorry. I'm sorry. They told me nothing. Just to be at the fort tonight."

"Any other rangers on the island?"

"No."

"Okay. You come with us. You know the island inside and out. That expertise may be critical. Can you do that?"

Santana shifts forward, elbows on his knees, hands cradling his head. "I must do at least that," he says, after a long silence. "This mess is my fault. All my fault."

He turns, lifts his head and stares at us. "My life is ruined," he moans. "Ruined."

* * *

No time to talk Santana out of his self-pity. We need to act fast before the weapons are moved.

I punch in Captain Catabegian's number, and catch him readying to leave the office for the day. He's not happy to receive my call. "This better be good Magliore. I'm heading home to sample some of my wife's famous pot roast."

I explain the situation and gain his undivided attention despite the lure of his favorite dinner. "Okay. You and Lopez go to Pemberton Point ASAP. I'll alert the Harbor Patrol and the Coast Guard. One of them will ferry you out to the fort. Hopefully, you can get there before those punks arrive and give them a warm New England reception."

Big Cat is decisive when necessary.

I punch off the phone and Lopez, Santana and I rush out of Mavis Fisher's office, startling the receptionist as we barrel by.

We take our unmarked vehicle, but employ our flashing lights to warn cars in front of us to move aside. Most pull over, but I'm forced to swerve around a couple of cars whose drivers act oblivious. I bellow a few choice expletives gleaned from many years of driving on Massachusetts roadways.

Lopez, in the" shotgun" seat, smiles and nods at my reaction, while Santana suffers in back, distraught and sobbing. Lopez and I concentrate on what might lie ahead, so we offer no words of consolation or encouragement to the poor guy. I'm pissed it took him so long to report what was happening. The delay may endanger all of us.

Lopez sits in her seat, body rigid, jaw set, eyes locked on passing scenery as we rush toward the unknown. I keep my eyes on the road. Traveling fast, I'm reluctant to give her a reassuring pat on the leg or shoulder.

I hope I don't regret that later.

Chapter 69

Lopez, Magliore and Santana

When we arrive at Pemberton Point, my phone rings with a call from Captain Catebegian.

"Bad news," he reports. "All Coast Guard ships are away on an interdiction exercise with the DEA along the Carolina coast, won't be able to help."

"Harbor Patrol?" I ask.

"That's the good news. They should be on the way now to pick you up."

"Okay. Thanks. I'll keep you updated."

A high-speed interceptor, nicknamed **The Persuader**, skids to a sidelong stop at the Pemberton Pier. The craft is manned by two officers in body armor. Shotguns and M-16s rest on the deck between them; their sidearms are Glock 23s. The boat, outfitted with dual 300 horse power Mercury outboard motors, is equipped with just four seats, so Santana scrunches down in the small space between the rear and front seats.

As we cast off from the pier and race through the Hull Gut, my heart sinks. A fishing trawler is tied up at the Georges Island wharf; no time to plan or organize a reception. Unfazed, the piloting officer cranks up the siren and sets a straight-ahead course; like the Marines, hi-diddle-diddle-charge-up the middle.

A risky practice at best; deadly at worst.

A half-moon casts some light across the water between us and the trawler. As we speed forward, siren whooping, the hull slamming the water, the trawler's crew, alerted to our arrival, throws off a tarp covering a .50-caliber machine gun. They crank off several rounds that sail above and around us. The deep thumping of the weapon as it spits fire towards us is frightening. I'm reminded of the scene from the movie, "Saving Private Ryan," depicting the Normandy landing in World War II. I don't dwell on the fact that many of the troops storming toward shore never made it out of the landing craft.

Shocked and scared, Santana loses it. He screams, "turn around, turn around," and lunges toward the piloting officer. I slam him back on the deck and jam my forearm into his neck to keep him down. Lopez reaches out to touch my shoulder, her face a mask of terror. I manage a smile, but I'm not feeling it. Bile rises to my throat.

Despite the commotion, the piloting officer maintains his composure. We execute evasive action by zig-zagging from side to side. We're thrown against each other, ocean spray soaking us. Then, as we zig one way, a dozen or more bullets smack into us broadside. One finds its mark. The piloting officer's head explodes spewing blood and brain matter everywhere. We spiral out of control, flip sideways, vault into the air and catapult end over end. We're all ejected, our bodies flying through the air like rag-dolls, arms and legs askew.

Somehow, I survive. The Atlantic is frigid, the cold rips through me like an electric shock; my teeth chatter. I shed my shoes and tread water searching for survivors among the now splintered remains of our interceptor. Blood seeps into my eyes from a head wound. I'm forced to duck underwater several times to avoid a searchlight from the trawler scanning our wreckage. The bastards continue to fire trying to ensure we're all dead.

In the glare of the searchlight, I spot two lifeless bodies floating ten feet away. One is the now headless Harbor Patrol officer and the other, Ranger Emeliano Santana. Poor bastard. He did the right thing in exposing the cartel's plans but it cost him his life.

After what seems like an eternity, the firing stops and the searchlight is extinguished. They're apparently convinced no one survived. I conceal myself behind a chunk of debris to avoid being seen in the sliver of moonlight that remains and paddle around looking for my partner and the other officer when a quivering, weak voice breaks the silence.

"Help me. Help me."

Theresa Lopez.

I dog-paddle toward the sound; reach her in a couple of minutes. She's draped over one of the floating seat cushions from our boat. Her injuries appear severe. Blood stains the surrounding water.

Fighting off the cold and a desire to just close my eyes and let the water engulf me, I consider my options. As a former lifeguard, I'm strong enough to drag her to Georges Island, but I can't go directly there for obvious reasons. I could maneuver her around the island and drag her to shore on the opposite side, but she might not survive that long. Ditto, if I try for another nearby island or go back to the tip of the Hull peninsula. Things don't look good. I'm shivering and becoming confused, a sign of hypothermia. If I don't reach land soon, neither of us will make it.

Frustrated and paralyzed by indecision, and close to giving up, my spirits are lifted when the cavalry comes to our rescue. Another Harbor Patrol boat, slower than the Interceptor, but outfitted with a machine gun on its bow, plows toward us, scanning the area with its own spotlight. Before they run us down, two officers, visually checking the water, spot me waving, yelling and hanging on to Lopez.

The two men jump into the water and, with others from the boat, pull and push us aboard. The 50-caliber from the trawler opens up again, and bullets ping off the superstructure of our craft.

But now we can answer.

Our gunner lets loose with a counter barrage as we haul ass out of there. The return fire silences the cartel gunners allowing us to make it to safety. Our rescuers place Lopez on a stretcher and cover her with blankets. I'm given a blanket to wrap around my shoulders, and a cup of coffee, as we're ferried to the **Guardian**, a 57-foot Sea Ark which serves as the command vessel for harbor patrol operations and contains a medical triage unit.

Lopez is carried to the cabin where an EMT officer attends to her. He determines she needs immediate surgery, dresses her wounds, and transfers her to a launch that speeds off to Rose Wharf in Boston where a medical team, alerted by the commander of the **Guardian**, is standing by.

None of us, including the officer who triaged Lopez, knows whether she will survive. My anger bubbles over. Wagging my finger at Sergeant Timothy McCann, the officer in charge, I shout, "We've got to nail those bastards. They killed two of your men and Ranger Santana. Let's move before they disappear."

McCann is not persuaded. "We don't have the manpower to storm the island, son," he retorts. "We're not the Marines. I don't intend to sacrifice more men for a futile, and unnecessary, assault. If the trawler sets sail, we can follow and note its location for the Coast Guard."

Makes sense, but I don't give up. I give him my best General Patton speech---or George C. Scott's from the movie---and plead with him to take action. Maybe I went too far with the "crap through a goose" line.

My appeal fails.

"I know how you feel, lieutenant," he says, his tone calmer now, "but I can't do it. We'll watch, wait and follow."

He puts his hand on my shoulder. "Go with Corporal Richards and put on some dry clothes."

Dejected, I nod and turn to see Richards standing by the door. He escorts me outside and to a cabin serving as a locker room containing extra uniforms.

"Grab one that fits," Richard says, as he retrieves a pair of black socks from a drawer attached to a bulkhead cabinet.

I wriggled out of my soaking clothes, drop them on the deck and try on a uniform, sans skivvies; no underwear available. The outfit is a tad tight, but will suffice for the time being. It feels good to shed my wet stuff.

Richards glances around to confirm we're alone. "Can you drive a boat?" he asks, in a voice just above a whisper,

I grew up in Hull where boating is a normal summer activity. I had maneuvered many outboard motor boats as well as a small cabin cruiser.

I nod.

"An interceptor is moored to this behemoth," he says. "I'll find you some body armor and an M-16 with extra magazines. I don't like the idea those cartel fucks can kill our guys and get away with it."

He pauses and looks me in the eye. "You're on your own if you do this."

The implication is clear. He will deny helping me if questioned.

"Point me in the right direction, Corporal," I say.

He smiles. "Wait here while I secure your gear and make sure we can make it to the interceptor without being seen."

"I appreciate this."

"Don't thank me pal. This is a suicide mission. You're no Audie Murphy."

I laugh. Murphy, one of the most decorated American soldiers in World War II, single-handedly held off a company of Germans during an assault and led a successful counterattack while wounded. He was a teenager at the time.

As a fledgling historian and World War II buff, I know this, but am surprised Richards does.

Doesn't matter. No doubt he's right. My chances of success are slim. If I survive, I could be booted from the state police for insubordination. Nevertheless, for Lopez, for Santana, for the slain officers, I gotta try.

I might even have an ally. A mysterious voice in the Fort Warren tunnels once promised, "I will save you."

Real or not, I can use all the help I can get.

Chapter 70

Miguel Chavez

Miguel Chavez is pissed.

He's in a tunnel at Fort Warren escorting four of his workers carrying pill machines to the trawler when the staccato report of the .50-caliber machine gun echoes through the night.

He's stunned. What the hell's going on? They're a few hours from getting away with their stash of guns and newly minted pills. They couldn't afford to be discovered now. He orders his people to stay put and dashes out of the tunnel and across the parade ground heading for the moored trawler. He's met half-way by his right-hand man, Luis Garcia. "What the fuck is going on, Luis?" he shouts, grabbing the man by the shoulders.

"A police boat approached the island with its siren blaring, our soldatos stopped them."

"Jesus Christ. Our operation is blown. La policia couldn't know about this without being warned. That fuck, Santana. I'll kill him and every member of his family."

Chavez and Garcia both speak English without an accent, but when talking to each other lapse into Spanish words like "policia."

Garcia understands his boss is capable of angry outbursts and will follow through on his threats. But Garcia needed to be a voice of reason. "Jefe. We must leave here now. The weapons are loaded. We can escape, find a cove along the coast to hide and offload our cargo. We can't outrun the Coast Guard."

"What about the pill machines?"

"Leave them."

Chavez nods. "Okay. Go back for our people."

"We can't risk it. Forget them."

Chavez shakes his head. "They know too much. Go."

Garcia gives in; races back across the parade ground to the tunnel.

He doesn't expect to encounter a man with a gun.

Chapter 71

Magliore

Corporal Richards doesn't accompany me to the interceptor. He can, if necessary, claim ignorance of my intentions. I understand.

I locate the boat, untie it and let the current carry me several feet away before I turn the ignition and jet away. The Guardian is stationed a mile and a half from Georges Island. I'll arrive there in a matter of minutes.

I have no plan; only rage.

Speeding toward Fort Warren, I flash back to those World War II movies with John Wayne at the helm of a PT Boat plowing toward the Japanese fleet, wind and ocean spray lashing his face, anger reflected in his eyes, intent on avenging some atrocity the 'Sons of the Rising Sun' had perpetrated.

Am I acting like John Wayne now, single-mindedly focused on exacting revenge for the loss of colleagues and a partner for whom I have developed more than professional feelings?

Guilty.

I angle toward an opening to Fort Warren on the northern side of Georges Island across a narrow straight facing nearby Lovell's Island. The access may be sealed off, but it's my best bet to slip inside and sneak up on the trawler undetected, assuming I arrive before they take off.

I beach the interceptor on a rocky area between huge boulders, hear a scrunching sound. They'll charge me for damaging government property if I survive my one-man assault. Never underestimate the bureaucracy.

Ha!

I grab the M-16 and a Maglite Richards loaned me, roll over the side of the interceptor and dash up the incline, the extra magazines jingling in my pockets. Entry is blocked by a single chain with a 'staff only' sign hanging from it.

I take up a position to the side of the tunnel and peer into pitch blackness. When my eyes acclimate to the darkness, I move ahead, mindful of depressions or holes in front of me.

The going is painfully slow. Too slow, I fear, to reach the cartel gang before they escape. I can see and hear nothing. No choice but to use the Maglite. I flip it on and crouch down to make a more difficult target if fired upon.

My lighting the way brings no response, so, channeling my inner Audie Murphy, I race forward following my flashlight beam. I emerge from a narrow corridor into a wider one and keep running, the M-16 in one hand, the Maglite in the other, good for balance but not for responding to gunfire if discovered. As I round a turn, I rush headlong into four men startled by my abrupt appearance behind them. Equally shocked, and unable to stop my forward motion, I stumble over a dip in the floor and fall flat on my face. My rifle flies one way, the flashlight another.

Three of the men scamper away, but one stays and plays his own light over my prone body. He holds a gun in his right hand aimed at me. He kicks the M-16 aside and approaches.

He stands over me, legs apart, ready to put a bullet into my brain. "I don't know who you are my friend," he says, "but you are one dead hombre."

I'm calm, though cold; accept my fate. My life doesn't flash before me like some have recounted during near-death experiences. I don't pray or curse, just wait.

The kill shot never comes.

Something like a feathery cloth or robe sweeps across my body. I raise my head to see a ghostlike form glide toward my would-be attacker. Distracted, he stumbles backward firing into the roof of the tunnel raining debris down on both of us. The specter hovers above the man for several seconds, then jerks away and melds into a wall.

I'm as stunned as my assailant, but seize the moment, leap up and jump on the dazed man before he can recover. We roll on the dirt floor; struggle for the gun he still grasps in his hand. I'm stronger, press my forearm into his throat until he stops struggling, his body limp. He may be dead or unconscious. Can't wait to find out which.

I rip the .45-caliber pistol from his fingers and put the barrel under his chin, poised to pull the trigger. It'll be an execution, like the one I pulled off in the San Bernardino Mountains when I killed the rogue LA cop.

But I hesitate; can't do it. Can't execute another man.

Instead, I hop up and kick him in the head. He'll be immobile for a while. Don't want him to sneak up behind me later.

Not sure how long the altercation with the cartel thug took, I fear I might now be too late to stop the trawler from leaving with its cache of guns and supply of opioids.

I pick up my M-16 and Maglite and set off at a dead run, exit the corridor through a narrow doorway, cross the parade ground and dash through a wood covered bridge toward the dock.

Not a tactically smart move as it turns out.

Blocking my way is a man with an Ak-47 assault rifle. But he's thrown off balance by my headlong rush towards him. In haste, he fires off a burst. One round slams into my left thigh spinning me around. I pirouette like a dancer in the grand finale of an opera, but land on my stomach still clutching the M-16 although my Maglite is lost. Fortunately, my attacker is silhouetted in the moonlight and slow to react. I press the rifle stock to my right cheek and fire two rounds, catching him in the upper body. He goes down. I push myself up and stagger toward him. He's lying on the ground face up, blood oozing from his mouth and chest.

He won't get up again.

* * *

I fish into the fallen man's pocket and extract his wallet. His driver's license lists his name as Miguel Chavez. May be valid; may not be. I don't care. Take it with me and hobble toward the moored trawler, rifle at port arms, my leg bleeding profusely, blood seeping into my eyes from a re-opened head wound received on our ill-fated earlier trip on the Interceptor. I'm woozy, disoriented.

The crew on the trawler doesn't take advantage of my condition. They watch me approach, but make no effort to stop me or uncover the .50-caliber. I can see wooden crates stored on the deck; the stolen weapons.

Four men descend the gangplank, hands raised. Without their leader, the man I killed, I presume, they're lost, lack direction and the will to continue the fight.

"Do any of you speak English?" I ask.

One man raises his hand.

"Do you have a cellphone?"

He nods.

I take it from him and punch in Captain Catebegian's number.

When he answers, his voice is gruff, tense. "What's going on, Magliore?"

I fill him in, request he contact the Harbor Patrol and inform them it's safe to land on the island.

I'm eager for news about my partner. Is she alive or dead?

Big Cat doesn't know. She's still in surgery.

Catebegian's response is not reassuring, but I can't do anything about that now. I usher the four men back onto the trawler, direct them to lie face down on the deck and await rescue.

I sit down on a box to guard my captives, but can't staunch the flow of blood from my leg, which hurts like hell. My rifle feels heavy; head is throbbing, vision blurred. The wailing sirens of approaching patrol boats resonate in the distance. I smile, relieved, until the deck of the trawler rolls like I'm riding waves. I fall forward, black out.

The last thing I remember---or think I remember---is a female voice sounding far away. "I'm watching over you. I have not gone."

Epilogue

The Rest of the Story

Three months later

I'm standing in front of the Anaheim Police Department Headquarters in southern California leaning on a cane rehearsing what I will say to the chief when I confess to murder. My therapist, Mavis Fisher, prodded me to come here, convincing me the way to achieve peace of mind is to unburden myself of guilt.

It's been an up and down three months. Theresa Lopez is still recovering from her wounds in Mass General in Boston, a renowned teaching hospital, and one of the best medical and surgical facilities in the country. She's in expert hands; projected to recover, though the likelihood of her being able to return to her old job is questionable. I'm not looking forward to working with a new partner, but depending on how my meeting with the Anaheim chief goes, that may be a moot point. I could wind up behind bars.

The good news is, Big Cat recommended Lopez and me for a Medal of Valor. The Harbor Patrol commander opted not to charge me with insubordination.

Guess the end justified the means?

My injuries are less severe than those suffered by Lopez; no vital organs damaged, though my head resembles a baseball from the number of stitches required to repair the slash across my forehead caused by a fifty-caliber bullet. I'm still in pain, but rejected any medication given my history of addiction.

I returned to work three weeks ago, though confined to a desk. The D.A. formally charged Hayward Paulson with the murders of Marsha Landry, Michael Dimick, Dakota Johnson and Andrew Rossi. His fingerprints at the Newport clinic synched it. Despite his earlier bravado and denials, he admitted planting evidence to incriminate student Rory Belanger and bragged about fooling incompetent police detectives. New Hampshire authorities ceded jurisdiction for prosecuting Paulson to Massachusetts.

Luis Garcia, the Mexican cartel henchman, and the man I grappled with in the tunnel at Fort Warren, survived my kick to his head. Garcia spilled his guts to DEA and Homeland Security agents and identified distribution houses and dealers throughout New England. He also named Willie Wilkins, the FedEx driver, and Bobby Walton, the Sturm, Ruger, employee who helped engineer the theft of guns. He led authorities to their bodies buried in a wooded area on the outskirts of Newport, New Hampshire. They were executed as liabilities.

The breakup of the Jalisco cartel dealt a significant blow to opioid operations in New England, but everyone conceded it was a temporary setback. Jalisco would recover or some other cartel, like the Sinaloa's, would take their place.

Not my problem.

I shake off these thoughts and enter police department headquarters. The chief's office and detective bureau are restricted by electronic gates, but the desk sergeant waves me through after some "long-time no see" chit chat.

The chief's realm is at the end of a long corridor, his name and rank emblazoned on the opaque glass door leading to a spacious reception area dominated by the solid oak desk of Ophelia Suarez, gatekeeper to the boss.

She smiles when I limp into the otherwise empty room; lifts her eyebrows but doesn't comment on my cane. "Magliore," she says, "long time no see," the universal response to someone who hasn't been around for a while.

"You look as ravishing as ever, O.S." I say, to the fifty-something plump woman in a loose-fitting flowered dress. She knows every officer in the department, and bullshit when she hears it. Nevertheless, her face turns crimson. She flicks her head toward the door behind her. "Go on in, he's expecting you."

Unlike my usual impulsive self, I called ahead and made an appointment, so I nod, knock and shuffle into Chief Virgil Alvarez's inner sanctum. He's sitting in his padded, black swivel chair, behind his department issue gray metal desk facing the window, staring on to Harbor Boulevard, a central thoroughfare zigzagging through Anaheim, Orange, Costa Mesa and other county communities. The well-traveled road is often jammed with traffic like most southern California roadways.

Perhaps Alvarez is planning his drive home, and dreading it.

He swivels in his chair as I enter. "Ah. The prodigal son returns," he says. "Come to reclaim your job?"

I shake my head. "Nope. To confess," I answer, causing him to recoil as if struck by a blow. His attempt at humor.

"I'm not a priest and this isn't the confessional," says the devout Catholic. "Can't offer absolution for whatever you've done."

"Three Hail Marys and four Our Fathers won't do it even if assigned as penance by a clergyman," I say.

He raises his eyebrows, leans forward, elbows on the desk. "That serious, huh?"

I nod.

He smiles again, spreads his arms wide, now my confessor.

"Okay. Unburden yourself, my son."

I tell him how, contrary to published reports, the rogue LA cop who terrorized southern California for several days over a year ago did not die by his own hand, but by mine. I provide details.

The chief's face transforms from one of mirthful forbearance to somber, the corners of his mouth turn down, his eyes narrow.

"Medical Examiner's official finding was the guy killed himself."

"He was wrong."

"Not officially."

Alvarez sticks to the party line. Irritated, I raise my voice. "I just told you how it went down."

Unmoved, the chief repeats, "M.E. got it right. The man offed himself as much as if he held the gun to his head. Suicide by cop any way you slice it. The bastard assassinated innocent people, civilians, cops, your partner, for Christ's sake. Had to know how it would end. Welcomed it. He's dead. Deserved what he got. Details don't matter. Nothing you say will change that."

My expression hardens. He interrupts before I can protest. "Forget it, Magliore. Nobody cares how he died. Only that he's gone, and we're all the better for it. You did your job."

He explains the reality to me. "No D.A. is going to want this shit-burger on his desk. And I'm not about to serve it up to ease your conscience, ruin the reputation of this department, and undermine the credibility of law enforcement in general. We've taken enough hits lately. Not going to happen."

He stands up and looks out the window, fingers interlaced behind his back. He speaks, still looking away, perhaps willing the traffic to disappear. "Go back to Massachusetts, be a good cop, catch bad guys. Forget about the past. Confess to a real priest if you must."

He turns around, smiles, makes the sign of the cross, and intones like a prelate on the altar: "In the name of the Father, the Son and the Holy Ghost. Go and sin no more…and don't darken my door again."

My Italian mother would shudder at such blasphemy. Not me. The message is clear. "Yes father," I say, steepling my hands as if in prayer and bowing my head.

Alvarez comes around his desk and wraps me in a bear hug. "Trust me," he whispers. "Walk away."

I extricate myself from his embrace, turn, open the door and leave his office without speaking or looking back; symbolically, I guess, shaking off the albatross that has dogged me since that fatal night in the San Bernardino mountains.

I lean on my cane limping through the reception area, wave to Ophelia with my free hand, don't stop to chat.

Once outside, I linger on the sidewalk. Consider my options. Take my story to the Orange County District Attorney or go to the press. The D.A. will be a dead end as Alvarez warned. The guy or gal will listen to my story, thank me for the candor, and bury the conversation like it never happened.

If I go to the media, the Fourth Estate will jump on it like a pack of hungry wolves thrown a piece of meat. Despite official denials, careers will be sullied, the profession besmirched. Protesters will hit the streets with yet another issue to harangue cops. Not my style or intent. I sought to punish myself, not others.

I take a deep breath, let it out. In my heart, despite what Mavis Fisher offered as a legal defense, I believe what I did was wrong. But the ruling authorities don't care. We got our man, avenged our brethren, satisfied the families of victims, reassured the public. Case closed. I did the right thing by confessing to my superior officer. It didn't work out. I can live with that now; my conscience clear.

I smile. That I live at all is thanks to the intervention of something or someone who, during my one-man assault on the cartel gang at Fort Warren, distracted a gunman seconds away from putting a bullet in my brain. Later, before I passed out from a loss of blood, I heard, or imagined, a female voice whisper, "I'm watching over you. I have not gone."

It was either a message from the Lady in Black confirming her spirit does exist and will forever linger in the place of her mortal demise---or the hallucination of a wounded man delirious with pain?

And how about the earlier episode in the darkness of a Fort Warren passageway when an otherworldly voice promised, "I will save you."

In the light of day, and without the stress of a near death experience, I view these occurrences with a more rational perspective. While recovering from my wounds, I researched the question of why people believe in the supernatural. Most writers on the subject offered similar reasons: When mysterious events occur, the human brain tries to find the cause and effect, and as philosopher Stephen Law concluded: "Invisible agents provide quick, convenient explanations."

I'm sure Law and others are right. I never revealed my encounters with the Lady in Black to any of my colleagues and never will. Whatever they were, they remain my secret.

I punch in the number of the taxi company I used earlier to get me to the Anaheim PD headquarters. I'm not an Uber or Lyft kind of guy. Don't have the apps on my phone. Wouldn't know how to use them if I did. Taxi drivers need the cash; squeezed by these part-time interlopers. The driver will get a big payday after taking me to my hotel in Anaheim, and on to the Long Beach airport where I hope to catch the Red Eye to Boston. I'll call to make a reservation on the way.

The yellow cab arrives after a short wait, ten, maybe fifteen minutes. I open the back door, throw my cane in and slide onto the seat pulling the door closed behind me.

"Where to" the cabbie asks, in a distinct East Asian accent.

"To my next life," I say, without hesitation.

He laughs, strokes his charcoal beard, catches my eye in the rearview mirror and says: "Hope we can find the way, sir."

I wink and reply: "Me too, my friend. Me too."

Acknowledgements

The idea for this story owes its existence to Edward Rowe Stowe an author, historian, raconteur, lecturer, preservationist, and treasure hunter. Stowe told the story of a mysterious Lady in Black haunting Fort Warren in his first book, <u>The Islands of Boston Harbor</u>, published in 1935. Later he repeated the story many times in guest lectures around New England and at the fort where he sometimes had young women leap out of a coffin he had placed in a dark corridor to frighten tourists.

Stowe might have adopted the idea of ghosts on Fort Warren from an account told by Colonel Francis J. Parker who was stationed there with the Thirty-Second Regiment of the Massachusetts Infantry during the Civil War. In his memoir, the Colonel noted that during "one dark and howling night" a sentry reported seeing a "white form" pass him twice and he didn't challenge the figure because he feared it was a ghost.

In addition, a reporter for the Gloucester Telegraph in 1862 recounted a tale by soldiers who claimed to have seen the image of an old woman flitting near the graves of some rebel soldiers.

There are many versions of this tale and to this day, some visitors to Fort Warren claim to have seen a Lady in Black or felt her presence. The rangers conducting tours often include the story in their narratives.

No book is the product of the author alone. My wife Carol has offered encouragement every step of the way. Faithful and insightful readers, Stephen Bricker, Debi Pavich, Jeanie Conway, Carol and Jack Curtiss, Bob McAlear and Barbara and Tom Gibbons offered many wonderful suggestions.

CPSIA information can be obtained
at www.ICGtesting.com
Printed in the USA
FSHW011254221121
86390FS